# SWEATER WEATHER

---

AN FU HOCKEY BOOK

MANDI BECK

Sweater Weather

Copyright 2023 by Mandi Beck

Cover Designer: Letitia Hasser, RBA Designs

Cover Photo: Lauren Perry, Perrywinkle Photography

Copy Editor: Jenny Simms, Edits 4 Indies

Copyright Law:

If you are reading this book and did not purchase it, this book has been pirated and you are stealing. Please delete it from your device and support the author by purchasing a legal copy. All rights reserved. Without limiting the rights under the copyright reserved above, no part of this publication may be reproduced, stored in or introduced into a retrieval system, or transmitted in any form, or by any means (electronic, mechanical, photocopying, recording, or otherwise) without the prior written permission of the above copyright owner of this book or publisher.

This is a work of fiction. Names, characters, places, brands, media, and incidents are either the product of the author's imagination or are used fictitiously. The author acknowledges the trademarked statue and trademark owners of various products referenced in this work of fiction, which have been used without permission. The publication/use of these trademarks is not authorized, associated with, or sponsored by the trademark owners.

*To Ran, always.*

*And to all of my readers. This story has been a long time coming. Thank you for sticking with me.*

## ALSO BY MANDI BECK

**FU Hockey Series**

Sin Bin

Arena Lights

Sweater Weather

**Caged Love**

Love Hurts

Love Burns

**Wrecked Series**

Stoned

Rhythm

Sugar

**Cherry Falls Series**

1228 Wanderlust Lane

1026 Wild Way

**Standalone**

Twisted

*"Again."*

*- Herb Brooks*

# 1

## LEVI

Bodies. Wall-to-wall bodies. Writhing. Grinding. Leaning. Dancing bodies. Some in way fewer clothes than Boston in January calls for, but I am in no way complaining.

With a drink in hand, I make my way through the crowd to my kitchen.

"Yo, Sexton! What's up, my man?" Murphy James—my friend, roommate, and the best damn goalie in the division—greets me. "You see your sisters and their friends?" He bites down on one of his knuckles. Homeboy has it bad for my little sisters' best friend. As long as it's not Millie, I'll let him live. I'm already down one roommate who thought it would be cool to date one of my sisters. I can't handle any more of that shit right now.

"No. What the fuck are they even doing here? You invite them, or did Benny?"

The guilty-as-hell look on his face gives me my answer. "I might have told them they could come if they brought Raegan." He shrugs. "Figured Benny would have told Maeve anyway, though," Murph says, referring to our traitor roommate and my other sister.

"And did they?" I question. Shaking my head at his dumb ass and trying not to growl at the mention of Benny Hayes and Maeve. Clearly still a wicked-sensitive topic with me.

"Oh yeah. And some other chick. Wicked hot, bro. Never seen her before. Cubbie called dibs," Murphy tells me with a grin, knowing damn well that I don't give a fuck what Cubbie calls.

Topping off my *drink*—juice since I gotta be on the ice early—I slap him on the back and go to find my sisters. I know they're safer here in Hockey House than anywhere else on campus, but still. You put a bunch of drunk college boys together, then throw in a set of twins, and you're asking for fucking trouble. Shit goes down at these parties that I like to pretend my little sisters don't know about, let alone participate in. Definitely shit I don't want them to see *me* participating in.

I catch a flash of red hair in the sea of people in the living room and weave my way in that direction, stopping to say hi to people along the way. Some with high-fives and a clap on the back, others with a wink and a slap on the ass. I need to find my sisters and get them out of here. I'm catching serious fuck-me eyes from Nora and her friend. Can't for the life of me remember her name, but I do remember that she sucks dick like a porn star and that she and Nora are always up for a good time. With that in mind, I point at the ceiling and the bedrooms up there and mouth to Nora, "Later." I grin when she nods her head. Yeah, my sisters need to go. I don't care what Benny says. He can go with them.

After a few more minutes of searching and stopping, I finally find them in the yard by the bonfire that's making their red hair look like it's literally on fire. Coming up behind the pair, I tug on Millie's ponytail, only knowing it's her and not Maeve by the number ten on the back of her Fulton University hoodie. The twins are identical. I'm not even sure my mother can tell them apart. Mill whirls around, ready to fight until she sees it's me.

"Levi, you punk! I almost hit you," she says, shoving my shoulder.

"Wouldn't have hurt, short stack," I tease before going all serious older brother. "What are you doing here? Does Dad know?"

"Hi, Levi," Maeve says sweetly, squeezing me around the waist. Maeve is sugar, all sweet and pure, whereas Millie is cayenne pepper and just this side of evil, always getting them into some kind of trouble.

"Hey, Maevey. Dad and Mom know you're here?" I question since the evil twin isn't answering.

Plucking the red Solo cup out of Millie's hand, I bring it to my lips for a sip to make sure it's not alcohol. She flips me off when I hand it back to her, satisfied that it's the same juice I've been drinking.

"Just checking, Mill, can't have any underage drinking here." That earns an epic eye roll, but I don't care. They won't be drinking here or anywhere else on campus. They're nineteen, which doesn't really matter in college, but it sure as fuck does when you have an older brother at the same school.

"Daddy knows we're here. He said we could come, but when you said it was time, we had to go straight home."

Millie rolls her eyes again. "Dad wanted me to remind you to be in his office at six."

"Yeah, I'll be there." I nudge Maeve. "Where's your boy? He not showing his face because I blacked his eye?" I ask smugly. To say I didn't take it well when I found out my friend and roommate was dating my sister is the understatement of the fucking year. He had it coming, though, and he knew it. He broke rule one of Hockey House, Thou shall not fuck with the Sexton twins. I'm the only one of the roommates with younger sisters, so that rule was sacred and taken seriously until Benny got my sister in a different state and away from my watchful eye. Fucker. I asked him to keep an eye on them. He took it a little too fucking seriously.

"He's not hiding, you bully. He's at the pro shop working for another hour. I told him I'd wait here," Maeve tells me.

I nod and I'm just about to ask if they know what Dad wants when Raegan walks up with some smokin' hot chick I've never seen before. Must be the new girl. Her gaze lands on mine. Bored gray eyes take me in for a moment, giving me time to do the same to her. She's a little shorter than the twins, way shorter than Rae, who towers over her, probably five-four at the most. Her honey-colored hair is tied back with a black ribbon, giving her a sexy schoolgirl vibe. She's dressed casually, more like my sisters and less like most of the girls here. Her jeans have holes in the knees, and she has a long-sleeved Tennessee Arrows shirt on, the number eight etched right above her heart, teasing over an awesome rack. Girl's got curves for days. "Oh my god, Becky," I mumble under my breath as my gaze lands on her rounded hips, and I catch a glimpse of a perfect bubble ass when I crane my neck a bit to see around her.

There's a chorus of throat clearing that finally has me bringing my eyes back up to her face. An eyebrow raised, a look of utter disgust on her face, her nose crinkled with it making me notice the light splash of freckles there and across her cheeks. Somehow, they don't make her look like a toddler, the way I swear my sisters' freckles make them look. No, these are sexy. Adding to that schoolgirl thing.

"You're new," I say, ignoring my sisters shaking their heads at me from behind her. They obviously appreciated me checking out their friend as much as she did.

"And you're an asshole," the new girl with the killer rack spits out, calling my attention to her full lips and the beauty mark above her mouth, Marilyn Monroe style. She's a fucking smoke show.

"Nah, not an asshole, doll. Just a guy who appreciates great tits and a stellar ass." I smirk, enjoying it way too much that I'm pissing her off.

"Oh my god, Levi!" Maeve admonishes.

"Saffie, I am so sorry. My brother usually saves his disgustingness for when we're not around and definitely for his skanks and not our friends," Millie explains, glaring at me. I can feel it. I've still not looked away from their stupidly hot friend, the one who's still shooting daggers at me.

"Saffron Briggs, meet my dumbass brother, Levi Sexton."

That caused her to break eye contact long enough to roll her eyes. "Let me guess, you're 'Sexy Sexton.' The one I've unfortunately *heard* about?" My sisters make gagging noises. They hate that nickname and the stories that go with it. But the way she says it in that hot little Yankee clip she has going on, definitely not from Massachusetts, has me forgetting all about the pain-in-the-ass twins and thinking way too much about their friend and what kind of things I'd like to do to her.

I shrug and tuck my hands in the pockets of my sweats. "So you've heard about me, then? Want me to show you how I got that nickname?" I offer, goading her.

She scoffs and then smiles sweetly. "No thanks. You're not my type."

With raised eyebrows, I nod in understanding. "Ooooh, you're a lesbian. That's cool. I'm all about one love, bi-love, self-love. Whatever." I grin, flashing my dimples in added innocence, letting her know that her ice queen bitchy attitude doesn't faze me.

"Oh, I like boys just fine. And even girls occasionally. It's you I don't like," she retorts smugly. "Plus, I have a boyfriend." I watch as she pulls a chain from the collar of her shirt, a massive ring hanging from it.

"Is that a high school ring?" I ask, just barely holding back my laughter. She's cute when she's pissed, and her boyfriend is clearly lame as fuck. "Do guys still do that?"

Her glare is enough to light my ass on fire right where I stand, but I don't care. I don't care about the tool boyfriend, either. If I want her, the boyfriend is her problem, not mine. And Cubbie can fuck off calling dibs.

Murphy comes up just then, slapping me on the back, drawing my attention. He greets my sisters using their hated nickname. "Hey, Off-limits, you two behaving?

They give him a double eye roll and laugh him off. "Raegan, how about you? You being a good girl?"

Blushing at him, she just nods. Rae *is* a good girl. She's been my sisters' best friend since they were tiny kids and a constant in my home. Aside from her pink hair and being so tall, she and the twins might as well be triplets. They've been attached at the hip since kindergarten.

"Good, good." Murph booms before turning to Saffron- Saffie, as my sister called her, who still has me locked in an epic *I hate your guts but refuse to look away first* stare down.

"Who's your new friend, Sexy? She looks like she really likes you," he says, laughing.

"That's enough, you guys. Leave her alone," Millie snaps. "She's Raegan's cousin, her name is Saffie, she has a boyfriend, and you can go now." My sister dismisses and waves us off.

I bark out a laugh. "Cool it, short stack. Saffie can take care of herself. I'm not gonna bite. Much," I add, snapping my teeth at her and then grinning when she rolls her eyes at me again. Between the three of them, their eyes are gonna fall right out of their damn heads from all the rolling they've been doing.

Murphy chooses that moment to say, "Speaking of biting, Nora and her friend Ava are looking for you. I'll keep an eye on these four."

I bet he will. Actually, he, Cubbie, and Benny, even if he is on my shit list, are the only guys on campus I would ever trust with my sisters. Not because they have some stellar reputation or anything. They're not even close to being fucking saints, but they do have mad respect for me, and that carries over to Millie and Maeve. Benny may have fucked up, but I would've done more than blacked his eye if I didn't think he had good intentions regarding Maeve. It would have been the last time he looked at my sister, let alone dated her.

"Ladies, behave please and remember not to take drinks from anyone you don't know and to kick anyone getting handsy right in the fucking balls. That goes for your little boyfriend, too," I order, pointing a finger back and forth between them. My sisters and Raegan promise. Saffie doesn't say a thing. I wave and leave them with Murph, then go in search of Nora and her porn star friend. It'll take the two of them to get my mind off the new girl. Saffron Briggs. Even her name is hot.

ABOUT AN HOUR HAS PASSED, and we still haven't made it upstairs to my room because Nora wants to wait for another friend of theirs who is "just *dying* to meet me." Who am I to deny her?

Kicked back in my oversized chair, Nora is tucked into my side, kissing my neck, while Ava, with her back to me, grinds against my cock to the beat of the music booming loudly from our makeshift DJ. She could teach a thing or two to some strippers I've seen. I let my head fall back and allow my mind to shut down and my body to just feel. The minute my eyes drift closed, a wicked-hot blond with flashing gray eyes and a smart mouth appears behind my lids. I groan. Fucking hell. Fighting with Saffie was hot. I'm so used to sorority chicks and puck bunnies just looking to score a hockey player that a little hard to get might be fun. Not that I don't love easy, because I do. But a little game of chase me is something I can get down with.

My eyes pop open when I hear a snort to find the gray eyes I had just been thinking about glaring first at me, then flicking to the girls draped all across my lap.

I smirk at her anger. Why she's pissed, I don't know. Dimples flashing, I wink at her before closing my eyes again. Oh yeah. She's gonna be fun.

## 2

## LEVI

I hoist my hockey bag higher onto my shoulder and pull my hood over my head. The sun's not even up yet, but I have to stop at the athletic building to see my dad before I can lace up and hit the ice.

Walking down the dimly lit halls to his office is eerie as fuck. Quiet as hell, nothing but the squeak from my gym shoes against the polished floors.

Before I can knock on the doorframe of the open office, he waves me in. His phone is wedged between his head and shoulder.

"Yes, sweetheart, I'll tell him." With the term of endearment, I know he's talking to my mom.

"Hi, Ma!" I call out as I fall into the worn chair in front of his desk. My dad grins.

"She says good morning, Levi."

They talk for a few more minutes. Right before he disconnects, he promises her we'll both be home for dinner.

"Son, good morning. Sorry to drag your ass out of bed so early, but I have a meeting, so this won't take long."

He's not sorry.

"What's up with that? It's still dark out," I grumble.

"Oh, quit your bitching. I need a favor." He leans back in his chair and props his ankle across his knee. "I just picked up a new pitcher from St. Claire."

"Cutting it close with your season starting in a couple of months. Classes have already started. How are you pulling that off?" I ask, confused as to why he would make this move now. I assumed he was looking for next season when he was out scouting.

"I know, but I got a call from her coach, and with Stella out for the season, this is perfect. Plus, she's got a rocket. In all honesty, this is lucky as hell for us."

I don't comment on Stella being out since it's kind of my fault. Well, not my fault, but when the mentor the NHL sends to check on you knocks up the school's star pitcher... "So what do you need from me?" I push the hood off my head, all warmed up now that I'm inside.

He starts to tell me, then stops abruptly. "Is that a hickey on your neck?"

Grimacing, I nod. Fucking Nora ended up leaving hickeys all over my chest and neck before I realized what she was doing and could stop her.

"Your coach will hand you your ass if he sees that," my dad points out.

"I know it. I'm hoping with all my gear on he won't see."

"Serves you right if he does. Your mom isn't going to be thrilled either."

Groaning, I agree with him again. "I know she's not." Trying to steer the conversation away from the mess on my neck, I ask, "So what do you need from me?"

"Well, I can tell you what I don't need," he says pointedly. He drops his eyes to my neck and then looks back up at my face, a dry look and pursed lips driving his point home.

"You don't want me to let her give me hickeys. Got it."

He glares. "You still need to tutor someone for your work program, right?"

I nod.

"I need a tutor for my new pitcher. They're letting her start classes now, although they began last week. She's taking a couple of accelerated classes to make up for some credits that wouldn't transfer. She'll need help getting up to speed."

"Dad, my season is in full swing. I won't have time," I argue. I do not want to be stuck tutoring anyone right now. Especially some uppity chick from St. Claire.

My dad raises a hand to quiet me. "That's why this is perfect. She won't need in-depth tutoring, and she's an athlete, so she'll understand your hectic schedule."

What he says makes sense. At least I don't have to put in a ton of work because she's failing or anything. "What class?"

"She's a sports medicine major like you so it's right up your alley."

I'm a double major—sports medicine and business. My class schedule is ridiculous, but my dad was adamant that I finish my degree before I enter the NHL. He didn't care that I was a first-round draft pick going into my freshman year here. Picked up by Chicago, I'll be heading there right after graduation in a few months to begin my career. Exciting and scary as fuck. I've only gotten better in my time here. Fulton University has one of the best hockey programs in the US. I've grown as a player here more than I ever thought possible. Cocky shit that I was, I thought I couldn't possibly get any better. I was wrong.

My dad cuts into my thoughts. "Anatomy. She had to drop the class last semester so she's taking accelerated A&P. Tough class on a regular schedule. Just help her to stay on track and make sure she doesn't struggle while she's trying to get acclimated to the new school, the new team. I know you already took it, so it shouldn't be a problem, right?"

I want to give him some smart-ass answer about anatomy

being my jam and not to worry, but I don't want another lecture this early in the morning, so I just nod.

"Good. And, Levi, I'm serious. Keep it in your damn pants. Don't think I don't know about you and Peta, Violet, Chandra, Ruby, and the rest of my fucking team." He's giving me the evil dad eye. I shrug sheepishly and grin at him. "You hockey players need to stay away from my softball players."

"What can I say? Your ladies love us."

He's not amused. "In your pants, Levi."

"Okay. Okay. So who is this totally off-limits star pitcher of yours?" I ask. Slouching down farther into the comfortable seat, I contemplate a nap.

He opens his mouth to answer when there's a light tap on the door. "Here she is now. Right on time."

I turn in my seat just as my dad says, "Saffron Briggs, meet Levi, your new tutor."

# 3

# SAFFIE

"You have got to be fucking kidding me." Oh shit. Did I just say that out loud? Shit. Shit. Shit. The look on Coach's face tells me I did indeed. He sits back in his chair somewhat deflated and pinches the bridge of his nose. "So you've met?" he asks with a sigh.

My eyes bounce back to Levi and his stupid cocky grin and roaming eyes, then back to Coach. "Sorry, Coach," I mumble, stepping fully into the office, taking the empty seat next to Levi that Coach gestures toward. He looks even more unhappy about this than I am.

"Hey there, Saffie. Long time no see," Levi says and then winks at me. He's really got a fucking winking problem.

"Not long enough," I sneer, then smile fakely.

Coach interrupts our stare down. "When did the two of you meet? And please tell me that's not where those came from," he says, pointing at the gross hickeys on Levi's neck.

"Absolutely not!" I shake my head emphatically. No way was I taking the blame for that mess. "We met at a party last night. This"—I waggle my fingers in disgust at his neck—"had zero to do with me, Coach. I can promise you that." The older man looks relieved. Levi snorts out a laugh.

"Just because you like girls." His lip pulls up in a smirk.

I huff. "No. Because you're not my type, and even if you were, I have a boyfriend and more respect for myself than to get mixed up with a player like you."

"You know what they say, right? Hate the game, not the player." He winks again. I'm pretty sure he has something in his stupid even-if-they-are-a-pretty-blue-color eyes.

"Um, I believe the only people saying that are actual players. But whatever." I don't know why I'm even engaging. He's infuriating.

"You two done now?" Coach asks. "I have a meeting to get to."

Levi smiles at me and says, "Not even close, Dad." Never breaking eye contact, I answer at the same time, "Yes." But then it sinks in. He called him dad. Shit. Why didn't I put two and two together? I knew that the twins were his kids. I must have blocked out the fact that he was related to them. Shoot me now.

"Saffron, clearly my son has made an impression on you, but I promise he will be on his best behavior while he's your tutor," Coach tells me, his tone stern.

"Sir, with all due respect. Isn't there anyone else?" There's a hint of desperation in my voice.

"You scared?" Levi taunts.

"Of you? Hardly. I just don't like spending my time with people I don't like."

"Because you like girls."

"For the love of…I don't like girls. Well, I do. I have. Oh my god, just shut up," I hiss, face flaming with absolute embarrassment. I not only just admitted to him but also to my coach that I've experimented with girls. Fuck this day. I mean, he coaches girls softball, so I'm sure experimenting is not new to him... but still.

"Coach clears his throat. "That's enough, Levi." Not that his asshole son cares. No. He's just sitting there grinning at me and my flushed face. He's getting off on this, I know it.

"Maybe she should be the one tutoring me. She seems to be an expert on anatomy."

I grit my teeth. I'm going to kill him. Beat him over the head with my favorite bat.

"Saffron," Coach says gently. "Forgive me. His mother and I really did raise him to be a gentleman." I slow blink the man, which causes him to smother a smile. I slow blink him once more. I'm pretty sure they failed. He clears his throat, swallowing what I'm certain is a laugh. "Levi will be able to get you all caught up and has a schedule and work ethic as grueling as yours. You'll work well together. I'm sure of it. And if he keeps giving you shit, let me know, and I'll tell his mom." His smile comes easily.

Groaning, I slump back in my seat. This is happening. There's no way around it. Suck it up, Briggs. You can handle one cocky jock who thinks you like girls because he can't possibly fathom the alternative. That you're just not interested in him and his stupid dimples. And now I'm giving myself a mental pep talk after five minutes in his presence. This is going to be a nightmare.

"Okay, Coach," I agree. Out of the corner of my eye, I catch the sly grin lighting up Levi's smug face and ignore it. And him.

"Good girl. Levi, you and Saffron figure out your schedules. Classes start back up on Monday. Make it happen," he commands as he stands. "Briggs, I'll see you at practice in about an hour. Levi, I'll see you at home for dinner before your game."

Levi nods. "Yes, sir."

We shuffle out of the office. Coach locks up behind us and

heads deeper into the athletic building toward the meeting he said he had. That leaves just Levi and me, standing there, him smiling and me glaring.

"What are you smiling at?" Why? Why do I hate him so much? Because I know him. His type. Total jock, manwhore, campus stud. Thinks he's God's gift and he can do anything he wants because he's Levi "Sexy" Sexton. Well, he can keep thinking that. It's not happening here. I'm not going to be one of the girls he's used to.

"Am I smiling?" he asks in mock innocence. "I didn't realize." Lifting his bag higher onto his shoulder, he smiles wider. No, not smiles, that's too innocent a word. What he's doing is cocky. Wicked. Dirty. It's all there in the playful, flirty lift of his full lip. Just the corner lifted makes him look like a modern-day freaking Elvis or something. Practically breathing fire now, I move to pass him, but he grabs my elbow, stopping me.

"You gonna give me your number or what, Briggsy?" His tone is gruff, but I can hear the teasing in it.

"You wish." I smirk. Take that, *Sexy*. Bet he's never heard that before. "And don't call me Briggsy." He's got some balls asking me for my number.

Running a hand over his lightly stubbled jaw, he watches me. Probably can't believe all his hockey boy charm still isn't working on me.

"Okay. Do you want mine, then?"

"Yeah, no," I deadpan.

"Gonna be pretty hard to tutor you if we don't get our schedules straight. I mean, we can give it a shot. You can just come to the rink and find me most days, but I'm sure you have better things to do than follow me around and wait for me to be available." He pauses dramatically. "Like your girlfriend."

"I. Don't. Have. A. Girlfriend." I seethe, just short of stomping my foot.

"Ahhhh, that's right. A boyfriend." Levi raises a finger as if he's remembering something important. "An Ivy League boyfriend." He whistles between his teeth. "Fancy, just like you."

"You're so obnoxious."

"Am not," he insists.

"Are too!" I counter until I realize he's playing me, and I just fell right into his trap.

He grins, causing a dimple to pop in his cheek, which does nothing but make my eyes narrow even more. Stupid dimples.

"So how about it, Briggsy? Am I calling you, or are you calling me?"

I refuse to give him my number on principle now. "Get my number from one of your sisters," I mutter, turning on my heel and stalking away as he stands there laughing at me. Fuck Levi Sexton and his stupid dimples.

# 4

## LEVI

God, she hates me. It shouldn't make me so happy but fuck me if it doesn't.

Chuckling to myself, I hurry toward the rink for practice. Suddenly being up this early isn't so bad.

The music is loud as fuck, blasting from the speakers around the locker room. The minute I hear the song, I know we're listening to Murphy's playlist today. He's the only motherfucker our age who listens to opera. Goalies are crazy superstitious, and when he was a kid, his coach played the shit before every game. He told them it was to keep them focused, and therefore, they'd be less likely to get injured and more likely to play to the best of their abilities. So Murph being the superstitious fuck that he is, listens every time he takes the ice. Loudly. If it's not his turn to control the music, he has his earbuds firmly in place. I won't admit it to him, but I've developed a fondness for the Three Tenors over the years we've played together.

Making my way around the team logo in the center of the floor, I stop in front of my locker and watch Murphy use his yellow bottle of powder as a mic. Eyes closed, he belts out the song that I won't even attempt to name in a respectable tenor. There are nine of us in the room, and we're all watching him, enthralled and a little horrified. Giving him an audience is never a good idea but come on! The guy is actually standing here singing to his ass and ball powder. I'm not sure if we're horrified about the mic choice or the fact that he's in nothing but a jock strap. Both are a straight-up tragedy.

He finishes with a bow and a flash of bare ass before going back to the rest of his crazy routine.

"What's up, Sexton?" my boy Jack calls from his stall across from mine. "Heard you had a party last night. I was worried you would come stumbling in late today." He snickers.

Pulling my hoodie over my head and hanging it on the hook, I glance over at him. "Nah, you know better than that." I grin, toeing off my gym shoes. "No hangover from too much pussy."

"Fucker," Jack huffs out.

"I did. All three of them." I brag as I drop my sweats. Laughing, he flips me off with a shake of his head.

Decker kills the music. "You mean three all day yesterday right? Like one in the morning and then one after class..."

"No, three at one time," Murphy answers. "Nora brought Ava with her and then their friend Jessica showed up. This asshole hit the fucking trifecta."

"Ava, she's the one who gives head like a porn star, right?" Jack asks a little wistfully.

Out of the eleven of us now in the room, nine of us nod our heads in agreement and appreciation. Benny is smarter than he looks and refrains from agreeing, although I know for a fact that he has firsthand knowledge. He probably doesn't want me to hit him again.

"Then his little sisters brought over fresh meat." Murphy,

the gossip, laughs. "Poor Cubbie called dibs, but I think Sexy will be overriding that shit."

"Speaking of the fresh meat, guess who gets to tutor the new girl?" I wait for them to put two and two together, cinching the waist of my hockey pants while they stare.

"Fuck you!" Murphy bursts. "How did that happen?"

"My dad. She's his new pitcher."

"You have a horseshoe up your ass. You know that, right?" Jack shakes his head in disgust.

"I'm gonna need it. She hates me," I admit, smiling at the thought.

This makes them all let loose. Laughing, whistling, and just being dicks.

"Wait. A chick who hates Sexy?" No way, man," Isaiah Decker says.

I'm about to tell them all to go fuck themselves when Coach Kiehn walks in.

"Are there strippers in here no one told me about? You fellas sure are chipper this morning." He blows on his ever-present mug of coffee. I've seen more of those mugs go flying in the past couple of years than I can count. He must have a stash of them somewhere. You'd think he'd use travel mugs or something that wouldn't shatter. I think he likes the sound of them breaking, to be honest. "Get your asses on the ice. I haven't had enough coffee for this happy happy joy joy bullshit from you guys," Coach grumbles as he ambles out.

Coach Kiehn is a bear in the morning. Hell, he's a bear all the fucking time. But he's the best coach in the NCAA, so we deal happily with his cranky ass.

"Let's go, boys!" I call out, following Coach with my helmet in hand. Brushing my hair back, I slip it on and fasten the cage. Morning skates before a game are pretty laid-back, but as the captain, I have to make sure we all show up. That we're here, and we mean business.

AFTER TWO HOURS of practice and three classes, I'm starving. I haul ass to my parents' for dinner, hoping my ma has everything ready. My game isn't until eight, but I have to be laced up by six for all the pregame bullshit.

"Mom, I'm home!"

"In here, Levi," she calls from the kitchen. Where the hell else would she be? I swear she sleeps standing up in front of the stove.

With my laundry in hand, I drop the bag in the mudroom on my way to the kitchen.

"Smells good, Ma," I tell her, pecking her cheek before I sit down at the island.

"Thanks, baby." She smiles at me over her shoulder.

"Whatcha makin'?"

"It's game night, so I made baked chicken parmesan with pasta and a nice salad. In fact, grab it out of the fridge and put it on the table please."

My mother's domain is the kitchen. She rules in here like a drill sergeant. With her red hair, matching my sisters', pulled back in a high ponytail, and her bright and cheery apron, she looks all sweet and innocent. More like my older sister than my mom. But dip your finger in her pot or be late to her table and she'll let that Irish temper fly.

I'm putting the last plate on the table just as the twins and my dad walk in. Raegan and to my delight, Saffie, are right behind them. A smile creeps over my face at her scowl upon seeing me. My grin slips a little when my dad catches my attention with a warning glare.

"Madeline, I've brought company," my father announces.

My mom turns from the stove, where she's pulling out a massive pan of chicken and baked pasta. "Hey, Rae," she greets before turning. "You must be the cousin, Saffron." My mom smiles invitingly.

"Yes, ma'am." Even now, her soft voice has a hint of underlying Yankee bitch that I dig for some reason. A little bit of ice queen and lord knows I love me some ice.

Sexy. As. Fuck.

"Girls, Dan, go get cleaned up. Levi and I will finish up here," my mom orders as she brings the bubbling pan to the table.

I watch the sway of Saffron's ass as she leaves the room. This girl has the most amazing ass.

"Levi." My mom's tone is harsh.

"Yeah, Ma?" I turn my grin on her, letting my dimples go to work.

"Don't 'yeah Ma' me. Your dad already told me you acted a fool with Saffron earlier today." She points a finger at me. "Best behavior at my dinner table, Levi. Not kidding."

The warning leaves no room for argument or wiggle room for me to charm her out of it. Let's just hope my hoodie stays in place and she doesn't see my neck, or she'll really kick my ass.

Mimicking Saffie, I say sweetly, "Yes, ma'am." She swats my arm, trying to hold back a smile. Clearly, she can't stay mad at me for long.

The girls and my dad file back into the room and take their seats at the table. My sisters, being the smart little shits that they are, make sure Saffie sits between them so I can't sit next to her. Millie flashes me an impish grin along with the bird, hurriedly busying her hands when my mom turns back to the table.

"This all looks amazing, Miss Madeline," Raegan praises. "I love game night."

"It does, ma. Thank you," I agree, kissing her cheek before taking my seat next to Raegan and right across from her cousin.

Her cousin won't meet my eyes even though I know she feels mine on her. The harder she works to ignore me, the harder I'm going to make it for her to do so.

Plates are passed and filled. The twins and Rae never stop with their chatter about this chick saying this, and this one cheating on that one, and the next party and on and on and on. I don't even pretend to try to keep up or pay too much attention until my mom speaks up.

"Maeve, is Benny not coming? You did invite him, didn't you?"

I mask my snort of disgust with an appreciative hum around a mouthful of chicken. Maeve isn't fooled, though, and glares.

"I did, Ma. He said thank you, but he didn't think you would appreciate breaking up a fight in the middle of your dining room."

"A fight? Who is going to fight?" my mother asks, glancing around the table. Shit. No doubt my sisters are about to rat my ass out, and my ma is gonna be pissed.

"Why don't you ask your precious, Levi?" Millie taunts. I knew it would be her. Even as mad as Maeve was with me, she still wouldn't snitch.

"Levi Daniel Sexton, you didn't!" My mother just busted out my full government name, and she only does that when she means business. There's no getting out of this one.

As nonchalantly as I can, I take a sip of my water to give myself a moment to collect my thoughts since it's obvious my dad, the only other man in the damn room, isn't coming to my rescue. The traitor. "I did. He had it coming, Ma. There's a code among friends and roommates and especially teammates, and he broke it." I shrug. "Blame him, not me." A muttered expletive comes from the other side of the table. Glancing at the twins, I see Maeve's flushed face, Millie's gleeful expression, and the look of utter disgust on Saffron's face, and I know immediately where it came from.

"A code, Levi? That's ridiculous." Mom huffs.

"Totally ridiculous," Millie quips. The brat.

"I think it's kind of sweet," Raegan says, patting my back. "A little caveman-y but still sweet."

Finally, someone's on my side. I smile at Rae in thanks. "You're my favorite."

"I know." She nods and goes back to her food. I'm just about to do the same, hoping to put an end to this whole thing, when Millie opens her snitching-ass mouth again.

"Poor Benny. I'll be surprised if he's even able to see out of his eye at the game tonight." Her tone is syrupy sweet and total bullshit. She's punishing me for sending Benny as a chaperone on their little trip in the first place. As if him dating Maeve isn't punishment enough.

"Oh, Levi! He's your friend."

"Still is. He's just my friend with a black eye who is now dating my sister and therefore subject to more ass beatings if I think he needs them." I point my fork at my ma. "This is all your fault anyway. You raised me to look after them and be the best big brother in the whole world. Well, this is me being big bro." Knowing that will give her something to think about, I go back to chewing, narrowing my eyes at my Judas of a father for not coming to my defense. He knows it too because he shrugs and gives me a "sorry not sorry" face.

Thankfully, that's that, and Mom moves on. "So Saffron, the girls tell me that you came from Connecticut."

"Yes, ma'am," she says softly. "My dad died, and my mom is moving here to be closer to my aunt, Raegan's mother, and to my grammy.

"You didn't want to stay at your school?" my mom questions, curious.

"I did, but Fulton offered me a full scholarship. I only had a partial scholarship at my school, and with my dad passing away, tuition was going to be tough." There's a sadness in her tone that makes me feel bad for giving her such a hard time. But then she goes and ruins it in her very next breath. "My boyfriend isn't too happy about the move. He misses me being so close by," she says, finally meeting my eyes. That last bit was for my benefit, no doubt.

"Oh, I bet he does," I murmur loud enough for her to hear.

Saffie stops glaring at me when my mom speaks in a gentle tone. "I'm very sorry for your loss." Her sympathy-laced voice reminds me that this girl just had her world rocked.

"Me too," I offer sincerely.

She nods in thanks, forking a bite of pasta into her mouth.

"So what school were you at back home?" My mom continues with her game of twenty questions. I'm grateful for her doing all the legwork for me. "I don't remember Dan saying, only that you are one hell of a pitcher and he got lucky. Especially with Stella being out."

I ignore the heat of my sisters glare boring into the side of my face at the mention of Stella. They act like it's my fault she and Jason hooked up and made a little Dagger! Seems like my mom and Raegan are the only women at the table who don't want me dead.

"St. Claire," Saffron answers once she's swallowed her food.

"Great school. Expensive," my mom acknowledges.

"Very. But the softball program is so much better at Fulton, so that's a huge plus." I'm not sure who she's trying to convince, my mom or herself.

"Madeline, let the girl eat. We don't have long before the game." My dad cuts in, sparing Saffie.

"You're all going?" I'm fishing. My family very rarely misses a game unless the twins are also playing. What I really want to know is if Saffie is coming along.

Raegan leans into me, putting all of her weight into it. "God, you weigh a ton!" She puffs out when she isn't able to budge me. "Of course, we're all going. My cousin has never been to a college hockey game. Can you believe that?"

My gaze falls to Saffie's bent head. I have a hard time thinking of her as Saffron. It sounds way too serious for a college student. "That true? How is that even possible?"

She shrugs, chewing and swallowing before rolling her eyes like I'm slow. "St. Claire's doesn't have a hockey team."

"Is it an all-girls school?"

"No. We just don't have a hockey team."

"Your boyfriend play any sports?" I take a bite of my pasta, licking a bit of sauce from my bottom lip. Grinning when I watch her eyes fall to my mouth and watch even after my tongue retreats. Her eyes narrow like she's just realized she was watching me with something other than dislike.

I cock a brow, "Let me guess, Quarterback? Frat boy?"

Maeve nudges my foot under the table. I ignore her.

"No. Golf. And not a frat boy, but he is Alpha Phi Alpha. The president actually," she says smugly as if that would shut me up. Put me in my place or impress me. It doesn't. Not even close.

"So a huge douche. Not just a normal one. Got it," I say, shoveling a bite of food in my mouth.

"Levi," my mom reprimands. "Leave her alone. It's refreshing to see a girl who doesn't fall all over herself the second you flash those dimples." Whose side is she on?

"It's okay, Mrs. Sexton. He's not used to it, either. Having to actually try to get my attention is making him act out, I think." Saffie joins forces with my traitor of a mother.

I glance up at my dad, hoping to catch a break there. No dice. He's enjoying this as much as the rest of the traitors at the table.

With a smirk, I push back from the table and stand. "Oh, you guys thought I was trying? That's cute." I chuckle. "Trust me, if I try, she'll know." Winking at an ever-glaring Saffie, I kiss my mom on the head, taking my plate to the sink. "See you all tonight," I call, whistling as I stroll out the front door, knowing that it will kill her that I got in the last word. Damn uppity ice queen. It'll be so fucking fun making her melt.

# 5

## SAFFIE

I'd rather be a million other places than in line for this hockey game. After the scene at the Sexton's house, I couldn't even bow out gracefully without them, and especially him, knowing he had gotten to me. Ugh, he's such an asshole. Something inside me must love fighting with him. I'm not sure what or why. It's exhilarating in a way, though. And just like that, I'm pissed at myself for allowing him to affect me in any way at all. I'm not this person. I don't let guys like Levi get to me. Must be all the stress of the move and transfer. Being away from home and Landon. Landon. Just thinking about him makes me smile. Taking out my phone, I shoot him a quick text while we stand in line, waiting to get into the arena. Knowing he won't respond during his class, I slip the phone back into my hoodie pocket and shuffle forward with the rest of the crowd.

"Is it always like this?" I ask Raegan, glancing around at the hordes of people slowly making their way toward the entrance.

"Hockey is life here," my cousin responds. The twins glance at us over their shoulders, nodding in agreement.

"It's true. You know how towns in the South shut down

when there's a football game? That's how we are when the Fire plays. It's like a religion," Maeve says with a little shrug.

"Really?" I don't get it. I mean, hockey isn't my thing, granted, but…I don't get it. Maybe I'm just bitter because hockey is, in fact, Levi's thing. Looking around, I see that they're not exaggerating. People are dressed in head-to-toe Fire paraphernalia. Painted faces, big foam #1 fingers in red or black, hats with flames sprouting from the top, and more than one shirt with Sexton across the back. Bewildered, I turn back to Rae. "They know it's just hockey, right?" The horrified look on her face causes me to sputter a laugh.

"You bite your damn tongue, Saffron Briggs. Just wait. You'll see once you get in there," she tells me confidently.

Whatever. I'd rather be watching Landon play golf, which is literally the most boring sport to watch. Raegan links arms with me, dragging me along as the line finally starts moving. "No worries, cousin, you'll get used to things here. And these hockey boys are pretty to look at." She bumps my shoulder and smiles when I make a little gagging noise. "Come on, wait till you see our seats. They're wicked!" Rae says excitedly. "Mr. Sexton likes to sit right on the glass. He has season tickets for us plus a couple of extra for when Levi's agent or whoever is in town. You see everything up close." She's practically bouncing, and as much as she says it's about the pretty hockey boys, I know it's her love for the game. She's played since she was little and is here at FU on a full hockey scholarship. She loves hockey as much as I love softball. I can't help but grin at her excitement.

After about thirty minutes, we make it to our seats. Raegan wasn't kidding. Even I can admit that they're amazing. We move along the glass, stopping when we hit our designated chairs. Once there, none of us sits, though. Our gazes focus on the players on the ice, whizzing by us in a red, white, and black blur. Raegan leans into me, her arm extended. "There's Levi, number thirty-one."

I shove her arm down. "Oh my god, Rae. Don't point." She looks at me and bursts out laughing.

"My bad." Her tone is amused as she looks at me like I'm half crazy. I am. I don't know why. It's him. He makes me stupid. I hate it. I also hate how good he looks on the ice in his uniform. He's tall as it is, but on skates...he's a giant. A broad-shouldered giant with sand-colored hair licking at the back of his helmet. Not that I noticed. As if he can feel my eyes on him, he glances in our direction. Even through the cage covering his face, I can see the flash of white teeth and disarming dimples. Of their own accord, my eyes roll and then narrow. At this rate, I'll be dizzy from all this damn eye-rolling. It's completely involuntary. Millie leans across Raegan, bringing my attention to her instead of the pain in the ass on the ice.

"We're going to go grab drinks and snacks. You stay here in case we aren't back before the game starts. You don't want to miss the intro! It's wicked cool." Motioning for Raegan to follow, the trio goes off leaving me to watch the skaters as they take shots at their goalie who I think is Murphy, though I'm not positive. It's super hard to tell with all of the equipment.

Coach Sexton doesn't sit. He stands at the glass, arms folded across his chest watching Levi intently. It gives me a little pang, reminding me of my dad. He never missed a single one of my games. He was die hard. A baseball player himself most of his life, he never had a son to follow in his footsteps, but I was happy to fill the space as best I could with softball. He loved it. Loved me. With tears pricking, I shake off the emotions and swing my gaze back to the players. I've seen Raegan play around in the yard with her dad, but we moved away before she started playing on an actual team or anything. The way these guys move is crazy. They're like fluid motion. They make it look so effortless. I'm kind of impressed. I wouldn't think that guys this big could be so graceful.

A horn blares, and the players file off the ice into a tunnel, the lights dimming as they do. People scurry onto the ice they just vacated, pushing huge...things. I have no clue what they are or what purpose they serve. Minutes tick by as more and more people shuffle onto the ice pushing large equipment into place in front of the doorway that the players had disappeared through just moments ago. I glance questioningly over at Coach, who still hasn't sat down. He smiles.

"Flame throwers."

At my startled expression, he laughs. "You'll see." As he says this, the arena goes completely black seconds before the jumbotron lights up in a countdown. The crowd chants along.

"Ten...Nine...Eight...Seven..." The numbers flick across the screen in succession. When they hit one, the arena explodes. Literally. Fireworks and flames light up the darkness from the ice to the rafters. Inside. Fireworks and fire. Inside the building. These people are fucking crazy. The flames dance across the shiny surface of the ice at the same time sparks fall from the ceiling, lighting up the space. I'm not sure where to look first. I'm not entirely sure the whole place isn't going to burn down. I mean, who does this?

*Light 'em up* starts playing, drawing my attention to the show and the pyrotechnics still happening on the ice. I almost miss the flashing of faces across the jumbotron. I smile a little when I recognize Murphy, who I sort of like. But my smile slips when Levi's dimpled face appears, bringing with it a rise in cheers and screams from around the arena. And there go my eyes, rolling around in my head like they're not even attached. Hockey player after hockey player lights up the screen, and while some get a louder response than others, none get the kind of response Levi did.

The flames get higher, the crowd louder, and then the

music stops. Everyone stands, whistling and cheering as the announcer starts introducing the players. One by one, he calls their names, and they come flying out of the tunnel through a canopy of flames. I'm waiting for one of them to catch fire.

"Annnnnd last but not least, captain of your Fulton University Fire number thirty onnnneeeeee Levvvviiii Sexxxttonnnn." He drags it out as the stadium goes absolutely insane. The entire place and everyone in it, including the twins and Raegan, who just got back to their seats, and is right this moment jabbing me with her bony ass elbow, erupts in deafening cheers. I turn to glare at her, but her smile is so bright I can't bring myself to do it. Does she like him? Oh god no. She can't. Can she? Deciding that there's no way, I lean in and shout.

"Isn't this a bit much? I mean, its college, not the NHL." I'm truly baffled. I mean, flamethrowers?

She moves closer and speaks louder so that I can hear her over the crowd.

"Maybe, but a few of these guys will go on to play in the minors if not the NHL like Levi."

I guess I didn't realize he was that big of a deal. Which is silly because since I've been here at Fulton, I've heard so much talk about him going pro. I must just have blocked it out.

The guys are all lined up on the blue line, except for Murphy who is standing a little ways apart from them and facing his goal. Everyone goes quiet and stands as skaters help a girl onto the ice to sing the national anthem. My cousin hisses, "Bitch," under her breath, and that's when I notice that the singer is, in fact, one of the girls who were all over Levi at his party.

"Nora," Raegan informs me, "or as we like to call her 'Whore-a. And not because she sleeps around but because she's so freaking nasty to everyone without a dick.'"

I can't help but laugh. My cousin isn't usually so hateful. She must *really* feel some type of way about this chick. The lighting in the arena changes, and the jumbotron turns into an American flag as Nora belts out a surprisingly beautiful rendition of the anthem. On her way off the ice, she blows a kiss Levi's way. There's no stopping my eyes from taking a trip around my skull, much the same as the twins can't stop their gagging noises, I'm guessing. The moment her feet are off the ice, the guys burst from where they were standing, making a circle against the glass before getting into position for the puck drop.

When Levi glides past, he taps a fist to his dad's through the glass with a little nod. Once he does, Coach sits down for the first time since we entered the stadium. It must be their thing, and I hate to admit it, but it makes me not want to punch Levi quite so much.

Seconds after that, the game starts and just like everyone else in the place, I'm riveted by the players flying around the ice like they run on jet fuel. Sticks clacking against each other as they fight for the puck in one of the corners. I jump a little when one of the guys is slammed into the glass in front of me by a player on the Fire. The twins beat on the glass in encouragement. Tiny little red headed savages. Not that my cousin is any better screaming out "Yeah! Put him into the boards, Fish! Don't take that shit from him!" Jesus. They're all a bunch of bloodthirsty animals. I'm not sure if I should be afraid of them or what.

By intermission, my nerves are shot, and I'm having a hard time sitting in my seat. I'm not sure if I love it or hate it. The game is tied. One player from the other team has been evicted for fighting, and Murphy had the wind knocked out of him by some asshat who obviously needs to be wearing figure skates since he doesn't know how to make a hockey stop, according to Raegan. I must agree because I just yelled at him to get some figure skates.

"This is the last period. They have to pull it together. We

can't lose to this team," Maeve says, passing her popcorn my way. Her eyes follow her man's movements as he goes back to the bench.

"We don't like them?" Three sets of eyes land on me the second the question leaves my mouth.

"We *hate* them," Millie says.

If it's one thing I can understand, it's sports rivalries. You don't even need a reason.

Mrs. Sexton pats her back and smiles. How she's still sitting there calmly, I don't know. Coach too. Although he's had some moments where I thought he was going to storm onto the ice and give the refs hell. They excuse themselves to go speak to someone a couple of aisles over, telling us to stay out of trouble before they move through the crowd.

Munching my popcorn, I watch the activity on the ice. The mascot, a giant flame, skates in front of the Zamboni, tossing shirts over the glass and acting like the driver is going to run him down. I've never seen a college sport get as much hype as this. I mean, this is the kind of stuff you see at pro games, not that I've seen any of those, really. It all just seems crazy. Beside me, my cousin groans. I look over, startled. "You okay?"

"Don't look now, but here comes Whore-a."

"Oh my god, you have got to stop calling her that. I'm going to slip and say it in front of her."

We laugh at the thought, the twins casting curious glances our way. "I'll tell you later," Rae says just as the pretty girl with the killer voice comes and stands in front of us.

"Raegan, you actually look like a girl today!" she says in a condescendingly sweet tone.

What the hell? I glance over to see if my cousin is going to set this chick straight. Face flat of any emotion, she says, "Not everyone has to wear their baby sister's clothes and clown makeup to get noticed, Nora." Nice, Rae.

Nora glares at her and then sets her beady-ass eyes on me.

"You're new." That's it. Not a hello or a welcome or an *anything* even remotely friendly.

"Aren't you astute?" I can tell she has no idea what the hell the word means.

"Levi invited her," Millie adds.

Nothing like hitting the girl when she's down and still trying to figure out what I just said to her.

I'm just about to correct Millie when Nora scoffs. "Her? I doubt it." Flipping her silky hair over her shoulder, she looks down her narrow nose at me. "He sure didn't mention you when I was with him last night," Nora says smugly.

"Oh, so you're the class act who left hickeys all over his neck."

"Gotta do what you gotta do to let everyone know he's not available," she says it so smugly, like it's something to be proud of.

"If you have to mark up your man to keep him from fucking around on you, you can have him."

"He's not my *man*." She sneers, digging herself a deeper hole for me to take advantage of. I'm guessing she didn't think about that before she said it.

I tilt my head and give her a questioning look. "Ohhhhhh, I get it. You want him to be, but he won't, so you have to stake a claim any way you can and hope that it will at least slow him down from sleeping with other girls." I nod like it all makes perfect sense. She's seething. I lean in, my face pulled into a fake grimace, "Just a heads-up, it won't slow him down."

Before Nora can come up with a response, which I would have loved to hear, Coach and his wife come back to their seats, and the guys start to file back onto the ice and get into place for the puck drop. "Better go take a seat, the game's about to start again," I say sweetly.

"Take several." My cousin calls after Nora as she storms off in a huff. I can't help but laugh.

"God, she's awful." That's met with head nods from not only the twins and Raegan but also Mr. and Mrs. Sexton. Seems like nobody's a fan of Whore-a. Well, except for Levi, but that doesn't surprise me in the least. Takes one to know one, I guess.

Just as I'm thinking that, the man himself is thrown into the glass right in front of me. The whistle blows, and Levi looks up at the exact moment I instinctively put a hand to the swaying barrier. It looks as if I'm reaching out to touch him, make sure he's all right. I'm so not, but of course he catches it and winks at me before skating off after the puck. He's lighting the lamp, which I learned means scoring, before I can even snatch my hand away from the glass.

The crowd erupts around me, everyone on their feet except for me. This time when Levi glides by to tap his dad's fist through the glass, he blows me a kiss and I think the whole thing between them is a whole lot less sweet.

## 6

## LEVI

Fresh from the shower, I walk into my bedroom, rubbing a towel over my head and across my chest before draping it around my neck. I go over to my desk where my phone is pinging and pick it up.

> 860-555-1212: I need to borrow a book
>
> Levi: Who is this?

I'M PRETTY sure I know who it is. I don't get too many texts from people asking me for books.

> 860-555-1212: Saffie

I was right. Must have killed her to ask one of my sisters or Rae for my number.

> Levi: Hey Briggsy. Knew you'd get my number somehow

> 860-555-1212: I just need a book.

I can pick up on her ice queen thing even through text.

> Levi: What book?

> 860-555-1212: Anatomy.

> Levi: The Kama Sutra?

I wish I could see her face right now. I palm my cock. Nothing else to do, so I might as well take advantage of the hard-on fucking with her gives me.

> 860-555-1212: If you need a picture book…

So she's got jokes.

> Levi: Some people are more visual.

> 860-555-1212: Forget it. I'll find another tutor.

> Levi: Calm down, Briggsy. I'm on my way to practice, and I can drop it by your dorm after. Is it the atlas book?

> 860-555-1212: I have practice, and yes, the atlas one.

> Levi: I'll bring it by there then. On the field or in the basement?

THEY HAVE a setup in the basement of the athletic building with batting cages and enough space for pitching and fielding drills. They can do just about anything but play an actual game down there.

> 860-555-1212: Basement. We'll be done around 7.

> Levi: I'll see you there.

SHE DOESN'T REPLY, not that I figured she would. She's a girl of few words, and it kills her to have to talk to me.

Looking at the time, I try to decide what the fuck I'm going to do with this hard-on. Knowing I don't have time to call anyone to take care of it without being late for practice, I groan in frustration as I head back to the bathroom for a cold shower. I don't even have time to rub one out. This chick is gonna be a pain in my ass. Fun, but still a pain.

∼

I SLIP QUIETLY into the basement training center, careful not to let the door make any noise behind me. My dad will kick my ass if I disrupt his practice. Making my way across the bright green Astro-Turf, I slide onto the bleachers scanning the space for Saffron. My gaze sweeps over the girls milling about, most of whom I've fucked around with, until my eyes settle on the hot piece of ass on the pitcher's mound. Saffron Briggs is wearing black spandex pants, a flame dancing up the side of her leg, a white tee with the sleeves ripped off, and a red sports bra playing peek-a-boo every time she lifts her arm. My interest piqued, I watch as she licks her fingers, adjusting her grip on the ball before letting it fly. The little grunting noise she makes on release just makes me wonder what kind of noises she'll make in bed. Not happy with that pitch, she makes an adjustment to her stance, licks her fingers, looks at the plate over the top of her glove, and lets it fly again. I look at the speed clock on the wall and let out a low whistle. Holy shit. Seventy-three miles per hour. My dad wasn't joking. Briggsy has a cannon! The world record is seventy-seven or some shit. That level of badassery just makes her even hotter.

"She's good, isn't she?" my dad asks from the bottom of the bleachers.

"You lucked out, old man. Stella was great, but that's some serious speed."

"Yeah, she throws at that speed no matter the pitch. It's impressive as hell." Propping his foot on the bench next to me and leaning on his knee, he narrows his eyes at me. "I know you're not here to talk about Saffron's pitching speed. What are you doing here, son?"

"Don't worry, Dad, I'm not here to take advantage of any of your players or convince them to skip practice and come back to my place, just bringing Briggsy a book she asked for." My dad doesn't look certain at first.

"Your lack of trust hurts, Dad," I kid, pulling out the

anatomy book from my bag. When he nods in approval, I snort out a laugh. "You're the one who asked me to tutor her. You know that in order to do that, I'm going to have to be around her, right?"

"Don't make me regret it, Levi. I mean it," he warns.

"I won't. Plus, she hates me, so you're safe there."

My dad snorts out a laugh. "Don't try to bullshit me, son. The chase is what it's all about. I was young once too, you know."

"You were?" I can't help but tease him.

"Yeah, you punk." He pops me in the arm. "All I'm saying is she has a lot going on in her life here lately. On top of losing her dad, she's playing catch-up with her classes and trying to get acclimated to a new team. You know how tough that is. Don't fuck it up for her. You have a way of making smart girls stupid." His pointed look has me grinning.

"Damn, Dad, tell me how you really feel." He's not wrong. I just like to bust his balls. As his only son, it's my job. With a shake of his head, he claps me on the back and walks back to watch the girls practice. I get a couple of flirty waves and air kisses from some of his team, which gets me a death stare from him. I just shrug and flash a smile as I lean back against the cool metal bleachers and wait on Briggs.

After about thirty minutes of me being mesmerized by all of her finger licking before every pitch—clearly, it's her thing—she goes over to talk to my dad, who points a finger in my direction. Even from here, I can see her shoulders tighten. When she turns, her eyes are already narrowed. I just flash her my dimples and try not to laugh. I haven't even said anything to her yet, and she's pissed. Saffie nods at something my dad says and comes over to where I'm kicked back, watching her move with a new appreciation for spandex.

"Why are you smiling?" she asks in a clipped tone.

"Am I? I didn't realize," I lie. "Would you rather I glare like you are?"

"I'm not glaring."

"Oh, my bad. Scowling, then? Or maybe that's just your face." My smile widens, and her face darkens as if a storm cloud is hanging over her head.

"Cut the shit, Sexton. Did you bring the book?" She plants her hands on her hips, drawing my attention to the curve and dip of her waist. Before I answer, I allow my gaze to travel over her. Sweat dampens the collar of her shirt, glistening across her collarbones and dipping down into the valley the sports bra creates. I find myself wondering if her nipples are the same dark pink as her lips. The need to find out is powerful and will most likely get me into a world of shit. Trying to hide my wince, I adjust my now semi-hard cock and drag my eyes up to meet her gaze. Gray eyes flashing like lightning in a storm, she holds out her hand. "The book, Levi. I have an exam before practice in the morning, and I haven't even read the chapter," she says impatiently.

"Well, then, we should go over it," I offer. The look on her face screams no before the word even leaves her pretty mouth.

"No."

"Come on, we'll go to my place and order takeout while we study." My offer is genuine. I'm not sure why, but her ice queen bullshit makes me want to be around her more. For some reason, I either want to be the one to make her thaw out or *really* give her a reason to be frosty toward me. Whichever. I think both will be fun. "I'm your tutor, after all. If you don't do well, it reflects poorly on me."

She rolls her eyes at me, but, to my surprise, she agrees. "Fine. I need to stop by my dorm and grab my notes and a shower first, though."

"I'll drive you."

"I'll drive myself."

A retort is on the tip of my tongue, but I know the minute I make even one sexual innuendo, she's done, and I'm not ready for her to be done before we even get started, so I just nod. "I'll see you in a little while then."

Not waiting for a response or to give her a reason to change her mind, I take the bleachers two at a time and wave to my dad on my way out of the basement. Keeping my dirty-ass thoughts about Saffron Briggs from slipping out of my mouth tonight is going to be hard as fuck. I'm seeing some more cold showers in my future. Unless of course I can convince Briggsy that I can teach her more than what's in those anatomy books.

## 7

## SAFFIE

"Wait, you're going over to Sexy's house? To study? Is that code for something?" my roommate Carrie asks.

Nose curled in disgust, I turn to her. "Ew. Don't call him that. And no, it's not code for anything. I have an exam tomorrow morning, and I'm not ready for it. My book didn't come in, and I have shit notes. He's my tutor. Coach told me to let him help me so I can focus on the team and finding my footing." Even to my own ears, it sounds like an excuse, but it's not. Not even close.

"Umm, that's his name. And I'm pretty sure it *is* code, so you might want to wear something else." Her cute heart-shaped face is scrunched up in what I think is sympathy? As if I don't know how to dress to catch a man. I guess it's a good thing I'm not trying to catch Levi or anyone else, for that matter.

"His name is Levi, it's not code, and I'm not changing," I tell her as I slip a hoodie over my head. My hair, in a messy bun, is even messier now. "And I have a boyfriend."

Carrie looks at me in horror. "You can't be serious about going over there like that." She flicks manicured fingers in my direction. A photography and film major, she looks more model than photographer with her long dark hair, almond-shaped eyes, and perfect olive skin. "And you cannot tell me that Levi 'Sexy' Sexton"—she puts extra emphasis on the sexy part—"does not set your skin on fire. That boy is so hot he should be illegal. And from what I hear, he's a beast in bed. He's straight-up ruining girls for all the mere mortals of the world." She's serious. What is wrong with the chicks here?

"He's not a god, Care! He's a jock. A braggy, entitled, fuck boy jock."

"I'd let him fuck boy me allllll day long and twice on Sunday." That's her response. "And you're a jock! You can't hate other jocks."

"I don't. I just hate ones like him who use it to get girls out of their panties."

"Oh honey, if you think that has anything to do with his hockey stick and not the one in his pants, you're so wrong."

Laughing at her ridiculousness, I grab the keys to my dad's truck, the one thing of his that makes me feel like he's still here. "I'll be back in a bit."

"I won't wait up," Carrie calls as the door closes behind me.

She can wait up or not all she wants. I'm going there to study for this exam. I wouldn't even be going if it wasn't for the little talk I had with Coach earlier. He's determined for me to let Levi help so that I can concentrate on my game instead of worrying about my grades. It's a "help me help you" situation. I can handle Levi Sexton. After a while, my resting bitch face should be enough to deter him. Right?

It only takes about five minutes to get to his place. A big Cape Cod-style house that he shares with three other guys, according to his sisters. It was hard to know who was who when we were here for the party the other night. Not wanting to take anyone's parking spot, I forgo the driveway, pull up to the curb, and grab my stuff before jumping out. As I get closer to the porch, I can hear music and people talking. Was that a moan? Oh my god. They're probably having a damn orgy in there. This was a bad idea. I'm just about to turn away and go back to my truck when the door flies open.

"Briggsy! I didn't hear you knock." Levi stands in the open doorway, shirtless with a pair of black sweats hanging low on his hips. I may not like him, but I can't deny that he's hot. The wicked gleam in his icy blues and the dimpled grin tells me he knows that I can't deny it, and that just pisses me off even more. Makes me want to kick him in the nuts just for the hell of it. That can't be healthy.

"I didn't want to...interrupt," I answer, hitching my bag higher on my shoulder. I'm no prude, but the thought of him doing whatever he was doing in there, knowing that I was on my way over, makes me mad. And *that* makes me madder. Pretty much everything about him makes me mad, obviously.

"Interrupt?" His brow is creased in confusion that turns into understanding when another moan cuts through the thumping bass to reach us. That dimpled grin widens. "You better get used to that, Saffie." He moves aside to let me in. I try my best not to brush against him when I pass, but he makes it impossible. Whether it's on purpose or because his broad shoulders and six-foot-four frame are just too damn big, I'm not sure. Probably a little of both. Completely ignoring the trail of heat left behind where my arm came into contact with his rigid abs, I hold my head high and try not to make eye contact with anyone in the room. I don't want to see anyone having sex or naked or whatever the hell is going on here. Levi chuckles, taking hold of my hand to lead me through the room. I tug, trying to dislodge my small, calloused hand from his much larger one, but he's not having it. "Don't worry, I'm not going to lead you into an orgy or anything, Briggsy. Not yet anyway." He tosses a wink at me over his shoulder as he continues through the room. I catch a glimpse of big guys and girls of all shapes and sizes and colors in various states of undress as we walk. Levi never breaks stride or seems surprised. As if there isn't a sex party happening in his damn living room.

Once we're upstairs, I breathe a little easier though I'm not sure why. A bedroom with Levi Sexy Sexton is in no way a safe place. At least he has more than just a bed in here, though. His room is twice the size of my whole dorm, with a connecting bathroom and a small sunken sitting room in front of a wall of high windows. Everything is dark gray and black with red accents, masculine and cleaner than I would have expected. In the middle of the room is a king-sized bed covered in a gray and black plaid comforter and a mountain of pillows. The desk in the corner is the only messy area in the room, and even that isn't bad. His scent, a clean, cool smell hangs in the air. Even Landon, who I always thought was a neat guy, isn't this neat.

"It's so clean." I let slip.

Levi shrugs. The muscles of his shoulders rippling under the lightly freckled skin that I tell myself I do not find attractive. "I pay my sisters to clean it."

Figures. Just barely stopping myself from rolling my eyes at him, I step down into the sitting area and drop into one of the comfy gray recliners, pulling my notebook, pens, and laptop out of my bag. Glancing up, I find him watching me, his bare chest drawing my eyes. Again. "Can you put a shirt on please? I don't need people thinking we're up here messing around." My voice drips with disdain. God, he brings out the worst in me.

"Don't worry, they won't notice that we're even up here," he answers, laughter in his own voice.

"So all you guys do is sit around here and have...have sex with girls?"

Levi bites his lip, I'm guessing to hold back a smile or to stop himself from laughing at me. Ridiculous that I notice his perfectly straight white teeth. Aren't hockey players supposed to be missing teeth or something?

"You say it like it's a bad thing, Briggsy."

This time, I don't try to stop the eye roll. "Is it going to be like this every time I come over?"

Shaking his head, he grins wide, both dimples flashing this time. "Yes."

"Oh my god."

"Probably. Maybe?"

He poses it like a question, and I can't help but laugh at him. "Holy shit. Is that a smile? Briggsy, you can't smile at me like that. I'll think you might actually like me, and you know what happens to girls who like me?" Before he can answer, I bean him with a pen.

"I don't like you, so don't worry."

"Whatever you say, Saffie. Whatever you say." He plucks a shirt from the dresser, finally, and pulls it over his head. The golden, muscled torso disappears underneath soft white cotton. I'm almost disappointed. Until he opens his mouth and I remember I don't like him. "You tell yourself whatever you have to. I'll break you down eventually."

Like hell he will.

## 8

## LEVI

Briggs has been here for a couple of hours and has finally started to relax. Enough that I've even been able to coax a laugh or two out of her. Man, she has this ice queen thing on lock. She's jotting down some notes when someone bangs on the door like they're the damn police, making Saffie jump.

"What?" I call, irritated. I told them not to even think about coming up here and to text me when the Chinese came. Not because I thought I was going to convince her to have sex and they might catch us, but because I knew she would be uptight enough as it was without the help of any of my roommates.

Cubbie pokes his head in. "Food's here, bro," he says, his eyes landing on Briggs, roaming over her in appreciation. I don't like it. "Hey, Saffron. Didn't know you were still here." *Liar.*

She glances up with a bland expression on her face. Briggs knows he's full of shit too. "Yup." Then she goes back to writing in her notebook. When he takes his eyes off her, and they land back on me, my grin is so smug he flips me the bird.

"See ya, Cubbie." I throw him deuces on my way to the

dresser to grab my wallet, grinning when I hear the door close a little more forcefully than necessary. If Briggsy wasn't sitting right here, I would ask him how the dibs he called was working for him. I'm not about to try my luck with that shit, though. She's liable to kick all of our asses.

Briggs grabs her bag. "Here, let me give you some money."

"Nah, I got it." I can see that she's about to argue. "You can get the next one." That seems to appease her. "Be right back."

The "party" downstairs is still in full swing. Not that it's out of the norm or even a party really. Just a lot of skin all over the place. Doing my best not to get distracted I pay for our food. As I'm closing the door, bags of food in hand I feel slender arms wrap around my waist, tits pressed against my back. I know damn well it's not Saffie.

"You sure that's what you're hungry for?" Nora purrs in my ear, her palm sliding over my stomach to grab a handful of my cock. I close my eyes and swear. Any other night, I'd be down. Probably right here in the entryway. As gently as I can, I step out of her embrace. I'm not trying to piss off Nora. She's up for anything at any time. I'm not sure who she's here to see. It might be me, but with her, you never can tell. We've all had a taste of Nora.

With an exaggerated groan, I tap her chin. "As good as that sounds, I can't right now. I'll call you later, though," I lie, watching a frown darken her face. She's not happy. That's too bad, though. Nora can be a little clingy, and I'm not about that. Plus, after the hickey shit the other night, I'm still pissed at her. I don't want her to know that. Just in case I really do call her later. Flashing her my dimples, I turn and take the stairs two at a time, making sure to lock the door when I enter my room.

"You get lost?" Saffie clips.

With a laugh, I set the bags down on the coffee table and start removing containers. When everything is laid out, I sit on the floor, my legs stretched in front of me. Saffie settles across from me, her legs folded as she leans against the chair. I watch as she opens all the boxes, placing mine in front of me along with a fork and a pair of chopsticks. I reach for my container of Lo Mein and the sticks. "Have you tried this place since you've been here?"

She shakes her head. "Is it really called Mr. Miyagi's?" Saffie asks, snapping her chopsticks apart, an incredulous smile tilting her lips.

"No, but the guy who owns it looks straight-up like Mr. Miyagi. It's what he told us to call him. He loves it. He used to enter look-alike contests. I'm not sure how the hell he found them." I laugh. "Has pictures hanging all over the restaurant."

"The menu is huge," she says as she opens her container.

"He calls it Tri-Asian. They serve Thai, Chinese and Japanese. It's the best and cheapest meal you'll get on campus."

"Good to know." I watch as she dips her sticks into the white box and pulls out a saucy piece of pork. I'm mesmerized by the way she wraps her tongue around it and pulls it into her mouth. Fuck.

"I'm surprised you know how to use those." I point at her with my own pair. Doing my best to make small talk and not allow my dick to get any harder.

"Chopsticks? Yeah. My dad was a foodie."

"Ahhh, so that explains the name."

She stops chewing for a minute and then nods. "Yeah. My sisters are Rosemary and Sage."

"You're shitting me, right?"

Saffie looks up at me, a mouthful of food. "Umm...no," she answers.

"Rosemary, Sage, and Saffron." I'm doing my best not to laugh.

"Yup." She's not amused.

"Was he a chef or something?"

"No. He was the fire chief."

"Well, I guess it could have been worse, and you guys could have been named like Smokey, Ash, and Fire Starter." Her face looks pinched as she tries to hold back her laughter. Finally, it bursts from her, the sound sexy and throaty. I decide I like making her laugh. A lot.

"He would have kicked your ass for making fun of our names. Everyone blew him shit for it," she says, smiling around her chopsticks at the thought.

"Gotta be tough if you're gonna name your daughters after herbs and spices, man."

"He was." Her tone drops an octave. The laughter turned melancholy.

"Did he die in a fire?" Saffie's face tightens, her eyes fluttering as if she's trying to fight back tears. Shit. It's too late to take it back.

"No. Believe it or not, he died while he was on a fishing trip with his buddies." She glances up at me before turning her attention back to her food. "They were out on the lake, heading back in because the weather was changing, when a young boy got caught in a rip current. My dad jumped in to save him." She stirs the noodles around, picking at them, thoughtful. "He couldn't save them both."

I'm sorry I asked because I don't like seeing her sad, but I'm glad she opened up and told me. I nudge her with my foot. "Your dad died a hero. Even if he did have shit taste in names." I wink, hoping to lighten the mood.

Saffie laughs and pegs me with a pea pod, the sauce leaving a brown blob on my shirt. "Ooooh, my sisters are gonna be pissed at you if that stains," I tease, reaching over my shoulder to pull my shirt off. I toss it toward the hamper, running a hand through my hair to try to tame it. Hockey season is in full swing, which means hockey hair is too. Your *flow* is as much a part of your uniform as your sweater.

I'm just about to ask her why she's so quiet when I catch her eyeing up my bare chest. Knowing that if I say anything, she'll crank up the ice queen thing she's working all over again, I give her a second to look her fill. She can deny her attraction to me all she wants. I know what she sees. She may not like me, but she wants me. And that's fine with me. I'm not looking for a girlfriend. I'm just trying to enjoy my last year before real life starts.

With a shake of her head, she returns to eating her food. "Tell your sisters you deserved it."

"They'll never believe that," I tease, smiling around the mouthful of egg roll.

Saffie scoffs. "Oh, they'll believe it! They know all about you, Sexy." Her tone is snarky, not the way girls usually let my nickname fall from their lips. I shouldn't like that as much as I do.

"Believe me, Briggsy. They don't know the half of it." I reach and dip my chopsticks into her other container, the one with orange chicken, and pluck a piece out, flashing a dimple when she growls at me. "Easy, Saffron. Didn't your ma ever tell you that sharing is caring?"

"She did, but I don't play well with others."

"That's too bad. I play so nice." I let the innuendo hang between us. And just as fast, I change the subject on her so that she doesn't have time to get pissed off at me. "How's ball going? You ready for the preseason?"

Saffron seems confused by my change in topic but goes with it.

"It's good. The team is really supportive and welcoming, which, I'm not gonna lie, surprised me a bit. I know they miss Stella, but they haven't made me feel bad about it."

"Nothing to feel bad about. You didn't knock her up." I chuckle.

She looks up, startled. Her mouth forms a perfect *O* I would love to fill. "Is that what happened? Nobody has said why she wasn't able to play this season."

"It's no secret. They're just super protective. Chicago sends a veteran player to check on their drafts. My babysitter happened to have a thing for college-aged chicks." I shrug and smile. "Can't blame him."

"Wow. So your, what? Mentor? Comes here to see you and hooks up with Stella and gets her pregnant? Some mentor," Saffie says snidely.

"Nah, he's good people. She's living with him now in Chicago. Jason is happy as shit, and so is Stella," I defend.

"Good for them." It doesn't sound like she really means it, but I don't push her on it.

"You should be thanking him, really."

"What? Why?" Her brows draw down in confusion.

"Well, had he not come here and gotten Stella all pregalicious, you wouldn't be here now, and you wouldn't have had the pleasure of meeting me." I smile smugly and watch as her face melts into a bored, icy mask.

"Deny it all you want, Briggsy. I know you like me."

"Don't bet your hockey career on it, Sexton," she says dryly.

Making Saffron Briggs admit she wants me just became a challenge I'd be crazy to ignore. She doesn't want to let herself like me, and she for damn sure doesn't want to want me. But she does. And it makes her inner ice queen pissy. I can see it in that wicked glimmer in her eyes, right before she rolls them. Game on, Baby. Game on.

# 9

## LEVI

Six o'clock practice comes early as fuck, even when you manage to get to bed before midnight. With a groan, I strip down and start dressing for the ice. Half-asleep, I plop down on the bench and chug my protein shake willing myself to wake up.

"Morning, Sexy," Murph says as he walks the locker room all chipper. He's the most morningest morning person I've ever met in my life. Been here since four in the gym, I'd bet money on it.

I manage a grunt and go back to drinking.

"Cubbie said Saffron was up in your room last night. You guys smash?" His lips twist in a *bow-chicka-wow-wow* smirk.

"Nah, bro. She's not ready for Sexy," I joke, although it's no lie.

He scoffs. "More like Sexy ain't ready."

Now *that's* no lie. Saffie is no Nora. She's commitment and monogamy and all that other shit I want nothing to do with. The only things I'm committed to are hockey, my bed and my mama. "You're right about that."

"Plus, doesn't she have a boyfriend back at her old school?"

He lays his gear out on the ground, making sure he has everything.

"Because I give a shit about that? He's not my fucking boyfriend." I don't make a habit of going after girls with boyfriends, but I don't make a habit of not going after them if they're willing. Again, I'm not the one in the relationship.

"True. True. She does, though."

"For now," I say smugly.

Murphy gives me a knowing look. "You only like her because she doesn't like you. Been a while since someone challenged you. They all just fall into Sexy's lap, hoping to land on that D."

I can't help but laugh. "You're so stupid."

"Whatever, bro. You know that shit's true. Speaking of chicks, Nora was pissed when she found out Saffron was up there last night. Like crazy eyes pissed. Like...stage five clinger pissed. Better be careful, eh? I heard that her and Saffron had words at the game the other night."

"About me?" My eyebrows shoot up in surprise. "They had words about me? How do you know?"

"I was talking to Raegan, and she told me. I guess your sisters were telling Nora that Saffie was invited by you, and Nora tried to lay shit down like you were her man. Saffron called her on it, then told her some shit about having to mark a man up to try to keep him not being her style." He points at my neck, and the now nearly faded hickeys. "Basically, Nora got put in her place, and then she found out that you had her up in your room last night and..." He grimaces. "You might have lost your Nora side piece."

I laugh at him. "Doubt it." I'm more interested in Saffie having words with her about me. Nora wants a meal ticket, she's not going anywhere unless she thinks she can find a different ride and right now I'm the hottest prospect on campus and she knows it. Not that there's any fucking way in hell I'm taking her to the show with me. I'm not taking anyone to the pros with me when I leave. Like I said, hockey, my bed and my mama. Drake knows what's up.

"You're right. Nora thinks you'll put a ring on it one day," Murphy says, doing the little Beyoncé dance.

I throw my glove at him and laugh. "Never gonna happen."

"Oh, I know it. Cubbie even knows it and he doesn't know shit. But Nora, Nora *thinks* she knows what's up. Just watch yourself. She'll be faking a pregnancy by graduation if she thinks she has to."

Just as he says that the rest of the team starts filing in and the noise level in the room makes it impossible for us to discuss it any further. He's right though. I'm gonna have to be a little more careful about how much time I spend with Nora. I'm not trying to fuck around and pull a Jason Dagger. Although it worked out for him, I'm not about that life.

An hour later my legs feel like jelly and my breaths are coming in short puffs. Coach doesn't give a shit that it's only seven in the morning. He's trying to kill us with these drills and the fucker is enjoying it if his smile behind the whistle is anything to go by.

"He's a sadistic fuck." Decker pants, making me grin.

"Yeah he is. But we keep coming back for more." The whistle blows and I burst from the blue line gaining speed as I corner around the first set of cones, dropping to my belly to slide under the hurdle before popping back up as quickly as I can, racing to the finish and coming to a hockey stop in front of the boys. A fresh shower of snow falling over them making me laugh as they shove me to the end of the line to finish up our drills. We usually spend the mornings scrimmaging, but a couple of the players showed up for practice hungover so we're all paying the price. It's my responsibility as the team captain to keep these guys in line and on time and all that shit. If their punk asses didn't look so tortured I'd be giving them hell after practice. Seeing as how they look ready to puke I'm going to hold off 'til later. I'm not looking to get thrown up on.

"Sexy!" Murphy calls, catching my attention. I look over at him and he jerks his head up toward the stands. A quick glance and I see that Saffron is sitting there watching. She gives a small wave and then a shooing motion like she's telling me "Get back to work." I grin and give her a salute. No clue what she's doing here or how long she's been watching, but all of a sudden I'm ready for practice to be over. And that's saying a lot since if I had my way I'd be on the ice just about every waking moment.

About twenty minutes later, Coach blows the whistle signaling the end of this morning's torture session. Everyone skates off breathing heavily, some a little worse than others. I stand at the open door leading off the ice and wait for Saffie to make her way down. The door leads into a tunnel, so I meet her at the glass, looking up at her. "Stalking me?" I joke as I take off my helmet.

Saffron snorts. "Hardly." She leans her arms atop the angled glass and looks down at me. "This was in my mailbox, I thought you might need it for class before the weekend." With a flick she hands me a folded piece of paper.

"What is it?" I shake my glove off to take it from her.

"Oh my god, what is that smell?" Saffie asks, wrinkling her nose.

A smile lifts the corner of my mouth. "That's called hockey, Briggsy."

"Hockey smells like shit," she fires back.

"It smells like success." I wink and flash her my dimples.

"Whatever you have to tell yourself, Levi. Anyway, I filled it out and I wanted to get it to you."

Unfolding the paper, I see it's the form that I need to hand in to my professor for tutoring her. "Thanks for this. I forgot all about giving you a heads-up. You didn't have to bring it all the way over here though. I thought we were studying tomorrow?" I ask, with a swipe of my sweat soaked hair.

"That's another thing, I'm not going to be there. Coach was able to get a preseason scrimmage set up between us and the Cougars in their new fancy dome. We're leaving this afternoon, won't be back until late tomorrow probably."

Happy that she's still standing here willingly talking to me, I widen my stance on my skates and lean on my stick. "You nervous?" It's gotta be hard coming to a new school, new team. They haven't even been practicing together long enough to really form an opinion of her, let alone any kind of loyalties.

Saffie shrugs. "A little. Your sisters make me feel a little more at ease. They act like they've known me forever. They're way nicer than their older brother."

We both smile at that. Partly because it's true. My sisters are the shit.

"Well, you smell and I have stuff to do. I'll let you know what my schedule looks like when I get back." With a choppy wave she turns and picks her way down the rest of the stairs. I think she gets pissed at us both when she finds herself not hating me as much as she wants to and races to get away.

"Briggsy!" The shout echoes around us in the empty arena.

Her head shoots up, startled. "Yeah?"

"Good luck."

Instead of a thank you she scrunches her face and sticks her tongue out, making me laugh at her need to dislike me.

# 10

# SAFFIE

Thank god for the Sexton twins. Not that everyone on the team hasn't been great but there's nothing like boarding a bus and feeling everyone watching you, hoping you won't sit next to them. I'm sure it's completely in my head, but I still feel like a bug under a microscope. Head down, I am just about to slip into an empty seat behind Coach Hayes when I hear my name shouted from the back of the bus. Up on tiptoes, craning my neck, I see Millie standing on her seat waving like a mad woman. Relief washes over me. It's been a long time since I've felt like the odd one out. They haven't treated me like the *new girl* since I started, but bus rides are different. Everyone is focused on the game coming up and they've been riding with the same chicks for a couple of years already. I was so preoccupied with Levi and getting him the paper, I never even thought to ask the twins if I could sit with them beforehand and didn't want to just assume. I'm not used to feeling this off kilter and I know it's more than just the bus ride. Landon and I keep seeming to miss each other's calls and when we do talk it's cut short because he has something going on or is on his way out or I'm on my way to class or practice. It's the distance and I'm sure it's nothing at all but I'm just not ready to delve any deeper than that right now. Not today. Side stepping down the aisle so I don't bump anyone, I make it back to the twins —along with Lakyn and Kenna— and squeeze onto the seat Maeve pats next to her.

"We were afraid you were going to miss the bus," Millie says, leaning over the back of her seat to talk to us.

"I had a class that I couldn't miss." This accelerated A&P class is no joke, even with Levi's help.

"I heard you were at the rink today." Maeve's voice is twinged with curiosity.

"Oh please do not tell me you have already been lured in by one of the hockey boys." Millie groans. "I had such high hopes for you." Her head falls forward, red ponytail flopping dramatically.

"Ew no, you're so crazy. I was just dropping off some papers that your brother needed for the tutor program."

"Oh good! I was worried for a second there. Now that Maeve is part of the hockey hoochies club I can't afford to lose any more of my friends to it too."

Maeve swats at her sister as Lakyn and Kenna giggle snort over Millie's dramatics. "Tell me you're not a hoochie for Benny so I can call you a liar!" Millie dares.

"Shhhhh! If daddy hears you I am going to tell him all about that frat party you snuck into the other night."

Millie's eyes go wide. "You wouldn't!" She doesn't sound very sure.

"If he overhears you talking about me and Benny I totally will." Maeve schools her features into a stern glare, I've never seen her look so...tough. It's almost comical because she's so not. Maeve is soft spoken and laid-back, very much like my cousin. Millie on the other hand...

"Ugh, finnnneee. I'll be quiet. But seriously, Saffie, protect yourself at all costs. Those hockey boys have a way about them that makes smart girls act stupid." That last parting shot was totally for her sister who flipped her off amid our snickering. These girls really are so much fun. They make me miss the easy friendships I left behind at St. Claire.

"Speaking of Benny, "Lakyn cuts in, "Is he coming up for the game?"

"He said he would try but that it all depended on if they scheduled another practice or not." Maeve shrugs. "We'll see."

"Oooh, maybe he'll bring some of the guys up with him," Kenna adds. "Why is it that all the hot guys like, know each other?"

"You say that like it's a bad thing," Lakyn says puffing out a little laugh. "At least if they stick together we don't have to look so hard for them."

We all laugh and nod our agreement. She makes a solid point.

"What about you, Saf? You got your eye on anyone? What your man doesn't know won't hurt himmmm." Millie sing songs, waggling her perfectly sculpted copper color brows at me.

"Nope. I plan on staying faithful and giving this long-distance thing a shot. I mean, it's not forever and we are both so busy with school and sports anyway." I don't bother mentioning that we haven't even had time to talk lately.

"Do you really believe that he'll behave? You know how guys are, out of sight out of mind," Kenna says, a sympathetic look on her pretty face.

"I totally do! Lan loves me, he would never cheat on me." I truly believe that or I wouldn't bother trying. Regardless of how often we get to talk or not. I trust him.

"Well knock on wood girl, because you just jinxed the shit out of yourself," Millie says knocking softly on the top of my head.

Before I can reply Coach stands up at the front of the bus,

raising his hands to silence the chattering that has gotten louder by the second.

"Ladies," he booms over the noise. Immediately everyone quiets. "Thank you. We have a couple of hours before we get to the hotel, let's keep the noise level a little below window shattering and get comfy." He smiles good-naturedly, like a man used to dealing with twenty plus girls at once, all the time. "You know the rules, no flashing cars, that goes for boobs, butts or any kind of sign language." His brows raise, disappearing under the brim of his FU Fire hat, as he looks around the bus at each of us. Driving his point home. "If you snap gram, insta chat, Twitter book, Ticky Toky, what-the-hell-ever, make sure you do it responsibly. Remember that anything on the internet stays there and will get you in a shitload of trouble if it is inappropriate or paints you or FU in a bad light. Be smart ladies." This is met with giggles over the butchering of every social media platform he's probably ever heard of. "Stay put and rest up, we'll be there soon enough." With a nod he goes back to his seat behind the bus driver and we're off.

My stomach lurches right along with the bus. I haven't felt this nervous before a game in forever. I close my eyes and lean my head back just listening to the conversation around me. This will be the first game I've played without my dad being there to cheer me on. I know it's the *real* reason I'm so out of sorts and nervous. I glance at my phone for the millionth time today looking for the text he would be sending me before an away game. Knowing it won't come but still hoping it will. My mom sent me one earlier wishing me luck and telling me she loved me but, it's not the same. The girls are talking among themselves laughing at something Kenna is saying. With them preoccupied I open the messages on my phone and scroll to the one I'm looking for. My hands tremble a bit as I click on the name *Big Papa*.

> Big Papa: Sorry I'm missing this one, kiddo! Give it hell. Don't drop that shoulder and remember that a walk is not the end of the world. The guys at the station said good luck! Love ya Saffron Sauce!

Swiping my thumb over the message I close my phone before the tears I feel pricking have the chance to fall. "Hey, you okay? You're quiet." Maeve asks, concern marring her face.

"I'm good. Just nervous about the game. It's been a while." It's a lie and the truth all at once.

"You got this girl. This is our year," she beams. "I've seen you in action, I'm not worried."

"How are you related to Sexy? You're too nice to be blood." It's not the first time I've wondered.

Maeve laughs "Levi isn't so bad once you get to know him. A player? Yes. But not a bad guy. He's actually pretty fantastic. Just don't tell him I said so. It'll go right to his head, and he doesn't need the ego boost." We both nod in agreement over that statement. Levi has confidence in spades.

"I'll have to take your word for it. I don't plan on getting to know him well enough to find out." I want one thing, and one thing only from her brother and that's help passing my class. Nora and the rest of the chicks on campus can fight over him all they want. I won't be a *"hockey hoochie,"* as Millie put it. Not for Levi "Sexy" Sexton, or his damn dimples.

## 11

## LEVI

My duffel in my hand, I close my bedroom door and head down the hall, banging on doors as I go. Once I hit the landing, Benny and Murph are both thundering down the stairs shoving each other and nearly toppling all three of us down the rest of the way.

Safely at the bottom, I turn laughing. "You fucking animals."

"Sorry, Sexy. It's a two-hour ride. I don't want to be stuck in the back seat of your truck the whole way and you know first one down gets shotgun," Murph says, a victorious smile splitting his face.

Benny grins slyly and turns to me. "We picking up Raegan, or is she meeting us here?" He knows he just won this battle. No way is Murphy going to let Benny ride in the back with Raegan, whether he's with my sister or not. That's two hours he can spend not flirting with her. I've never seen a guy with so much game have absolutely no game at all when it comes to Rae. It's comical, actually.

"Fucker. Why didn't you tell me Raegan was coming?"

"My bad, bro. She texted me a little while ago to see if we

were going. Told her she could ride with us." I decide to fuck with him a little bit. "Should I tell her we don't have room?"

He looks at me like I'm an idiot. "Do it, and I'll invite Nora to ride with us."

After our little talk the other day, he knows I'm trying to keep her at a distance. I'm not trying to catch a case right now. And while she's usually just down for a good time, she sees Briggsy as a threat and has been putting the heat on me. Texting and popping up more often and shit. Not what I need.

"Why you gotta be so mean, bro?"

"You two done?" Benny calls from the open door, the cold air filling the entryway.

"Let's roll. We won't be able to meet up with them tonight. They have curfew, and my dad won't hesitate to kick our asses if we mess with that." None of us want that, especially me. He's still giving me shit over the Benny thing.

∼

SINCE WE ROLLED up after curfew last night, we didn't get to talk to anybody. We got to the hotel and, after making sure Rae was *alone* in the roll out cot we had them bring up for her, we were all asleep within minutes. Now after taking turns in the shower and hitting the free breakfast, we're on our way to the new enclosed dome the Cougars just finished building. They're one of our biggest rivals for hockey as well as softball, so this dome is a sore spot for us as well as my dad. I don't doubt for a minute that he'll be working the board over to get one for Fulton real soon.

"Holy shit, will you look at this thing." Murphy whistles in disbelief. "It's fucking huge!"

"It's a bit much for softball isn't it?" Rae asks. Softball rolling off her tongue with a note of disgust. Spoken like a true hockey player.

"Right? Wonder if they'll get a new rink now?" Benny cranes his neck to get a look through the window at the giant bubble-looking stadium.

"Whatever. They still won't be able to beat us on their home ice, even if they do get a new one," Murphy chirps from the back seat.

"Got that right," I reply as I whip my truck into a parking spot. The game doesn't start for another forty minutes, but they wanted to get here early to see if we can peep the girls before they hit the field.

Murphy helps Rae down from the back seat as Benny and I round the front of the truck. His beanie is pulled low, matching mine and making us look like freaking twins. The only difference is he's got a black eye that is turning a nice green and yellow. Hate to admit it, but it kind of makes him look like a badass. Fucker. As we turn to go into the stadium, I realize we're all wearing FU hoodies and sweats. The Cougar fans are gonna love us. I might get a black eye to match Benny's, after all.

"Do they even know we're here?" Rae asks once we're inside. "I wasn't sure if Benny was trying to surprise Maeve, so I didn't say anything to my cousin."

"I told my dad that we might be coming up but didn't let him know that we actually did."

"I didn't say shit about shit." Murphy shrugs, knowing he doesn't have anyone on the team to really tell anyway.

"No shit." Benny laughs. "I didn't say anything to Maeve. I wanted to surprise her."

My face pulls in disgust. "That's fucking adorable. Now shut up before I black your other eye."

"You can try. I gave you the first one, bro. The next one you'll have to work for," Benny taunts.

"Hayes, you better quit while you're ahead, man. Sexy was nice enough to let you live last time." Murphy claps him on the back. "That was him being easy."

"No fighting, boys. Let's just go find them or some seats." Rae whips her hat off. "It's so warm in here. I'd rather watch them play outside and be cold."

"Without a doubt. They would shrivel up and die, though. Softball players aren't built like us hockey players. Just don't tell them I said that." My beanie pushed back on my head now because of the overly warm stadium, I turn and lead us down to the first level. "We can grab some seats and then see about the locker room." Since it's so far from home and a last-minute scrimmage game, we're literally the only people from FU here. Hell, we're so early we're just about the *only* people here.

"Looks like we're basically the first ones here. Where do you want to sit? The visitors should be in the dugout down the first base line. We can sit facing them down the third base line, or do you want to sit at home plate?" Everyone knows behind home plate are the best seats in the house. But at home games, we'll sit on the third base line to be closer to Millie and Maeve.

"I doubt many people will be here at all. Let's sit on the baseline, though. We'll be able to see all three of them pretty well from there," Raegan suggests.

All in agreement, we pick our way over to the club seats there. They're raised off the field and definitely the swanky seats. "We'll sit here and see if we get kicked out." I shrug and plop down in the padded chairs. Much nicer than the ones we have at our stadium. Hockey or softball.

"I'm going to see if I can find Maeve and wish them luck. You coming?" Benny stands, waiting for us to decide.

"Yep. Should someone stay and save our seats?"

"I'll stay. You three go, but bring me back some food, eh? I'm starving." Murphy slouches down in the chair, getting more comfortable.

"Deal. Even though we did just eat," Rae says as she heads back the way we came, shaking her head in amusement.

"I'm a growing boy, you know!" Murphy calls after us.

After about ten minutes, we finally make it to the visitors' locker room. A finger to my lips, I shush Rae and Benny and put my ear to the door. I just want to make sure my dad isn't in there giving some big pregame speech. When I don't hear his booming voice, I nod over at Rae. "You go in and see if it's clear. I don't hear my dad, but if he's in there, he won't be pissed at you for interrupting like he would be at us." I grin. "Plus, if the girls aren't dressed and I walk in, they might be late to the field."

"Oh my god. There's something wrong with you," Rae says on a huffy laugh as she pushes open the door and sticks her head in. There's a loud squeal that I'm pretty sure is Millie at the sight of her friend. Raegan pulls her head back. "All clear." And practically bounces through the door and over to my sisters.

Holding the door open, I let Benny pass through but stop him with a hand to his chest before he gets any farther. "No kissy shit in front of me. I'm not ready for any of that noise." The dick just smiles at me and pushes my hand away, heading straight for Maeve.

Millie looks just as disgusted as I feel when Benny calls over his shoulder, "Look away bro, I'm about to kiss my girl." The locker room is filled with girly sighs and a chorus of "aw."

Turning my back on them, I scan over the rest of the players looking for the one I really came here for, though I'm not sure why. No way in hell is she going to be happy to see me. My eyes land on her just as Rae releases her from a hug. Saffie's eyes look puffy, her face splotchy like she's been crying. Rae links arms with her heading toward me and the door.

"What's the matter, Briggsy? You sad because your little boyfriend didn't call?" I joke. Her eyes flare, the gray looking like a wicked storm brewing, cold and dangerous like the waves that crash against the jetty when the winds kick up. I'm so focused on her and her stormy eyes I don't catch Rae trying to get my attention until Saffie bites out, "Not my boyfriend, jerk. My dad." She brushes past me, Rae shaking her head, her glare murderous.

"Your dad?" My confusion lasts about a second before I put two and two together. Briggsy said her dad hardly ever missed a game, that he was her biggest cheerleader. This will be the first game she's played since he died. Fuck, what a dick I am. I couldn't imagine playing hockey without my parents there. My ma especially. She dragged my ass around to every rink in the damn state growing up while my dad stayed behind, working to pay for it all. But Ma? She never missed a game no matter where it was. I'm lucky now that he gets to see me play as often as he does because we're at the same school. Man, to hockey without them...that would be so hard.

"Shit, Briggsy!" I'm able to catch up with her just outside of the door. Gently, I pull her to a stop by her elbow. Rae looks nervous. I know how she feels about confrontation, and the way Saffron is looking at me right now, shit just might get confrontational. With my eyes locked on Briggs, fearlessly meeting her cold stare down. "Rae, go make sure Benny keeps his hands off my sister." She looks at her cousin for guidance. Saffie, arms crossed tightly over her chest, gives an imperceptible nod. Reluctantly, Rae leaves us but not before poking me in the arm in warning. I wait until the door swishes closed behind her to speak. "Briggsy, I'm sorry. I didn't think."

"What else is new?" She huffs, looking past me. I'll allow it. I deserve it. And if she's upset about her dad not being here, never again being here to see her play, I'll let her take that out on me too.

"Listen, I know you hate me, and I don't help with that, but I'm here if you want to talk." Words I've never said to another chick before in my life, and I'm not saying them now for my own benefit. Not trying to score some ass. I'm being sincere. Why? I'm not entirely sure. I'm probably the last person she wants to confide in, but I mean it. "This is your first game without him, isn't it?" She nods, not meeting my gaze. I bend slightly to look at her under the brim of her hat. Anger rolls off her in waves mixed in with a whole lot of hurt. I'm not sure if the anger is because I'm seeing her like this or that the *ice queen* is feeling feelings and she hates it in general. I get that, though. Feelings aren't my thing either. My sisters start crying, and I'm out! But the raw emotions I can see on her face, in her eyes, make me want to stay and reassure her. "Briggsy, I know that this sucks, and you're hurting, but I'm going to tell you something my ma always says to me, and it will be okay for you to listen because it's coming from her and not me." That brings the tiniest smile to her face. Had I blinked, I would have missed it. "This is some profound shit. Are you ready?" I don't go on until she nods that she is. "The oh so wise Magdeline Sexton says that if you love a person, you carry that person with you. So no matter where they are, they can't be further than your heart." She sniffles and jerks her head in a nod, pulling the brim of her hat down lower but not before I see the tears fall. I can't handle it. "Now stop being a pussy. Rub some dirt in it or whatever you chicks do and kick the shit out of these fuckers." A snort-laugh slips out as she dashes her hands over her cheeks.

"You're such a prick." There's not a whole lot of heat behind her words.

With a shrug and a flash of dimples, I don't disagree, "At least I'm consistent, right?" As expected, she rolls her eyes at me and tugs the brim of her hat down. Before she can respond with whatever smart-ass thing she was going to, the door opens, and the girls come pouring out, blocking Saffie from my view.

"Okay, ladies, let's get on the field and get warmed up!" someone says from just behind me. Benny slides in next to me, probably hoping my dad didn't see him come out with Maeve.

"You two, glad you could make it. Stay out of trouble," my dad warns as he walks by us, clapping me on the back as he does.

The girls bounce by full of excited energy, their voices ringing through the empty hall. I bop Millie and Maeve on the head as they pass, wishing them both luck. Maeve tries to be sneaky and give Benny a quick kiss on the cheek, but she's shit at sneaky. I push her along. "Get out there before I tell Dad," I threaten. Benny flips me off and walks to catch up with her. Briggsy and Rae are bringing up the rear. I lift my hand for a high five that she grudgingly returns with the back of her mitt. "Remember what I said," I call after her. If she hears me, she doesn't show it, not that I expected her to.

"What was that all about?" Raegan asks, falling into step behind me.

"Oh, nothing, just trying to make your cousin not hate me so much. Or more." With a grin, I shrug. "Whichever."

## 12

## SAFFIE

"Come on, Saffie. We're going to be late," Rae calls from the sitting area of my dorm.

"Is that Raegan? Tell her I love her and can't wait to see her," my mom says from the other end of the phone line.

"It is. She's dragging me out with her and some of our friends."

"That's good. You need to enjoy your life, Saffron Sauce. You know that's what he'd want," she reminds me gently, using the nickname my father had given me practically at birth.

"I know, Mom. I'm trying," I answer quietly.

"Me too, baby. Me too. Now go and have fun but be safe! I love you."

"Love you too, Mom." I disconnect the call and look down at the screen for the time. Landon was supposed to call over an hour ago. Sure I didn't miss it, I check the call log just in case. Nope. Blowing out a resigned breath, I shout so that Rae can hear me. "Tell me again why we're going?" I've tried every excuse I could think of to get out of this, and she's not budging. I just want to lay around and be sad tonight.

Her voice is softer now as she stands in the doorway of my room, watching as I ruffle through my closet. "Saff, it's your dad's birthday. The other day was your first game without him. A lot of shitty firsts. You need to get out and have a good time."

She's right. I know she's right. Her and my mom. "Yeah, but why Levi's?"

"Hockey House is the safest place on campus if you plan on drinking." She nudges me out of my bedroom, leading me to the front door.

"Do I plan on drinking?" I'm not sure I do.

"You totally plan on it. You have been wound so tight since you've been here. Between your heavy class load, softball, missing your dad, and waiting on your mom to arrive, leaving Landon. It's been a lot. It's time to just have fun. Forget everything." I get my hand up just in time to catch the hoodie she throws my way. "Now come on, and let's go. You probably won't even see Levi."

I snort-laugh at her. "It's a party at *his* house, Raegan."

"Ummm, yeah, but we're late, and the party started a while ago, which means all the hockey hoochies have already descended on him. Seriously, though, by this time, if you do see him, you won't be able to *unsee* him," she says with an exaggerated shudder.

"Gross." The thought of seeing him in a...compromising position with anyone makes me want to throw up.

"Gross is right. Especially because it will probably be Nora." Raegan's face pulls into a scowl.

"Whore-a? Why? I don't get it. She seems awful." The cold air hits us as we start walking the few blocks to his house.

"Oh, you know why." She laughs.

"I guess I do. But still. What a bitch."

"I'm pretty sure she's reaaaalllyy nice to him," Raegan says before making gagging noises.

"I don't even want to think about that." And I don't. It makes me feel...I don't know how it makes me feel. I don't necessarily like Levi, but I don't necessarily *not* like him either. After my game last week and him being understanding and actually not his typical cocky asshole self, I don't hate him like I used to. But that could all change. In fact, I'm betting it will. Guys like Levi can't help themselves. They're too hot, too popular, too talented, too just...everything, and they know it. Before I can think about how annoying that is, my phone buzzes from my pocket. My breath makes little puffs in front of me as I pull it from my hoodie and let out a little squeal. "It's Landon. I haven't been able to talk to him all week. He probably knows what today is." Without giving my cousin a chance to respond, I swipe across the phone and answer.

"Hey, you!" The smile on my face slips a little as I hear what sounds like a party on the other end of the line. My voice rises so that I can be heard over the music. "Hellllooo?" I wait a beat. "Hello?" I repeat.

"Hello? Saffron?" His voice sounds a million miles away instead of the two hundred or so he actually is.

"Landon, I'm here!" I've stopped walking now, my cousin watching me, her brows disappearing underneath her hat in question.

"Hey! I didn't even hear the phone ring." I can barely make out what he's saying.

"It didn't. You called me." The excitement I felt just moments ago is quickly replaced with disappointment. He didn't mean to call me.

"Oh! I must have ass dialed you. My bad, angel."

"It's okay. I'm glad you di— "

"Yo! Save me some of that!" He shouts to someone, cutting me off. "Sorry, this party is wild. I can barely hear you. Can I call you when I get back to my house?"

"Yeah. Sure. I'm on my way to a party anyway." My disappointment turns to anger. "You go have a good time." I try to keep the bite from my voice. I don't care that he's at a party, just that he hasn't called me and didn't mean to now.

"You too. Make sure those FU guys know that you've got a man. I don't want to have to come there and beat any of those chumps up." Someone is yelling for him in the background, and I don't bother trying to talk over them. This whole phone call has done nothing for my mood. "Shit, I've gotta go. The Kappa Delta guys just showed up. Call you later."

He doesn't wait for me to answer, Doesn't say goodbye or I love you, or be safe, or any of the things he usually does when we talk on the phone. I try not to be upset about it, but today has been a shit day already and his non-call just made it worse. Not wanting to ruin Rae's night, I tug her arm and get us walking again. "You know what? You're right. I do plan on drinking tonight."

∼

Hockey House is packed. It had started to snow just as we were walking up, and already, everyone has abandoned the firepit in the backyard for the warmth of the house. We've been here about five minutes and thankfully haven't run into Levi yet although we did find the twins, Kenna, Lakyn, and even my roommate, Carrie. Rae hasn't said anything about my phone call with Landon, for which I'm grateful. Instead, she pulled me right to the kitchen the moment we came through the front door and poured me a glass of Pink Whitney, what she claimed was the nectar of the hockey gods, and added some lemonade.

"Just go easy because it sneaks up on you," Rae warns.

I extend my pinky to her. "I promise!" With a grin, she hooks hers with mine before leading the way back to the living room and our friends.

"Is that a drink?" Lakyn asks. I nod and take a sip of the surprisingly delicious concoction. It tastes like really good pink lemonade. "Bad day, or are you just in the mood to party?" That makes me laugh. I'm not a partier by nature.

"Well, between it being my dad's birthday and my boyfriend being an asshole, I'll go with bad day." I'm usually not such an open book, and I haven't even started drinking yet.

Kenna raises her red Solo cup to mine. "Well, happy birthday to your dad and screw your boyfriend! I'll hold your hair if you puke." She smiles. "But please don't puke because I will too." That pulls a laugh from me.

The girls all tap their cups to mine, and we drink. Just as I'm about to lower my cup, Millie waggles her finger at me and tips it back up, encouraging me to finish. Once I've emptied my drink, Rae takes it from me with a smile, turning to the kitchen for a refill.

"Does she have you drinking the Pink Whitney?" Millie asks.

"Yeah, she said it's for hockey players or something?"

Mill rolls her eyes. "So they keep saying."

"Maybe if I drink it, I'll catch a hockey player," Kenna says, biting back a smile at the look of horror that crosses Millie's face. It's no secret how she feels about the hockey boys. We all burst out laughing when we're sure smoke will start pouring from her ears.

"Speaking of hockey boys, is that where Maeve went?" I stand on tiptoes to look around the crowd for Maeve and my cousin.

Millie grimaces as if she's in pain or about to be sick. "I don't want to know what they're doing, but yes, she's with Benny. Somewhere." Lakyn bumps Millie with her hip.

"Girl, be happy for her. If it were anyone other than Benny, you would be. You've been pushing her to get some side action for ages."

"I know, I know. I just don't understand why it had to be him," Millie whines.

"I can give you a few reasons," Kenna joins in. "They all have to do with how damn fine he is, though, and you're not trying to hear any of that."

"No. No, I'm not," she says firmly, making me laugh.

"I'm gonna go see what the hell happened to Rae," I tell them.

Millie slaps my ass as I pass by her. "Don't get lost like my sister has."

Laughing, I agree, "I'll find you."

The house is packed, even more so than the last party I attended. Doing my best not to touch anyone, I squeeze between people dancing, talking, making out, and practically dry humping. When I finally get to the kitchen and don't see Rae, I make myself a drink. I'll probably regret it when I have to make my way back through all the writhing bodies everywhere without spilling it. Scanning the crowd, I see a tall blond guy who looks a lot like Landon. "Asshole," I murmur, downing my drink in a couple of big gulps. Rae was right. This stuff was so smooth. Ice clinks in my cup as I slam it down on the counter a little harder than I intended. "Oops. Slow down, Saffron." Awesome. Now I'm talking to myself. I glance around to be sure nobody has witnessed my little chat.

Happy that nobody has, I finish making yet another drink and set off to find Rae, a happy buzz starting to replace the sadness and aggravation from earlier. Carefully picking my way through the clusters of people grouped around the beer pong table set up in the dining room, I smile when I make it past without spilling a drop. Still no sign of Rae. "Where the heck is she?"

Out of places downstairs to look, I turn toward the staircase by the front door that leads up to the bedrooms. And that's when I see him. Levi "Sexy" Sexton. His hair is messy, his white T-shirt stretched tautly across his broad shoulders, and his gray sweatpants slung low on his hips. Gray. Sweatpants.

Doesn't he know that men shouldn't be out in public in them? They're like boy's lingerie. Not that he looks good in them or anything.

Okay, who am I kidding? Of course he does.

Well, he did, until I realize that his head is bent as he says something in someone's ear. No. Not *someone*. Nora. My eyes narrow as I watch her hands gliding under the hem of his shirt, tracing the waistband of his pants. He doesn't stop her, just smiles down at her, his dimple flashing in his cheek. Ridiculous for a rough, tough, six-foot-four hockey player to have dimples like some innocent schoolboy. Taking another sip of my drink, I don't realize that he's caught me staring at them until my gaze clashes with his, and he winks. The slowest, cockiest smile kicks up one side of his mouth. Before I can turn and hide, he peels Nora's hands from him and heads my way. "Dammit," I mutter.

"Hey, Briggsy. Didn't know you were coming." He talks loudly to be heard over the music, and still, I strain to hear him.

"Yeah. I didn't want to come. Rae made me," I bite out, hiding my...anger? Behind my red Solo cup, I pull in a deep gulp.

"Is that right?" His eyes roam over my face. What he's looking for, I have no clue.

"Why don't you go back to your little girlfriend before her head explodes?" Over his shoulder, I see Nora, arms crossed, causing her breasts to nearly tumble out of the low-cut top, staring daggers at us. I can almost feel her glare.

"She's not my girlfriend, and I don't care if her head explodes."

I shrug, ignoring the little zip of petty happiness his words give me, and take another sip.

"You drinking?" Levi asks casually.

I shrug again. "Maybe."

"Should you be?" He watches me warily as if he's waiting for a fight.

Defiantly, my eyes locked on his. I raise my cup, never breaking eye contact, even over the rim, and drink deeply until I've emptied it. Smacking my lips in exaggeration, I go a step further and let out an "aaaahhhh" as if it was the most refreshing, thirst-quenching drink I've ever had. Clearly, my petty is not just for Nora.

"That's some flex. You mad at me for something?" he asks, crossing his arms over his barreled chest. Of their own free will, my eyes dart over at Nora to where she still stands glaring. Levi glances behind him, following my gaze. "Oooh, you're jealous. I get it now. Well, Briggsy, just say the word, and I'm yours." His smile wide, dimples on full display. He really is *sexy*. A little dazed and a lot buzzed, it takes my fuzzy brain a bit longer to remember that I don't like him.

"In your dreams, Levi." I scoff.

"Oh, you have no idea," he says, his voice teasing.

Thankfully, I don't have time to figure out what he means by that because my cousin chooses that moment to appear at my side with another drink in hand. As if summoned, knowing I needed her to save me. I'm just not sure who she is saving me from. Levi or myself.

## 13

## LEVI

I can't help but admire the sway of Saffie's ass as she's pulled through the crowd by Raegan. It had only taken me a moment to realize that she was standing and watching Nora and me. Her laser-beam glare was a beacon drawing my eyes to hers. I never understood people saying shit like "I felt it before I saw it." I mean, not off the ice. But I totally did. I felt Saffie and her gaze on me before I saw her standing there. How long had she been there? Was she able to hear anything that Nora and I were saying? If she did, she would have heard things that would have no doubt made her blush. Nora had been telling me all the things that she wanted to do to me and how much she's missed me the last couple of weeks. I've done my best to avoid her without making it seem like I was avoiding her. Kind of hard to do at a party in my own house, though. Especially since any other time, we would've already been up in my room fucking.

The crowd swallowed them up, making it impossible for me to see where they'd gone. Clearly, Saffie has been drinking. I'll have to find her later to make sure she's okay. We always made sure that everyone at Hockey House feels safe no matter how much or how little they've had to drink. Bedroom doors stayed locked unless we were the ones using them, people checking the bathrooms, shit like that. Knowing that Saffie was in the house and drinking had my over-protectiveness kicking into high gear. Not the kind that my sisters cause either because I don't feel even a little brotherly toward her. Before I can think any more about how unbrotherly I feel about Saffron Briggs, Nora is beside me, looking mad as hell.

"Are we going upstairs or are you going to chase after Raegan's cousin?" she snips.

I know that the decision I'm about to make will have consequences I probably won't like later on, but it's not as if Nora is the only no-strings chick on campus. Although she seems pretty fucking *attached* lately. Not appreciating her tone, I just shrug. "I don't chase after anybody, Nora. You should know that better than anyone," I tell her before walking away without a backward glance to go find Saffie. Totally okay with the fact that I have time to make sure she stays out of trouble now that I've blown Nora off.

It doesn't take me long to find the group of them all huddled on my couch with their heads together, laughing and smiling, unaware of the guys hovering just behind them hoping to get some action. Making eye contact with one of them, I narrow my gaze and give a shake of my head. Not gonna happen. My face set like granite, I stare until they pick up what I'm throwing down and walk away. Satisfied, I turn my focus to Saffron. It doesn't take me but a second to notice her smile doesn't quite reach her eyes, and a pretty pink flush covers her cheeks. I make my way over to them and perch on the arm next to Millie, tugging her hair.

"Hey, ladies." I greet them all, but my eyes never leave Saffie. This close I can see that hers have that fuzzy glazed-over look you get when you're hella lit, and she is. Clearly. How much has she had to drink?

"Hey, Levi," my sister greets unenthusiastically.

"Saw the game the other night. Looking good, Sexy," Lakyn says, drawing my attention her way.

"You trying to get me naked, Lakyn?" I tease.

"Is it working?" she volleys, causing my sister to stick her finger in her mouth and make gagging noises.

"Not with so many people around. Don't want to make anyone jealous, right, Briggsy?" I wink at Lakyn and turn my attention back to Saffie, who is scowling into her cup.

"Yeah, Whore-a would *not* be happy about that," she says before taking a big swig of her drink.

Did she just say "whore A?" A shocked laugh slips out. "Did you—did you just say...Whore-a?" I glance at the faces of the girls sitting around the couch. Some averting their gazes, others with eyes as wide as hockey pucks. Holy shit, that is what she said.

"Oh my god, Levi, she said Nora. Don't be stupid," Millie says, pushing at my leg.

"You bunch of prudes. What about girl power and never slut shaming your fellow sisters?" I tsk. It's probably not the worst thing Nora's been called. She's literally the mean girl on campus.

"We don't slut shame," Rae insists.

"We Nora shame because she's a bitch," Saffie interjects. Yeah, she's definitely lit.

"She's only a bitch to people she doesn't like," I tell her, not even bothering to hide the smile her pinched, "I hate Nora," face brings to mine.

"So anyone who isn't you?" Saffie fires back. "Because she for sure doesn't like me. She acts like I'm going to steal you away from her." She snorts a little laugh and rolls her eyes.

"Are you?" Her gaze flies to mine, brows drawn low over her stormy gray eyes. My question lingers in the air wavering there like it's being carried by the beat of the music. The *thump thump* of the bass wars with the beat of my heart in my ear. I can feel the looks of the other girls bouncing between us, but I'm dialed in on Saffie. Like we're in the face-off circle, and I'm waiting for that puck to drop.

Her mouth opens and closes and opens again. "Eww, no. I have a boyfriend, remember?" she says, snarkily.

"Oh, I remember. Does he?" I glance around like I'm expecting him to appear. "Is he here? I'd love to meet him?" My smile is smug. Sparring with her is like foreplay, and I love it. Only instead of popping off, she stands up, a bit unsteady, and walks away without a word. Rae's right behind her, giving me a solid shot to the shoulder as she passes.

"Real nice, Levi," Millie says, her voice heavy with disdain.

"What?" I'm seriously confused.

Millie just shakes her head at me. "Didn't you notice she's drinking? Like, a lot."

"And?"

Kenna leans across the couch, her blue hair falling over her shoulder. "It's her dad's birthday, and her man is out partying. Butt dialed her on accident, she thought he was calling to check on her, but he didn't even say anything to her about it." She winces. "She's only seen him twice since she left St. Claire, and both times, it was because she went there." I typically don't give a shit about gossip like this, but I'm soaking up every word like a thirteen-year-old girl.

"Yeah, and the last couple of weeks have been really rough on her with the game and now her dad's birthday," Lakyn adds, her eyes narrowed into slits. "I think we need to take a road trip and beat his punk ass." There's so much heat in her words I think she might be serious.

"So that's why she's drinking? Because her boyfriend is a dick, and it's her dad's birthday, and he didn't say shit about it?" I just want to make sure I understand.

"Are you even listening, Levi?" Millie asks, totally out of patience with my ass.

"I was listening, but then I got a hard-on when Lakyn mentioned going to whoop his ass and forgot what Kenna said," I tell her, grinning and not entirely full of shit. I'd fight him. Not because he didn't call on purpose or whatever, but just because. I don't even care what kind of person that makes me.

Kenna giggles, and Lakyn points at me and winks. "Yes! That's what I'm talking about." Every team needs an enforcer, and clearly, Lakyn is theirs. She's down to fight for her friends, and I dig it.

"Oh my god. First, gross, Levi. Second, be serious. She's wasted and sad. That's never a good mix, and you just made it all worse," Millie accuses.

"I made it worse?" My voice rises to be heard over the music. "I'm not her fucking boyfriend. I didn't forget to call her." I shrug, glancing over my shoulder to see if I can find where they went. I can't, not her or Rae. Fuck. I school my features into a bored look just as one of the girls from Sorority Row walks by me, letting her painted fingernails skate across my back. I watch as she glides past and stops at the other end of the couch. She blows me a kiss right before she lifts her shirt and flashes me her red lace-covered tits. Usually, I'd be vaulting over the couch and burying my face between her perfect D cups before I even got her up to my room, but not tonight. God, what the hell is the matter with me? First Nora, now this chick who is obviously down to fuck. And for what? The ice princess? "Fuck me," I mutter as my bored expression becomes just that.

"Eww. Put your titties away!" Kenna shouts, jerking her thumb to the side. "Girl, bye. We're talking," she says, shooing her away before I can object even though I'm pretty sure I wasn't going to.

"She seems nice," Millie says, sarcasm dripping from every

syllable. Her eyes making their usual trip around the inside of her head.

Fucking with her, I smile. "I thought so." She would have been way nicer to me than Briggsy, that's for sure. Not wanting to talk about Briggsy and her boyfriend anymore, I stand. "Well, as much fun as this has been, I'm gonna go up to my room away from you bunch of cock blockers." Pointing at Millie, I use my big brother tone. "Don't get into any fucking trouble." Now that Maeve is splitting her time between the evil twin and their friends and Benny, I worry about Millie even more. The girl needs a keeper.

"Yeah, yeah. Don't have to worry about that here. There are snitches everywhere," she huffs.

"Watch out for your drunk-ass friend too. Come get me if she needs a ride back to her dorm."

"Be careful, Levi. If I didn't know you any better, I would swear you care about what happens to her," Lakyn says as she twirls one of her long braids around a finger, her smile smug.

I don't offer up a response because I can't deny it, but I'm not about to admit that to them either. With a finger wave over my shoulder, I pick my way through the crowd and up to my room. Alone. Probably for the first time since I moved into Hockey House.

## 14

## LEVI

Fresh from the shower, I run the towel across my chest and shoulders, catching the droplets left by my hair. Hockey season is in full force, which means the flow is too. And everybody knows that a hockey player is only as sick as his flow. Tossing the towel over the chair, I pull on my boxer briefs and a pair of FU Fire sweats. My body is loose and relaxed after the hot shower and self-love I had to resort to tonight. Contemplating sending a text out to Nora or one of the other hookups I have saved in my phone, I jump a bit when there's banging on my door. "The fuck." I laugh at being startled. I'm thinking about ignoring the knock, not really wanting to deal with anyone tonight no matter what I was trying to convince myself I wanted to do just a moment ago.

"Levi, it's Rae. Open!" Her voice is muffled, but I can still hear its urgency. Knowing that she wouldn't come up here and chance me being with anyone if it wasn't important, I hurry to the door and throw it open. She's not there but standing at the landing, looking over the rail down to the bottom of the stairs.

"Raegan, what's up?" She exhales a relieved breath.

"I need help. It's Saffie." She doesn't say anything more, just heads to the stairs. Moving so quickly I would swear she had her skates on. My heart pounds as I follow her. "I left her at the bottom of the stairs. I couldn't get her up them."

"Alone?" As the words leave my mouth, I see Saffie sitting, hunched a bit against the wall at the ground floor landing with Davey from the JV team standing over her. Not thinking or seeing past the adrenaline rush propelling me, I leap down the last few stairs and shove Davey. "Back the fuck up, bro!" He stumbles and hits the wall hard, drawing attention from people in the foyer. I ignore their curious looks and murmurs of "what the fuck?"

Saffie darts a glance up at me, messy bun more mess than bun, with an exasperated look on her face. "Hey! He was being nice." Her words are slurred. I bet he fucking was.

Davey holds his hands up, "Sexy, I was just waiting for you, I swear. Raegan told me to wait with her so she could get you." His voice cracks on the last word sounding like a thirteen-year-old going through puberty. "I would never fuck around like that, especially here."

He knows if he did and I found out, I would end his hockey career at FU so fucking quick. I don't apologize to him, just nod my head curtly. Let Rae console him. My focus is on Saffie. Squatting down so I'm eye level and don't need to yell to be heard, I ask, "Can you stand?" She glares at me with fire in her eyes. The gray looking misted over like fog on the harbor. I always love seeing that fire, but it brings some relief with it now. At least I know she's not gonna die of alcohol poisoning on my watch. My heart rate falls back into a normal cadence, and I smile at her anger. I can't decide what she's more mad about, me being here coming to her rescue or the fact that she won't be able to stand upright without my help. Without waiting for her to answer, I scoop her under her legs and around her back and stand. I fully expect a fight, but she must realize it won't do her any good.

"Do you ever wear clothes?" Her voice is sleepy but still full of fight and dislike for me.

"I try not to." I look down at her and wink, my dimples flashing with the smile I hit her with. It's not a lie.

She snorts a breath of disgust. "You really should at least wear a shirt. Especially when you're wearing sweatpants. It's... indecent." The last word slips from her lips as her eyes flutter closed, her head resting against my shoulder as I take the two flights of stairs to my room, laughing all the way and loving that she thinks me shirtless is indecent.

When I get to the door, I ease us through without pinging her head against the frame and lead us to my bed. Rae rushes past me to throw back the covers. I had forgotten all about her even being there.

"You gonna stay here too?" I ask quietly as I ease Saffie down, careful not to jostle her too much.

"I can't! I'm freaking out right now. I have to be on the ice by five o'clock because of half the team breaking curfew on Friday, and now here I am, breaking curfew *big time,* and my cousin is passed out drunk. Like, are you kidding?" she all but screeches.

"Rae. Holy shit, girl. Slow your roll." I pull out my phone and text Murphy. "Take her shoes off for me," I instruct to give her something to do other than tweaking.

> Me: Hey, you drinking?

> Murph: You know better.

> Me: yeah, I do. Sending Rae down. She needs a ride home. JUST a ride home.

> Murph: I got her. Tell her I'll meet her by the front door.

> Me: she'll be there in two.

"Murphy will drive you to your dorm so you're not walking back by yourself," I tell her, tossing my phone on the foot of the bed.

"Thank you! But what about my cousin? Your dad finds out, and she's dead." Her brows are pulled in worry, her pink hair looking like she's stuck her finger in an outlet. "I'll cover for her. If my dad finds out, I'll say we were studying, and she fell asleep." I shrug. "No big deal. It was his idea for me to tutor her anyway."

"I can't leave her here by herself!" Rae whisper-shouts frantically.

"Ummm...why? She's safer here than she would be passed out drunk in her dorm." Rae knows me. "I don't need to take advantage of anyone, Raegan. If I want ass, I'll go downstairs and get ass."

She gnaws on her bottom lip. "You're right. She'll be pissed that I left her with you, though."

"She'll get over it. Now go before Murphy comes looking for you. I've got her. I promise."

Raegan finally relents. I know that she's not worried about me but worried about how mad her cousin will be that she left her with the big bad hockey player. Anybody else, and this would be the worst idea in the fucking world. Rae knows me, though, and knows my ma raised me to respect women, and that goes double when they're drunk out of their fucking minds.

"Okay. Tell her not to be mad at me when she wakes up. Thank you!" With a quick hug, she dashes out of my room like Saffie might all of a sudden jump up and chase after her swinging. I watch her go down the steps before closing and locking the door, turning for the bed and my dinging phone.

> Murph: Got her
>
> Me: That was quick
>
> Murph: That's what she said *winky emoji*

I LAUGH at his dumb ass. That's what she said jokes will never get old.

> Me: Sorry to hear about that, bro.
>
> Murph: hear Briggs is up there. She good?
>
> Me: Yeah. She's OUUUTTTT.
>
> Murph: damn

AS IF SHE knows we're talking about her, she lets out a sleepy sigh.

> Me: Gotta go. Thanks for taking Rae.
>
> Murph: *deuces emoji*

PADDING over to where Saffie is lying sprawled on my bed, I contemplate my choices. I can sleep in my recliner, though at six-foot-four, that would suck ass. Or I could keep my sweats on and sleep next to her with the extra blanket. It's a king-sized bed with plenty of room. After convincing myself that it'll be fine, I go to my closet and grab the extra blanket before turning back to her. She has black leggings on, super comfy to sleep in, but her hoodie looks as if it's about to strangle her and smells like shit. Not *shit,* shit, but like vodka, beer, and bad decisions.

"Fuck," I mutter. Grabbing the hem, I lift to be sure she has a shirt on underneath before I try to wrestle her out of it as gently as I can. Satisfied that she at least has a tank top underneath, I start removing her arms from the sleeves, one by one and ever so slowly. All I need is for her to wake up now and think I'm some kind of fucking perv undressing her while she's unconscious. I mean, I am undressing her and she is unconscious, but I'm doing it for her, not me. There's a first time for everything, I guess.

Arms successfully uncovered, I try as best as I can to stretch out the neck and get her head through the hole. With only minimal tugging, I slip it over her head. As much as I want to just take her in, I don't allow my gaze to linger.

"There." I huff, tossing the sweatshirt onto the chair. Her phone falls out mid throw, landing with a thud on the plush carpet. I walk over and scoop it up, scowling when it lights up with a picture of Saffie and some douchey-looking guy I'm assuming is her boyfriend. "Asshole." Not just because he has Saffie. I mean, does he have her? Whose bed is she in right now? Not that she's in it for the reasons I wish she were, but I hate him for disappointing her. Which is pretty fucking funny coming from me. Other than my parents, coaches, and teammates, I've never cared about disappointing any-damn-body.

Not wanting to go there and dissect what that means, I put her phone on the nightstand and go get a Gatorade from the mini fridge. If she wakes up in the middle of the night she's going to feel like shit. With that thought in mind, I head to the bathroom for some ibuprofen and a trash can. Snagging my towel from earlier, I place it on the floor next to the bed and put the trash can on top of it, and the pills next to her drink. I've never played nurse in my fucking life, yet here I am doing a damn good job of it. And for someone who doesn't even like me.

Laughing at myself, I grab the corner of the blanket and pull it over her sleeping bag style to create a little more of a separation between us. Spare blanket in hand, I climb in next to her, wincing when the bed dips, and she rolls to her side. I do my best to get comfortable without disturbing her. My hands stacked under my head, I stare at the ceiling, wondering how the fuck I'm going to be able to sleep with her next to me. Even through the blankets, I can feel her heat, the sweet honey scent of her hair hovering between us. As I'm contemplating how the hell I thought this would work, Saffie rolls my way, out of her protective blanket, crossing onto my side of the bed. Head on my shoulder, hand splayed across my chest, heat-throwing pussy pressed into my thigh, and her leg tossed over my waist about two inches north of my now hardening dick.

Worst. Fucking. Idea. Ever.

Knowing that I'm only torturing myself, I bring my arms from behind my head and tuck her in even tighter to me, careful to keep my hands from the places I really want to grab, like her leggings-clad ass, the one she's wiggling back and forth the same way she did when she was up to bat. With a low and long, tortured groan, I close my eyes and just accept my fate as the dumb bastard I am.

## 15

## SAFFIE

The pounding in my temples feels as if someone is using my favorite bat to bash me upside the head. Over and over. Not even wanting to attempt to open my eyes, I snuggle deeper into Landon's arms. He must be really hitting the gym since I've been gone. His pecs are way more defined where my head rests, thighs hard under my leg, arms like steel around me. I run my nose along his collarbone, inhaling before pressing a soft kiss to his warm skin. "Mmm." He feels good under me. It's been so long that being in his arms like this again feels brand new. Feels right. I inhale again. He must be using a new soap too. Instead of the woody scent I'm used to, he smells cool. Like a winter breeze or like ice. Ice. He smells like ice. My eyes fly open, and my head comes up with a snap. Not Landon, Levi! I'm in Levi "Sexy" Sexton's room. In his bed. In. His. Arms. Holy fuck. I look down, hands patting at clothes. Okay, I'm fully dressed. But he's not. My gaze darts to his chest, bare except for the gold chain and medal resting where my head had just been. Blanket low on his waist but not low enough to tell me if he's dressed. I gingerly lift the edge and peek under, relieved when I see that he's wearing sweats, although they're not doing a very good job of keeping his massive hard-on in check. Jesus. It's as big as the rest of him.

"Like what you see?" Dropping the blanket as if it's burned me, I whip my head to his face, and the wicked smirk lifting the corner of his mouth. "Morning, Briggsy." His dimples flash along with his ridiculously perfect white teeth.

"What in the fuck?" I croak out. Literally croak. Like a frog being strangled.

"How's the head?" he asks, concern in his voice. How does he sound so normal right now? My brain feels as if it's in quicksand. I just stare blankly, trying to string sentences together in my mind to ask more questions. Like "how did I end up here?" "Why am I in your bed?" Why, oh why did I freaking like it so much?" It doesn't happen, and he doesn't wait for me to get my shit together. Instead, he rolls over, pressing me into the mattress and pinning me with his massive body. *All* of his massive...body. Propped on his elbows, he focuses his eyes on mine. His fingers make their way into my hair, massaging my scalp, then down to the base of my neck and back again.

"Get off me," I splutter, though it's halfhearted at best. My head is in a fog, and my body is aching...in all kinds of ways. Ways that I am going to ignore from now until forever.

With a smile that tells me he knows exactly why I want him off, he stays put, instead reaching for something on the nightstand. Before I have time to think about what he could be grabbing, he brings his fingers to my mouth. "Open."

Like hell. I shout silently to myself even as I do exactly what I'm told. Levi places two tablets on my tongue, reaching again onto the nightstand and returning with a bottle of Gatorade. He squeezes, squirting the liquid into my mouth the whole act impossibly sinful even in its innocence. "Swallow," he murmurs, his voice gruffer than it was just a moment ago. The two commands shouldn't sound as dirty as they do. Maybe it's the way he's watching me as I do what he tells me to. Or the way I can feel his dick against me growing with every breath I take.

"Good girl," he rumbles.

I blink slowly, trying to focus. This is Levi, I remind myself. You don't even like him.

"I don't even like you." Shit. That was out loud.

Levi smirks. "Whatever you need to tell yourself, sweetheart."

"Uggghhhh, you're so infuriating." I push at his rock-hard pecs, knowing that if he didn't want to budge, I couldn't do anything about it. For some reason, the thought doesn't worry me as much as it should. With his weight off me, I can think a little more clearly. "What am I even doing here with you?" My voice is less croaky than it was but still a little weak because of the marching band in my head. Not letting that slow me down, I kick free of the covers and stand, looking for my things. "Where's Rae? I'm going to kill her." I don't ask the question I really want the answer to. Mostly because I don't know how to even approach the subject and also because of my body's reaction to him, I'm almost afraid of the answer.

Levi just sits propped against his headboard, watching me rant and stomp around the room without actually getting anything accomplished. I still don't have my hoodie, my phone, my shoes, or answers. "Well? Are you just going to sit there, or are you going to help me?" I huff. I know I sound like an ungrateful bitch, but he's got me flustered and clearly when Levi has me this way, I act out.

"Nah, you're doing a stellar job all on your own," he says cooly. Enjoying this way too much.

Pissed at him and myself for letting him get to me, I spin. "You know, you could at least tell me what happened last night. Did we?" I flap a hand between us, not finishing the question, hands planted on my hips as I glared at him, pretending my heart wasn't thundering against my rib cage.

"Did we what?" Levi locks his fingers behind his head and settles deeper into the bed and headboard. The movement causes his muscled chest to ripple, the gold charm on his chain sliding to the side, his biceps bulging. Why does he have to look like...that? I don't even want to know what I look like. I wasn't winning any beauty contests when I got here, and that was before I drank myself stupid and slept it off in Levi's bed. Lovely. I fight the urge to lift a hand to check my hair. What was the question again? Oh right.

"You know what, Levi. Don't be a dick."

"Did we sleep? We did. You a little better than I did since *somebody*, I'm not naming names, was over on my side of the bed the whole night." He looks so pleased with himself over that little tidbit. "Wiggling her ass around like she does when she's up to bat."

"I do not wiggle my ass." The words are pushed past clenched teeth and stiff lips.

"Oh, you wiggle." Levi waggles his eyebrows at me, his lip pulled between his teeth.

I'm not willing to argue whether I do or don't because I need to steer him back on track. "Did we do anything else?" I prod. He's going to make me say it. I know he is.

"We didn't get a chance to talk really if that's what you're asking." The ass.

"Oh, for the love...fine! You win. Did we have sex last night?" My teeth are clenched so tight I think they might shatter as I stare him down, pretending like my insides aren't all wishy-washy right now.

Levi rises from the bed like he doesn't have a single care in the world and like I'm not standing there waiting for an answer to a very important question. When he still doesn't answer, I fume.

"I have a boyfriend, for shit's sake. This is not funny." It's not funny, but not because of Landon. I'm still so pissed at him. My mind is fuzzy. I might even be a little drunk still, but I vaguely remember calling him again and some chick answering, "Landon's phone, he's not available right now." That's when things get reeeaaalllly fuzzy. I started drinking even heavier than I had been. Totally unlike me and probably why I can't remember shit after that. And why I feel like I got hit by a truck.

He turns to face me, a bored expression on his face. The scar on his lip a little less noticeable than usual under the scruff of facial hair he's sporting. "Always the boyfriend with you, Briggsy. Is it me you're trying to remind or yourself?"

My eyes narrow. "I'm not reminding anyone, just stating a fact."

"You state it a *lot*." When he's being like this, it makes it easier for me to dislike him and ignore the way he had my body tingling just a few minutes ago. And he still hasn't answered the question.

"Just answer the damn question, Levi."

"What do you think?" His legs are planted wide, his arms folded across his chest, and his dirty-blond hair flopping over one eye, looking like he didn't have a single care in the world. I hate him.

"I don't know what to think! You're...you." I flick my hand in his direction.

"I am...me. And being that I am, I can promise you two things. One: I'm all about consent. Because consent. And No ass is worth going to prison for or losing my ride to the show. Even yours. And two: if we had fucked, you'd know. There wouldn't be a question in your mind. You'd feel me still in places you didn't even know existed. You wouldn't have to be reminded of anything or even have to ask." His voice is sure as if he's speaking from experience. Which he probably is.

My mouth opens and closes like a fish, my eyes wide and unblinking, watching him watch me, the smugness of his promise oozing off him. I guess that answers that. Thankfully, someone knocks on the door, saving me from having to come up with something to say after his little speech. Not wanting anyone to find me in here, though I'm sure they all already know I spent the night, I grab my phone off the nightstand and dart into the bathroom, slamming the door behind me. With my breathing erratic and my heart racing, I go to the sink and try to forget what Levi just said to me and how it had me hotter than I'd ever admit. I groan at my reflection in the mirror. "Wonderful. He's out there looking like he just walked off the cover of some hot guy sports magazine, and I look like I was mauled by a damn bear," I whine, totally aware that I'm talking to myself. Just wanting to get the hell out of here, I do my best to wash off the smudged eyeliner and fix my knotted bedhead. My hands still when I hear voices. Tiptoeing to the door, I press an ear against the cool wood to listen.

"How was practice?"

"Brutal. Where's my cousin?" I fumble with the lock at the sound of Rae's voice.

"Hiding in the bathroom," Levi responds.

He's such an ass. "I am not hiding," I shout as I storm into the room, finally free of the bathroom and its tricky door. Eyes on Rae, I keep my focus there instead of on the half-dressed jock who just had me feeling as if I had played seven innings in the hot sun.

"Saffie! You look...good," my cousin says, trying to lie straight to my face. "How do you feel?"

"I feel fine. Can we go?" The clip in my tone isn't really for her. Well, it is because she is the one who left me here with him, but it's my fault I drank so much and gave her no other choice.

"S-Sure," she stammers, looking worried.

"Don't be hard on Rae, Briggsy. It's not her fault we didn't hook up. Maybe next time, don't try to seduce me when you're drunk. The outcome will be better for both of us." My head whips in his direction, causing my vision to go a little spotty from the pain.

"In. Your. Dreams." Twice in one week, I've uttered those words to him. I don't think I've ever said them before a day in my fucking life.

"You're the one with the ass wiggle and soft kisses, so probably in yours." He winks as he walks past us into the bathroom, dropping his gray sweats at the open door and kicking them away. Rae yelps behind me at the sight of his bare ass, grabbing my wrist and dragging me out of the bedroom before we see even more of Levi Sexton than *she* wants to.

# 16

## SAFFIE

It's been five days since that little scene in Levi's room. Thankfully, I've managed to avoid him pretty easily on a campus as large as Fulton. I never would have been able to at St. Claire's. Now, with an important exam looming, I need his help. As much as I hate to admit it, this accelerated A&P class is hard as hell, and Levi is crazy smart. I honestly don't know if I would be passing without his help. So, with my A on the line, I've sucked it up and asked him to study with me. I've insisted we meet at the library instead of his house. There's no way I'm ready to be locked in a bedroom with him again so soon. I still feel guilty about that. I mean, who am I to get all pissy with Landon for a girl answering his phone, which he explained and was totally no big deal, and there I am, sleeping in someone else's bed! Not just someone else either, Levi's bed. Hockey stud, on his way to the pros, hottest playboy on campus, Levi Sexton. Literally anyone else's bed would have been better. Thank god Landon doesn't know where I was that night or who Levi *really* is, other than my tutor. I mean, even the most secure guy on the planet would feel some kind of something if they knew their girl spent the night with the guy on campus they nicknamed *Sexy*. Not that Landon has anything to worry about. All that silly tingly, light-headed stuff I was feeling was totally because I was still drunk when I woke up. Simple as that. I'm too smart to catch feelings for him, especially when I have a boyfriend and especially *especially* when I don't even like Levi. Not his cocky smile or the dimples that should make him look innocent but fail miserably instead, adding to the wickedness that oozes from him. Not the scar through his lip that makes him look a little wild and a lot dangerous. The one I refuse to ask him about. And I definitely don't like that my cousin trusted him enough to leave me with him, totally wasted, without a second's hesitation about my safety.

"Nope. Don't like that," I mutter. I don't want to think of him as some chivalrous guy who everyone can see good in but me. But that would be a lie, wouldn't it? Because I have seen good in Levi. He's come through for me more than once, and that makes me madder than it should. Not willing to ask what kind of person that makes me, I focus on what matters. Which is one, I don't like Levi. He's my tutor, and that's all. And two, I have a boyfriend who I *do* actually like. A lot. The other day was nothing, less than nothing, and I've been stupid to avoid him over it. That thought puts a little bounce in my step instead of the dragging feeling I've had over our first face-to-face. Amazing what a brisk walk in the cold Boston air and a pep talk with yourself will do for your mood.

Lighter now, I tug open the heavy ornate library doors and let the quiet and warmth blanket me. I love the smell and feel of libraries. It brings me a sense of peace. Almost like the mound does. Softball and books, my two loves. The study room log book is on the desk. I make my way over to it to look for Levi's name. *Room 107*. I didn't realize there were that many.

"Excuse me?" I say quietly to get the librarian's attention.

With her easy smile and funky style, she looks as if she could be a student here. "Can you tell me where study room 107 is?"

"Are you meeting Levi?" she asks, her tone curious bordering on dubious.

"Yup." *Not that it's her business but whatever,* I think irritably.

"Room 107 is upstairs in the science wing. He got here a little while ago," the nosy librarian, who I was thinking complimentary things about moments ago but now think maybe she's a lot older than I originally thought, says. I give a wave of thanks and head the way she indicated. I haven't been up here yet, and realize now that the floor is separated by major. There's business, science, communications, and arts sections that I can see from here. I make my way to the science area, appreciating how easy it makes studying. Everything right at your fingertips with models and study guides available as well. Our study room is the last one, tucked back away from the others. Windows line the wall leading to the room, and I can see Levi at the table...along with three girls I don't recognize. One sitting on the table in front of him, swinging her leg back and forth so that it brushes against him, the other two huddled around them giggling and murmuring god only knows what. Wonderful. Everywhere he freaking goes, a trail of girls follow him like cum-thirsty, lusty-eyed little zombies. I contemplate not even going in but talk myself out of it just as quickly. "Screw that." I open the door and let it close behind me with a loud bang that makes me cringe inwardly. I'm going to get us kicked out of the damn library over *his* ridiculousness. All heads turn my way, only one of them happy to see me.

"Hey, Briggsy," he says, a dimpled smile lighting up his face. "Ladies, my study date is here. Maybe some other time," he tells them, his tone full of what sounds like chagrin. His announcement is met with pouts and simpers. I can only imagine what they had been offering. Doing my best not to roll my eyes or say anything hateful, I come fully into the room and drop my bag down on the table.

They walk by, not missing the chance to glare at me on their way out.

"You know, hanging out with you is making it really hard for me to make female friends here," I say as the door closes behind the entourage, not even a little upset about them leaving or by the fact they don't want to make friends with me.

Levi laughs. "Don't let them get to you, Saffie. They all just want a ride to the show, and they think they'll get there on my jock." For a minute, I think that might upset him.

"Is that what you think?" My hands still, my brows drawn as I watch him and wait for his answer, still trying to decide if he's upset about it. To anyone looking in, Levi is carefree, a player, and someone who, as I've heard him say, only loves hockey, his bed, and his mama. But maybe that's just what he let's us see.

"It's what I know. Don't get me wrong, I'm a fucking catch. I mean, look at me." He holds his arms out to the side to give me a better glimpse of him in all his glory. And I do. My eyes touch at the top of his head, baseball cap flipped backward, the dirty-blond strands licking at the brim, black T-shirt stretched tight across his muscled chest and arms, the gold chain and medal he always wears bright against the dark material. "I know what they see." His voice snaps me back to his face, his blue eyes twinkling at my ogling. "They don't seem to understand, though, that no amount of tits and ass they throw my way will have me pledging my undying love for them and taking them with me when I leave."

"Charming," I say, my tone dripping in sickly sweet sarcasm.

He shrugs. "It is what it is, and I am who I am." There are no apologies in his words.

"And who's that, Dr. Seuss?" I tease, unpacking my notes from my bag.

"I've been known to play doctor a time or two..." He bursts out laughing at my look of disgust. "Don't knock it till you try it, Briggsy."

Refusing to even let myself think about playing doctor or anything else with him, I change the subject. "So how well did you do on this chapter? Because it's kicking my ass so far."

"You have Canerday, right? She breaks it down into two parts so you don't have to do the muscular and skeletal at once, which makes it a little easier."

"Thankfully. I don't think I could do both at once," I admit, lining my pens and highlighters up in front of me.

"You'd do fine. We would just have to study more. Bet you're glad she doesn't. All that together time would make it so much harder for you to hate me," Levi says.

"Or easier." I snort.

"You wound me, Briggsy." He stands and moves toward the door.

"Are you—are you leaving? I was just kidding." I didn't think I could actually hurt his feelings. Wasn't sure he actually had any.

Levi turns, his face screwed into a comical expression. "Umm, no. It'll take a lot more than that to chase me away. I'm wicked tough." He stands straighter, puffing out his chest a bit. It elicits an eye roll from me, which I know is what he expected. "I'm going to grab Bob."

"Wait? Who? I don't want to study with anyone else."

"What? Like I'm gonna share you with anyone." Levi shakes his head like I'm silly for even thinking such a thing and leaves the room.

"*Like I'm gonna share you...*" I know he didn't mean it that way, but it had me feeling a certain way, and I didn't like that it did. I wasn't Levi's to share or not share. And I didn't want to be. I have a boyfriend. And he is *not* Levi. He's nothing like him, as a matter of fact. The thought didn't give me as much comfort as

I hoped it would. Before I can dwell on that any further, there's a clatter at the door. I turn to see Levi rolling in "Bob."

Laughing, I get up to hold the door for him.

"Briggsy, meet Bob." He holds the skeleton's hand out for me to shake.

Taking the bony extremity, I can't help but smile. "Nice to meet you, Bob."

"This dude is a lifesaver. It really helps to have more of a visual for you to actually put hands on. As much as I would love to be your Bob, I figured you wouldn't be down for feeling up my bones."

I choke out a laugh. Does he know what B.O.B. stands for? By the glimmer in his eyes, I'm guessing yes.

"Get your mind out of the gutter, Briggsy."

"Me? You're the one offering yourself to be my battery-operated boyfriend!"

"Trust me doll, you'd throw Bob and all his buddies right in the trash if you gave me a chance."

Give Levi Sexton a chance? Not gonna happen. I like my heart in one piece. Not that he's serious. But still.

"You don't want a chance. You want some ass." Why am I engaging? I know better than to encourage him.

"I can get ass all day long without even trying. Don't tell me what I want, woman." His tone is half serious, half teasing and all the way truthful. Hell, he just sent three girls I know for a fact would have screwed him right here in the library, on their merry little way.

"As tempting as that offer *isn't,* I'm more interested in your brains than your body," I tell him. Meaning it. Mostly.

"That's a first," he says on a laugh, rolling the skeleton to the head of the table so we can start studying.

THREE HOURS LATER, a light comes on in the room, drawing my attention. "Time's up, Briggsy." Levi starts gathering his stuff, sliding my things over to put away.

"Is that what that light is?" I ask, snapping the lids on my highlighters.

"Yeah. This way, they don't have to come up here to kick us out."

"Makes things easier. Although I'm sure the librarian wouldn't mind coming up here to talk to you." Damn, I didn't mean to let that slip out in *that* tone or at all really. I have to be careful around him. He makes me act irrationally.

"Miss Tate?" he asks with a devilish gleam in his eye. "Yeah, you're probably right. She has a sweet spot for me." Levi just shrugs it off as if he's used to it.

I'm taken aback by his admission, glad he didn't call me out on my noticing. "Must be so hard being you," I say, slipping my bag over my head, the strap cutting across my chest.

"Oh, it's hard all right," he quips smugly. I walked right into that one. He barks out a laugh at my deadpan expression. "Come on, Briggsy. It's game night, and I have to get home for dinner."

I hold the door, allowing him to roll Bob through. "Another one? Didn't you play last night?"

He glances back over his shoulder. "Were you there?"

"Uh, no. Rae was, though. I was at the batting cages."

"For a minute there, I thought you were stalking me." His lips break into a grin.

"You wish, Sexton." I scoff. "No really, though, isn't that a lot?"

Levi trots down the steps on his way to the front desk, waving to his biggest fan, Miss Tate, as he holds the door open for me to slip by. "It's Sweater Weather, Briggsy," he says like that explains everything.

I glance around at the fat floating flakes. "I mean, yeah. It was cold when I got here, but at least it wasn't snowing then," I respond, regretting letting Rae borrow the truck. Walking back to the dorm in this will suck. Not sure what it being cold out has to do with a heavy game schedule, though.

Levi stops in his tracks, causing me to run right into him. "Oomph." My breath whooshes from between my lips. He's like a damn mountain. Reaching out to steady me, he says slowly as if it will make it easier for me to understand.

"No, I mean it's *Sweater Weather*."

I blink and stare at him. Am I the dumbass or is he? "Yes, it is. It's winter." I draw the words out as slowly as he did.

"Seriously, Briggsy?" At my blank look, he goes on, "A hockey jersey is called a sweater. Sweater Weather is hockey season...get on my level, girl." He chuckles.

"Speak a language I understand. Hockey speak makes no sense unless you're a hockey player." In the short time I've known him, I've discovered that it is literally a language all its own. One I will never understand.

"All you have to do is spend a little more time with me, and you'll be speaking Hockey like a natural. I'll teach you all the things, Briggsy." He waggles his eyebrows at me suggestively.

"I'm good," I respond, laughing when he grips his chest as if my words wound him.

"Where's your truck?" Levi glances around the parking lot.

"I let Rae borrow it to go see her mom." I shrug. "I needed to study and didn't want her to Uber it or anything. No big."

"Come on, I'll drive you."

"You don't have to. I'm fine." Even as the words leave my mouth, the snow starts coming down harder, blowing in all directions like we're in a snow globe, and someone just shook the hell out of it.

"It's freezing and snowing, and you don't even have a jacket." He grabs my arm and practically drags me over to his truck parked right in front in the preferred parking lot.

Knowing there's no way he'll let me walk, I go along. "Are you supposed to be parked here? Isn't it for teachers and library staff or whatever?"

Bottom lip caught between his teeth, his smile mischievous, he shrugs.

I can't help but laugh. "Let me guess, Miss Tate?"

"I can't help who finds me irresistible and who doesn't, Briggsy. It's a gift."

"It's something all right," I quip, shaking my head at him and his massive ego. He surprises me by opening the truck's door, then standing back to let me get in. "Thanks." I hop in and let him close the door, taking a second to look around the clean yet slightly stinky, but not *so* stinky cab. I recognize the smell immediately. It smells like Levi and hockey, and I realize two things. One, I know his scent, and two, I kind of like it.

## 17

## LEVI

With Briggsy safely in my truck, I walk around the front and climb in. Firing it up, I crank the heat for her. "Are you cold? It should warm up in here in just a minute."

"Thanks. I feel like it gets colder here than it did back home," she says, rubbing her hands together to warm them.

"Maybe? I typically don't notice the cold all that much. You spend as much time as I do on the ice, and it's weird not to be surrounded by cold. It's like a security blanket. Does that make sense?" I let a little self-conscientious laugh escape. I've never tried to explain things like that to anyone. My friends all got it, but they played hockey. The chicks I hung out with...well, we weren't doing a whole lot of talking. But with Briggsy— I liked talking to her. She barely tolerated me most days, but when she did, she was a good time. Hell, even when she didn't, she was a good time.

She nods. "It makes total sense. The cold is a part of you, like an old friend or something. I get it." I believe that she does, and I appreciate her not making fun of me for it.

Not wanting to make shit awkward, I don't say anything and

put the truck in reverse. Before I get it in drive, the cab fills with the ringing of my phone, startling Briggsy. I laugh and pat her leggings-clad thigh, the heat of her skin meeting my palm. It takes everything in me not to keep my hand there, even more not to slide it up farther and settle it more snugly between her thighs to *really* hit her hot spot. Reluctantly, I take my hand away and accept the call.

"Hey, Ma." I stop moving and lean on the steering wheel. Selfishly, I don't want to be on the phone with my mom for the entire ride over to Briggsy's dorm.

"Hi, baby. You on your way?" I can hear the clank of glass plates and silverware in the background.

"Yeah, I have to drop Briggsy off first, and then I'll be there."

"Shh, Millie, hush!" she admonishes. "Who? I'm sorry, you're on speaker, and your sister is making crazy faces and won't be quiet long enough for me to hear you."

I'm sure Millie heard exactly who I said I was with, which is why she's losing her damn mind. "Hi, Mill!" I say sweetly to goad her. "I said I'm with Briggsy, Ma. Saffron Briggs. We've been together all afternoon." I look over to where she sits in the passenger seat, shaking her head at my embellishment. She too knows that my sister's head is in danger of exploding after I dropped that little nugget.

"Saffie! Saffie, get out of the truck and run!" My sister's yells make me cringe as her shrill voice takes up way too much space inside my truck.

"Millie Margo Sexton. Get ahold of yourself!" Ooohhh, my mom means business. She busted out Millie's government name. "Levi. Bring Saffron here for dinner. She's going to the game, right?" I glance over with my brows raised in question.

"Well, Briggsy?" I ask, putting her on the spot.

"Oh! Am I on speaker too? Saffron, can you hear me?" my ma asks, done talking to me apparently.

"Hi, Mrs. Sexton," Briggsy says, giving me the finger. She knows there's no way she'll be able to say no now.

"Hi, doll. I'll set a place at the table for you." She doesn't bother asking.

"I really shouldn't. I don't even have any team swag or anything to wear to the game," Briggsy tries lamely. I have to roll my eyes at that and mouth, "Nice try." That earns me the finger again.

"Oh sweetie, we have more clothes with Levi's name and number on them than the pro shop has of the whole team combined. I'll just go grab you something from the closet." Again not asking or waiting for an answer, my ma goes on, "Hurry up, you two, we don't want to rush dinner on game night. You'll skate like garbage. See you in a few. Bye." And just like that, she was gone.

"Well, you heard her," I say, glad my ma called and laid it down.

"Yeah, I did." She looks a little shell-shocked. "She's a force."

I shrug and smile. "That she is and she doesn't play when it comes to me and my game." And that's no lie. She's the first to tell me I play well and also the first to tell me if I've played like shit. She would look at me and say, "How do you think you played?" and I would know that she thought I hadn't played my best, and she was always right.

"I can tell." Briggsy laughs. "As soon as she said 'hi, doll,' I knew she meant business."

"My ma always means business, but you know when she really, *really* means business?" I prompt glancing over at her with a smile as I slip the truck back into drive.

With a deep sigh and a reluctant smile, she answers, "When it's *Sweater Weather*."

"When it's *Sweater Weather*." I grin, loving that she was paying attention. "I told ya, Briggsy. Stick with me, and I'll teach you all kinds of new things."

## Sweater Weather

~

STANDING at the doorway of the locker room, leading out to the tunnel, I fist bump each player as they go through. It's a ritual that brings me a sense of calm. It's my time to connect with each of them as their captain and also helps me to find my center and think about the game ahead. Tonight, though, I find myself thinking about Saffie. How she laughed at my mom's lame-ass jokes at dinner and rolled her eyes at me when I told her she looked good wearing my number. I know that now is not the time for that shit and I have to focus on the game. It's the same team we played last night, one of our biggest rivalries after Boston College. They're a tough team, fast and aggressive. We won last night but only barely. I want us to play harder and win bigger tonight. And not just because Saffie is here. I mean, it has something to do with it, but I always want to win. Always want to do better than the game before. Her being here is just a bonus.

Murphy is the last one out the door. I fist bump him and slap his well-padded ass. "You ready, Murph?" I fall into step behind him, laughing at his goalie waddle.

"I'm ready, Sexy, are you? You gonna show off all your tricks for Saffie tonight?"

"I'm me. I don't have to show off. That shit comes naturally." I grin, flashing him my black mouthguard with SEXY painted on it in red. He laughs, knowing damn well I'm right, and whacks me with his stick.

We step out onto the ice, all talk stopping as the noise from the crowd and the video montage playing above us rise to deafening levels. We go separate ways, him to stretch it out and me to shoot around a bit with the boys, run some easy warm-up drills until the horn. Benny skates next to me with a shit-eating grin on his face. "How'd you get Saffie to wear your number, bro?" He takes a pass from Decker and slaps it at Murph. "I would've bet money that she would rather die than wear anything of yours."

I just shrug and laugh. "You probably would've won that bet last week. I'm growing on her." I call as I skate across the ice to take a clapper at Murph, blowing him a kiss when it whizzes by him. If he could, he would've flipped me off for the kiss and the goal.

We each take a couple more easy shots at Murph before the horn blares, signaling the start of the player intro that Fulton University is notorious for. Skating off the ice and back through the tunnel, we gather in the locker room for Coach's pregame pep talk. We all stand, leaning on our sticks, as he steps up on the bench so that he doesn't have to look up at any of us as he delivers his speech.

"All right, you guys, last night they nearly handed us our asses. They played rougher than we did, smarter and skated faster. Tonight, it's our turn. There's no reason in the goddamn world they should beat us or even come close. We're better than they are in every way. Be better. This is our house. Don't let them come here and take a shit in it." He looked at us all pointedly and then gave a curt nod and yelled out, "Whose house?"

We yelled back louder, "Our house!"

"Whose house?"

Louder still, we yelled, "Our house!"

"I said whose house?" he shouts, making the coffee in his cup slosh over the rim and onto the floor.

"Our house!" we boom, our voices bouncing off the lockers and walls around us, putting our chant in stereo.

"Let's go, then!" Coach pops the now nearly empty cup on top of the locker nearest to him and hops down. He leads us back out through the tunnel to wait for them to introduce us one by one. As they do, he slaps us on the back and offers up words of encouragement before we skate through the flaming archway.

"Skate hard.

"Use your body.

"Keep your damn head up!"

Something different for each of us that he shouts over the noise and chants from the crowd. When he gets to me, he claps me first across the numbers and then on the back of my helmet.

"Give 'em hell but keep your cool, Sexton."

Now that everyone is announced, we're lined up shoulder to shoulder on the blue line as the crowd settles and waits for Nora to make her way onto the ice for the Anthem. Hand over my heart, I scissor on my skates back and forth, thinking about the game ahead. This is my calm before the storm. The time I need to tune out everything and everyone around me and focus on what comes next. Tonight, though, I'm fighting the urge to look over my shoulder at Saffie. I can feel her here in a damn arena with about ten thousand people in it. I've never in all my life been more aware of a person, especially before a game. I need to shake this shit off before the puck drops. Doing my best to shift my focus, I close my eyes, even out my breathing, and think about the plays we've been running all week. About what we need to do to beat these assholes tonight and not about the girl sitting in the stands behind me with my name and number all over her body like I want to be.

My eyes open as Nora sings the last note. Without giving her a glance, I put my helmet on and skate off the line to do my usual warm-up laps. I always start with a couple passes around the ice, past the puck bunnies typically sitting on the glass in the section right next to the bench. I usually take time to give them a wink and a wave. Sometimes that gets me a flash of titties, sometimes it gets me sucked off after the game, and *sometimes* it leads to one hell of a party at my house with very little clothes. Today, I barely glance their way, eager to get to where my family is sitting with Saffie and Raegan, who made it to my house just in time for dinner. I breeze around the rink, the air ruffling the hair at my nape, the smell of the ice, the feel of it under my blades, the sounds of the arena the energy of it all feeding my own. I make it over to the crease where my parents are. I smile at the four girls as I glide past them, my sisters and Rae waving like crazy people, and Saffie *trying* to look unimpressed. With a smirk and a head shake, I continue bumping the glass with my fist where my dad stands waiting like he does every game. As he sits, my ma raises her hand and gives me a little Shaka wave like she's done since I was ten years old, new to playing on a team. I asked her why once, and she said "so you know I see you, that I'm watching, and that I know you will do and *can* do what you need to." And that was enough for me. Though I've never doubted that and have always sought her out in the crowd before every game, every shit-ass play, every goal, and penalty for that little hand gesture to ground me. I nod when I see it and skate off to the bench, ready for the game to start.

By the end of the third, we're winning three to two, and I'm one goal away from a hat trick. Benny and I are sitting on the bench next to each other waiting for our shift when Cubbie takes a hit right in front of us that sends him over the boards and into our laps. The crowd is on their feet shouting in dismay. They've played like this all night. The hits got dirtier as the game went on, and we held our lead. We scramble to right Cubbie and help him back onto the ice. As Coach yells at the refs and then the other team's coach about the dirty hit, a scrum has started on the ice between our defenseman and the other players. Benny and I are just about to jump over the boards to intervene when Coach Kiehn grabs the backs of our sweaters, jerking us back onto the bench. "You two hotheads keep your asses put! I don't need you getting ejected!"

"Coach—" He cuts me off.

"I'm telling you, Sexton, Hayes, don't either of you step foot onto that ice until I say to. You beat their asses up there," he says, pointing at the scoreboard.

Pissed but knowing it won't do us any good to argue, we sit back down.

The refs get everyone separated and put the players in the penalty box, leaving us both short handed. Finally, we get the go-ahead with less than thirty seconds left on the clock and burst off the bench like we're on fire. Meeting Sperry, their captain, at center ice for the face-off, I get into position. My hands are low on the stick, skates set wide. I jerk my chin at Benny to let him know that I'm sending the puck his way.

"You crybabies ready to play, or should we fight over what a bunch of pussies you are some more?"

I don't bother answering, just grin, flashing him my SEXY mouthguard. I could chirp back and say some smart-ass shit, but Coach is right. I'm going to kick his ass by scoring my third goal of the night against him and his weak-ass line. The ref releases the puck between us, and I drop my shoulder to block him out and throw him off balance. It works, and before he can recover, Benny has the puck, and I'm on my way around Sperry to the net. Benny is skating up the middle, drawing two of their players, so I break off and burst up the ice on his side, wide open to receive the pass I know is coming. The second it does, I reel back and fire, not giving any of them a chance to shift my way. By the time they make it to me, the horn blows to signal the end of the game, the band plays our fight song, and the puck is buried in the back of the net. I glance over my shoulder, a wide smile splitting my face to see my family all on their feet screaming and cheering. I can hear them over the rest of the crowd when I'm this close. And the one yelling the loudest... Saffron Briggs.

## 18

## LEVI

"Hey, bro, you gonna be okay if we get out of here?" Cubbie calls from the bench he's sitting on, taking off his skates. He, Murphy, and Benny came out to help me finish the setup on the outdoor rink. Every winter, the team sets it up out behind the actual arena as a fundraiser.

"I'll be fine. I'm just gonna do a couple more things here."

"You're sure, Sexy? I don't want to leave you hanging," Murphy says, not looking convinced.

"Like he'd be letting us leave if he still needed help." Benny scoffed, already putting his skates in his bag.

"He's not typically right about shit, but he's right about that." I laugh as he shrugs off the jab.

"Go, I'll catch you guys back at the house later." I wave them off and skate over to the opposite end of the ice to the Zamboni doors to make sure they're locked. That's all we need is some dumbass taking a joy ride on the Zam. A lesson we've learned the hard way. The next time we open the outdoor rink will be for rat hockey, so I push the nets into place. I'm just securing the second one when my phone buzzes in my pocket. I pull it out and can't help the smile that splits my face.

> **Briggsy:** Where are you????? I just went by the house, and nobody was home.
>
> **Me:** You stalking me?
>
> **Briggsy:** Hardly. It was super weird that nobody was there since the house is always packed. And seriously, lock your damn door, you weirdos!
>
> **Me:** We never do. Nobody ever just walks in. Usually…

I tease her. I kind of like that she felt comfortable enough to just walk into my house. I'm not sure why, but I'm not going to look too deeply into it.

> **Briggsy:** Your sister told me to! She was with me.
>
> **Me:** Just kidding, Briggsy. You can come right in whenever you want. Just be warned that you might see shit you don't want to see.
>
> **Briggsy:** There's not enough eye bleach in the world for the things I've already seen going down at your house!
>
> **Briggsy:** ANYWAYSSSS. Where are you?
>
> **Me:** I'm at the outdoor rink.
>
> **Briggsy:** We have one of those?!?!
>
> **Me:** Yeah, back behind the arena.
>
> **Briggsy:** Cool! Be there in a sec. Dropping Maeve off.

I don't tell her that I was just about to leave, happy to have her to myself for a while. Something else I'm not going to look too deeply into. Instead, I go over to the skate rental area and flip on the lights I had just turned off. I'll get her out on the ice, maybe teach her how to skate. I'm not sure why she's even coming, but I'll keep her here for a bit.

> Me: What size shoe do you wear?

> Briggsy: 7 why?

> Me: Just get here. I'll see you in a few.

I put my phone away and reach for a pair of size 7 skates off the shelf. I rub my thumb down the blade, checking that they're sharpened well. Putting them on the counter, I reach into the cabinet and pull out our makeshift stereo system and plug my phone into it. Scrolling through my playlists, I settle on one that has a little bit of everything on it and set the volume. While I wait, I grab my stick from the corner, shot targets from the shelf, and some pucks. Dropping them on the ice, I go over and attach the targets to the net. I don't even get a dozen shots off before Briggsy pulls up. Skating over to the door, I open it up and wait for her to make her way over to me.

"This is so cool!" she says, pulling a hoodie over her head the thick material muffling her words a bit.

"We do it every year as a team fundraiser. We rent out the ice for rat hockey and some classes, sometimes a tournament." I point at the bench for her to sit. "Plus on the weekends when we don't have games, we do open skates with music and shit." I drop to my knee in front of her and begin taking off her shoes. "We all pitch in to help out, drive the Zamboni, work the skate rental, whatever it takes. It gets pretty busy and makes us a ton of money. Then at the end of season, we vote on what we use it for. Equipment, a party, new sound system for the locker room." Once I've removed both her shoes, I grab an ice skate. Loosening the laces and spreading the boot, I slide her foot in. My grip on her muscular calf is soft and lingers longer than necessary.

"I can do that, you know." Her voice is a little breathy. Not as much *ice queen* in it as it usually has when she's talking to me.

I ignore her and move to her other foot. "Do you know how to skate?"

"I do, actually! I mean not as well as you can, but I thought I wanted to be a figure skater once a looonnnggg time ago." She laughs, and as if she summoned it with the lighthearted tinkling sound, it starts snowing. Big fat perfectly formed flakes swirl around us on the cold air.

"The twins too. I wanted them to play hockey, and they wanted to do silly-ass twirls and spin until they were nothing but a blur," I tell her in mock disgust.

"Yup! And it got even worse when I watched this one movie with my sisters. After that, all my little ten-year-old self wanted was to be a figure skater in the Olympics."

I can hear the happy in her voice. It isn't something I've heard a ton from her since we've met. I don't know how much of that has to do with her dad and all she's been through lately or if it's just her, but I like this side too. I have her foot sandwiched between my knees as I pull the laces tight but glance up at her to ensure I'm not hurting her. I'm used to tightening my skates until my blood flow stops. "That okay?" She nods, and I get to work on the other.

"It's been forever since I've skated, though, so I'll be rusty. Don't go being a show-off and skating circles around me," she admonishes.

"Don't worry, I won't let you fall."

"I didn't say I was going to fall." Saffie huffs.

I release my hold on her foot and place it on the ground. She stands and immediately wobbles. Reaching out, I steady her. "Good thing you're not going to fall." My lips curl into a smirk. She sticks her tongue out at me before stepping past me to the open door. The quick flash of pink making me hotter than it should. Hell, *she* makes me hotter than she should. Before I follow her, I adjust my growing hard-on. If just that little flash of tongue has me hard, I'm fucked. Or need to get fucked more like. With a shake of my head, I watch as she steps gingerly onto the ice, a hand holding firmly to the low wall.

Wanting to distract her so that she's going off muscle memory to skate, I prod, "So this movie, which was it that had you wanting to be in the Olympics?" Lazily, I skate backward in front of her as she gets used to the feel of the ice underneath her.

"You've probably never seen it. It's an older movie, but my sisters loved it! They would watch it every chance they got, and since I'm the youngest..."

"You didn't have much of a choice." I chuckle.

"Right! At least they had good taste. It totally could have been worse."

"Don't ask my sisters what I made them watch. They'd probably bitch about the number of times we've watched *Miracle*." I shake my head, not even able to fathom someone ever being tired of watching the best hockey movie ever made.

"I don't think I've ever seen it. I take it you like it, and they don't?"

Her words have me coming to a stop, mouth agape. She loses her balance at my abrupt switch, making her reach for me. Saffie's long fingers wrap around my forearms. The heat of her touch seeps through my hoodie, sending a little zing through me. Never has a touch zinged *anything* unless the touch was to my cock. Instead of shying away from her touch and the feelings it invokes, I find myself leaning into it, hoping to prolong the feel of her hands on me, wishing she'd never stop touching me.

"Oh," she yelps. "Levi, you can't stop like that. This isn't a hockey game, I need warning." Laughing, she rights herself and drops her hands. I instantly miss the feel of them on me. "And you can't be mad a me for not seeing your movie when you haven't seen mine." Saffie harrumphs triumphantly.

"For one, who said I never saw *your* movie? You never even told me what it was. And two, *Miracle* is only the best movie ever in the history of ever."

"Whatevvverrr." Moving backward again, Saffie grins. "Just because you say so I'm supposed to believe you?"

"Ummm, yes," I say emphatically. "Would I lie to you?"

"I don't know, would you?" Briggsy asks, her tone soft. Wind whips around us making the snow dance faster, sticking to Briggsy's long lashes and landing on her full lips. My eyes focused on the quickly melting specs I manage, "Nah. Not to you." I mean it too. I'm honest by nature, but I don't think I could ever lie to her. She'd see right through my ass. Shaking my head, I ask, "So what's this movie?"

Briggsy answers quickly almost as if she's glad for the subject change. "*The Cutting Edge*. It's about a figure skater and a hockey player actually," she says, almost as if she had forgotten that part.

Trying to hide my grin I widen my legs and bring them back in as I glide along the ice, making C-cuts. A hockey basic that they taught us back in the very beginning.

"Stop being fancy," she admonishes, pointing at my skates.

I laugh. "You ain't seen shit, Briggsy." Letting the grin slide across my face with a flash of a dimple. "I mean I can't Pamchenko twist you like her boy Douglas can, but I can Alex Ovechkin the hell out of you," I tell her, the grin spreading even wider into a cocky smile at her look of surprise. Like there was a hockey movie on the planet that I haven't seen.

"What in the world does that even mean, Sexton?"

Without warning, I pick her up, making her yelp in

surprise, her legs automatically going around my waist. She angles her feet away from me so as not to dig her skates into my ass. "That's where I put you into the boards." I skate over to the plexiglass partitions and slam us both gently into the boards, making them rattle as if hit by a train. She squeals and lets out a peel of laughter, so I do it again. Her arms are tight around my neck, crushing her into my chest so there's no space between us. My eyes land on her lips, full and tinted the slightest shade of pink, and this time, when I press her against the glass, the air changes around us. It's charged, hot and crackling even in the frigid cold. Funny, I never felt this way putting any of the guys into the boards during a game. Slowly, the smile falls from her lips, her mouth open slightly, her chest rising and falling against mine as her breathing quickens.

"Levi..." She trails off, and before she can say anything else, my mouth is covering hers, swallowing her breaths and the soft moan she lets slip. With her pinned against the glass, my hands full of her perfect ass, I widen my stance for balance and let my tongue tease the seam of her lips, begging for entrance. When she gives it, I reward us both by angling my head and deepening the kiss, fingers kneading over the soft material of her leggings and pressing her even tighter against me. Saffie's fingernails rake against the back of my head, tangling in the longer hair at my nape. I ease us away from the glass and slowly, carefully, slam us back against it. The way it imitates fucking makes me harder than I've ever been in my entire life. Fully clothed, drilling her into the boards, the head of my cock brushing lightly against her ass every time I press her to the glass means I'm dangerously close to coming in my pants. Reluctantly, I pull my mouth away to take in a deep, Saffie-scented breath. Her eyes open slowly. Eyes that are soft, vulnerable, and a bit dazed roam over my face as little by little recognition and what looks a little like regret blossoms in the gray depths.

With her remorse dawning, I try to pull her back into the moment. "Briggsy—" She shuts me down with a shake of her head, her hands falling from me as if I were on fire. Well fuck. Guess that's that.

"*Toe pick*," I mutter under my breath.

# 19

## LEVI

The bus leaves in an hour for our away game. My sisters are on their way over for my laundry now. Typically, I would drop my clothes off and grab a road snack from my mom. I'm not even sorry about how much of a mama's boy I am. I'll miss this when I'm in Chicago. Wonder if I can get her to move with me? Probably not. My dad might not appreciate me taking his wife away so she can make me pregame meals and road snacks.

"Levi!" Millie yells from the bottom of the stairs, as what sounds like a herd of elephants stampedes its way up them.

"Holy hell, Mill, why the fuck are you so loud?" I ask as I open the bedroom door wider for her, Maeve, and Rae. I'm disappointed that Saffie isn't with them, though I'm not surprised. I haven't seen her since the kiss that rocked my fucking world.

"I'm not about to walk in on you up here with one of your hockey hoes." Millie snorts out like I'm an idiot.

"That's fair," I admit, grinning.

"Mommy said to give you this and she'll see you at the game. Also to skate hard, play like you're winning, and that you owe her two." Maeve smiles as she hands me a paper bag that smells like heaven.

Ever since forever my ma has said this to me before my games. It was her little pep talk. *"Skate hard and play like you're winning, Levi. Even when you're not, you play like you are. Got it? Good, boy. Now how many goals do you owe me? Yup, two. Love you, baby."* Every game without fail. I call it "Mama Mentality" instead of *Mamba Mentality*. She has always said that when we're winning, we play with a different mindset than we do when we're losing. I told her it's called big dick energy to which she told me to watch my mouth. And the two goals, well she said it was more attainable than a hat trick every game so that I should aim for two for her and any others after that were for me. Hockey moms, it seems, are as weird and superstitious as hockey players.

"You're playing Rhode Island today, right?" Rae asks as she plops into my chair.

"Yup. First time this season. They had to cancel the first game for some shit. They look good, though."

"Dirty?" she asks, brows raised.

I shrug. "As dirty as they've always been." They were known for their hard hits and landing ones that weren't always legal, especially when the officials weren't looking.

"You guys coming?" I ask that question instead of the one I want to ask. I'm hoping that Rae will tell me that Saffie is coming without me having to actually ask her.

"Of course." Maeve answers before Rae. "Like Ma is going to miss a game when it's within driving distance." Millie scoffs. "She had me get tickets as soon as the schedule went up. Right up front."

"Just you guys, Ma, and Dad?" I prod.

"Who else would come?" Millie looks at me like I'm an idiot before she figures it out. "Ooooh, you're wanting to know if

Saffron is coming? Stay away from my friend, Levi. You'll get your hockey boy cooties on her." my sister warns.

Laughing, Rae shakes her head. "No. She's actually in Connecticut this weekend helping her mom and visiting Landon at St. Claire for some...thing. His birthday? Their anniversary? An awards dinner?" Her faces scrunches in thought. "I don't know. It's something. I kind of tune anything that has to do with him out."

My hands are still on the laundry basket I was pulling out of the closet. "She's in Conneticut? When did she leave?" I try to make my voice sound nonchalant when I feel anything but. With my back to them, they can't see the muscle in my jaw ticking at the thought of her there with him. Her boyfriend. Fucking hell, Sexton. Get ahold of yourself.

"Ummm...day before yesterday, I think. It was a last-minute thing," Rae says.

"Why do you care?" Millie cuts in. "She doesn't even like you," she digs.

*Oh, little sister, if you only knew...*So she left the day after she came to see me at the outdoor rink. The day I kissed the hell out of her, and she kissed me back. I let her leave, lying about having practice because I knew she needed to escape as much as I wanted her to stay. That can't be a coincidence. "Just asking. We're supposed to study for the second part of her test." Not a lie. Just not why I was fucking asking.

"I'm pretty sure she's coming back today. She has practice in the morning. I can call her if you want? Your ma said she has an extra ticket, and it'll take her the same amount of time to drive there," Rae supplies without any prompting, not deterred by Millie trying to shut us down.

So she's been with him for a couple of days now, probably fucking him. The anger that washes over me at the thought is... new. Scary as hell. And new. It's more than just jealousy and so far from anything I've ever felt in my life. So here I am, big mad over the fact that Saffie is in Connecticut with her bitch-ass boyfriend, and I'm here feeling shit that I don't want to be feeling. At least I don't think I want to be. I'm not sure which pisses me off more. Her being there with him or that I feel a certain type of way about it. Not wanting to let on that I'm pissed, I relax my face into a neutral mask and hand them the basket. "It's whatever. We'll meet up when she gets back." I jerk my chin toward the door and ask my sisters, "You want me to carry this out for you?" Maeve watches me with a pensive look on her face as if she wants to say something, ask a question, but is not sure if she should. I meet her gaze and will her not to. I don't even want to answer my own questions right now, let alone my sister's. Millie breaks in, saving me from Maeve.

"Of course we do." Holding out a hand, she helps Rae out of the chair.

I lead the way down the stairs in a rush to get them out of here before Maeve has a chance to grill me like I know she wants to. She's turned into a bit of a romantic since her and Benny got together. Before, she was just cool doing whatever, watching over Millie and letting everyone else just do their thing. Now, though, it's like she's on the lookout for a happily ever after for every mofo she knows. It's fucking terrifying. And if that look on her face earlier is any indication, she's setting her sights on me. I don't know whether to shudder at the thought or ask her opinion on the fucked-up headspace I'm letting Saffie occupy.

Once I have the basket loaded into their trunk, I turn and gather all three for a tight squeeze, making them squeak in protest. "I'll see you at the game. Make sure you remember that *I'm* your favorite player," I tell the girls, looking pointedly at Maeve before turning to head back into the house and waving over my shoulder.

∽

THREE AND A HALF HOURS LATER, the bus is pulling up in front of the stadium in Rhode Island and my mood over Saffie being in Connecticut has gone from bad to worse. I'd had a two-hour bus ride to let shit simmer. And it did. About half a dozen times, I pulled my phone out to text her. To see what she would say, if she would lie to me about where she was or if she'd reply at all. Not that she had a reason to do either. And still I don't understand why the fuck I care. Do I like her? Have fun pissing her off? Love spending time with her? I did. All of it. A lot. Did I want her to break up with her boyfriend? Yep, sure as shit did. But for what? To smash? She doesn't have to be single for that. To date her? Do I want to fucking date her? I don't think I want to date anyone. Never have. But I've also never sat by myself on the way to a game, any game, and got all in my feelings over a girl either. And for fucking sure, I've never been jealous at the thought of some other guy being with any of the girls I hooked up with. More pissed off than I was even just a minute ago, I grab my shit and start making my way off the bus. I need to get my head in the game we're about to play and not focus on Saffie.

"Yo, Sexy!" I look up to see Murphy and Benny standing at the bottom of the stairs, arms crossed. "You good, bro?" Murphy asks, watching me as intently as Maeve had been earlier.

"Yeah. Why?" I ask, tucking my phone in my pocket.

Eyes narrowing, Benny says, "Oh, I don't know. Maybe because you sat by yourself the whole ride, didn't say fuck all to anyone, and look like you're about to punch people. You had your headphones in the entire time, probably listening to some fuck the world shit if your face was anything to go by. So, yeah, no reason." He shrugs.

"Fuck off." I brush past them and follow everyone else through the door that leads to the locker rooms—knowing that I just proved his point.

"Totally good," the smart-ass responds. He's lucky I

promised my ma I wouldn't hit him again until he and Maeve broke up.

"Sexy, he's right. You look like you're ready to throw hands. You get into it with someone?" Murphy asks—less of a smart-ass than Benny and actually sounding concerned.

"I'm good, really. Just ready to play these assholes," I lie. They know it too. Their looks tell me that they're not buying a single fucking word.

"Lie to us if you want, bro. It's cool. But we're here if you want to hash shit out before you take that mad out onto the ice," Benny offers as he puts his gear in the stall beside mine in the locker room.

"You better shake whatever off before the game. These guys are going to be all over your ass, and if you go out there pissed off, it's gonna get ugly quick." Murphy claps me on the back and goes off to start his pregame rituals, leaving me with Benny.

I turn to him and can't believe the words that fall from my mouth. "How'd you know you wanted to date my sister?"

Benny looks at me and blinks. Once. Twice. "Holy fuck, Sexy has girl problems," he says in a stunned tone.

"Forget it," I spit out, agitated with myself for asking and him being a dick about it.

"No, no. I'm sorry. You just caught me off guard. Way off fucking guard," he mumbles. "I'm assuming you're talking about Saffie and not Nora."

My head flies up. "Not Nora. Fuck no."

Benny chuckles. "I didn't think so but just wanted to be sure." He pulls on his shin pads, fastening the straps while he talks. "Well, with Maeve, it was a little different because we were away from everybody and everything, but I couldn't stop thinking about her."

I'm not sure I want to hear any of this, but it's too late now. I asked.

He stops dressing and leans his forearms on his knees. "I was legit terrified when she thought I was fucking around with Samantha. Hated that she was hurt because of some bullshit."

I cut in, not knowing all of this but some of it. "You weren't, though, right? Samantha was just trying to start shit?" There's a warning in my voice he must hear and realize I'd break my promise to my ma in a minute about hitting him.

"Nah, bro. I hadn't even talked to Sam since the last time I was in town. Anyway, as I was saying," he says with a grin, "I knew I would do anything to make her believe me and that I was done worrying about what you were gonna think, what Millie had to say, and everything else. I just wanted to be with her, and I was willing to let you beat my ass to do it." We both laugh at that. "What about her man?" Benny asks.

"What about him?" At the mention of Landon, the tension is back in my spine, a bite in my tone.

"Whoa, whoa." Benny raises his hands palms up, laughing. "I was just asking if he was part of the problem or whatever?"

"I mean, not for me really." That's technically not true. He is a problem. The problem is that she's still going to see him and shit when I just want her here with me. At my game. Sitting with my parents. Wearing my sweater, my name. *Fuck*. Like the lamp being lit and the horn blaring, it hits me. I want to get serious with Saffron fucking Briggs.

## 20

## SAFFIE

Rae lays across my full-size bed, head hanging off the edge as she picks at the ends of her newly colored lavender hair. "Let me get this straight, you went all the way to Connecticut to where your boyfriend lives, and you didn't go see him?" I can feel her eyes on me as I move around my room putting away my freshly laundered clothes.

"It's not that big a deal," I lie. It is a big deal, but I'm not ready to tell her *why* I didn't go see Landon or even tell him I was there. "I was there to help my mom with some stuff, plus Rosie and Sage came up, so I just spent time with them." At least that was the truth. My mom had called and mentioned that my sisters were coming to the house to tie up some loose ends, and I jumped at the opportunity to get away from Fulton...and Levi.

"Right, I get it. But you haven't seen him in a while, and your house is literally like ten minutes from St. Claire," she says as if I don't know.

"His house is on campus. I just didn't feel like going and possibly running into any of my old teammates and stuff." The lie rolls off my tongue without thought.

"Nuh-uh. Try again, Saffron Theodora Briggs."

"Ooohh, we're busting out government names, so Rae must mean business." Comes a voice from my bedroom door. I turn to see Millie, Maeve, and Kenna coming into the suddenly cramped room.

"What are you girls doing?" Maeve asks as they all pile onto the bed next to Rae.

"Well, I'm here trying to figure out why my cousin went all the way to Connecticut for almost three days and didn't see her boyfriend once while she was there. Since she didn't even tell him that she was in the same state, I'm wondering if we have to load up and go kick his ass or what?" Rae says, her tone letting me know she's serious.

Kenna pulls out her phone, her thumbs flying. "Lakyn will wanna ride. There's no way she won't. I'll get her over here."

"Oh my god, you guys. Nobody is kicking anyone's ass. I just...I just. I didn't go see him because I felt guilty, okay? I cheated on him and didn't know what to do." I pause in my ramble, stunned that I told them, but now that I did, I need clarity. "I mean I think I cheated." I toss the shirt I'm holding onto my dresser and look at them, their faces all varied masks of confusion, shock, and compassion. Compassion from Maeve, naturally. She might feel differently once she finds out *who* I maybe cheated with.

"Wait, wait, wait. What do you mean you *think*?" Millie questions. "You either did or you didn't."

"Well. Is kissing cheating? Because I kissed someone else. Someone who is not my boyfriend," I admit, not elaborating any further. I don't tell them that I haven't been able to stop thinking about that kiss since it happened. Or how it made me feel other than guilty.

"Girl." Kenna drops her chin to her chest and rolls her eyes up to meet mine. "If Landon was kissing on some girl up at St. Claire, would we or would we not be on our way there to beat his ass for cheating?" She gives me a knowing look. "The answer is yes, we would be, and he would deserve that shit. So yeah, kissing counts as cheating."

"Never mind that." Millie waves her hand. "We're not talking about him, we're talking about you and we don't care about you kissing someone else we care about *who* that someone else is." They all nod, four pairs of expectant eyes on me. Dammit. How did I think they weren't going to ask this?

"I mean if you're not at practice, you're with us somewhere else. Or with Levi study—" Millie stops midsentence, her eyes widening . "No. No. No. No. No."

Kenna jumps to her feet on the bed, her quick movements making everyone shift. When she starts jumping, I hurriedly move to close the door in case Carrie comes home. She's a great roommate, we get along well, and she's so, so nice. But she likes to gossip, especially if it has to do with Levi. I do not need it getting out that anything happened between us.

"Yooooo! You kissed Sexy?" Kenna screeches.

"Well. He kissed me," I correct.

"Wait, this wasn't when you spent the night there, was it?" Rae demands, all of the amusement falling from her face.

"Holy what? You spent the night with Sexy, *the* Sexy, and didn't tell us?" Kenna's voice goes up an octave with every word. It's impressive. "Girl, you better spill. This tea is too hot." Her eyes gleam with excitement.

"You slept with Levi, but you're worried about the kissing part?" Maeve asks, sounding a bit confused.

"No, I didn't sleep with him. Well, yes. But no. Not like that." I rub a hand down my face trying to get my thoughts in order to explain what happened.

"It's okay. Just start at the beginning," Maeve says gently, pulling Kenna down to sit

"Okay, the night of the party, I was a little drunk."

"Mmm, you were more than a little drunk. You were wasted," Rae corrects.

"Fine. I was wasted. Completely wasted. Rae apparently left me with Levi because she had practice in the morning, and she couldn't get me back here by herself."

"You left your cousin with Sexy, passed out drunk?" Kenna asks incredulously.

"Yeah, I thought I could trust him," Rae defends.

"You can. Levi would never take advantage of anyone. Especially drunk like that," Maeve insists.

Millie nods in agreement. "Yeah. My brother is an ass, but he would never. Plus, he doesn't have to. These hoes line up for him." She holds up a hand. "No offense."

"None taken. I don't think," I reply. "Anyway, I slept *in his room* and nothing happened. Rae came to get me in the morning and that was that. So yes, I slept in the same bed with him but did not *sleep* with him."

"So that's not when he kissed you?" my cousin asks even more confused.

"No. That happened the day I met him at the outdoor rink."

"Dammit! I knew I should have gone with you when you dropped Maeve off," Millie curses.

"Shhhh!" Kenna breaks in. "I need to know how this happened."

"I'm not even sure. One minute, we were skating and laughing and talking about hockey movies, and the next thing I know, he's lifted me up and crashed me into the glass wall thingy—"

"He put you into the glass?" Rae asks incredulously.

"Yeah. And it was…hot." My hands cover my face, which I know must be flaming red right now. I can feel the heat of my embarrassment across my cheeks, shooting down my neck and spreading across my chest.

"That sounds like some freaky shit. I bet it was hot as hell," Kenna says gleefully.

I drop my hands. "It was. And it shouldn't have been. When he did it again, that's when he kissed me."

"Did you kiss him back?" Millie questions, her words dripping with disgust.

I nod. "I did. I totally did. And then I made some lame excuse about having to go to practice and left." My face scrunches. "Do you know how damn awkward it is to try to make an escape while in ice skates?" That gets a laugh from everyone except for Millie.

She leans forward, her brow creased. "So let me get this straight. You slept with my brother but not really, then you kissed him, and then you went all the way to Connecticut but didn't go see your boyfriend because you think he'll look at you and know you cheated on him?"

When she puts it like that..."Basically."

"So now what? Are you going to break up with Landon?" There's a tinge of hope in Rae's voice.

"No," I answer quickly. This is met by raised eyebrows all around.

"Listen, this is Sexy we're talking about. It was a kiss. He's probably kissed five other girls since that day." The words taste sour in my mouth, but I brush it off and double down. "Hell, he's probably slept with that many. I'm not breaking up with my boyfriend for someone like Levi."

"That's not fair, Saffie. Levi is a great guy," Maeve admonishes in defense of her brother.

"I didn't mean it like that. Just that he's not about monogamy. I mean, he walks around in a shirt that says he's only committed to hockey, his bed, and his mama. It's not exactly a secret that he's not looking to get serious with anyone."

"Are you going to tell Landon?" Millie asks.

"I'm not sure," I admit. " I think I should, but I'm worried that he won't forgive me."

They look at me sympathetically, and then Millie sits up straighter as if electrocuted. "Oh my god, I bet that's what happened with Levi the other day at the game."

"Holy shit, I bet you're right," my cousin agrees.

"What are you talking about?" I look at them confused.

"The other day there was an away game, Levi ended up getting into a fight and got ejected in the third period. They gave him a one-game suspension," Millie explains.

"What the hell does that have to do with me?"

"He was asking about you before the game, kind of dancing around it. Millie was blowing him shit about it, and I told him you were in Connecticut seeing your mom and boyfriend. I had thought you went there to see him for some anniversary or something," Rae tells me.

"Oh, damn. So he thought she was up there smashing and got pissed," Kenna adds, a smile splitting her lips as the other three nod in agreement. "Giiiirrrlll, you've got Sexy acting out."

"I do not. I'm sure that had nothing to do with it," I reassure, though some small part of me is thrilled that he may have been jealous. It isn't fair of me, and I tamp it down, but the warmth of the thought spreads through me. "Do you think?" I direct the question at Maeve because she's the most levelheaded and realistic.

Her slender shoulders rise and fall under her yellow sweater. "Makes sense. Levi isn't used to girls not falling all over themselves to be around him. The fact that you guys had a moment and then you left to see your boyfriend..." She trails off.

Unsure of what to do with that, I flap my hands in the air as if I could flick the thought away. "Whatever. I'm sure he doesn't give a shit. It was just a kiss. Not like we had sex."

"Have you seen him since?" Millie asks.

No because I ran away like a giant wuss ass. "Not yet. I just got home. I'll catch up with him soon, though. I have another test coming up." My heart thumps harder in my chest at the thought. The mention of seeing Levi again has me on edge. I'm not sure if I'm worried that he might try to kiss me again, or that he won't. And I hate myself for both of those worries.

"I had such high hopes for you." Millie sighs. "You had me thinking that you didn't like him and here you are sleeping in his bed and letting him kiss you."

"I don't like him." Not even I believed that anymore. It had certainly been true before, but now I'm wondering if I didn't like him or if I just didn't like myself for reacting to him.

Millie gives me a dubious look. "Oh, girlfriend, you can go ahead and lie to yourself all you want. In fact, please do because then maybe you'll stay away from him, and I won't lose another person to the hockey boys."

"Nuh-uh. No way. Like him. Like the shit out of him. He's too fine not to, and you know what? Maybe he's ready for a real relationship and not just the smash-and-dash type thing he's been doing since he got here," Kenna says, her voice hopeful. "You never know. You might be the one to bring Sexy to his knees." She waggles her eyebrows at me suggestively, making the twins and Raegan groan.

"Saffie, just be careful. I don't want to see you get hurt, but I also don't want you to hurt my brother. He's an ass, but he's my ass." Maeve smiles. "If you don't have plans to break up with Landon or whatever, you should probably make sure not to kiss him again," she says gently. This is all making my head hurt. This should be a non issue, really.

"Look, my brother doesn't give a shit about your boyfriend. He will kiss you, sleep with you, whatever. Whether you're with Landon or not. *Trust me.*" Millie goes on. "I'm not worried about you hurting him, but don't let him get in your head and toy with your emotions. If you wanna break up with your man, cool. Break up with him. But don't break up with him because you think that's the only way you can be with Levi."

What the hell is she saying? Is Millie encouraging me to cheat on my boyfriend with her brother? Surely not.

"Oh my god, Millie, that is the worst advice ever," Rae chastises.

"Why? It's true. Levi doesn't give a shit that she has a boyfriend. Has it ever stopped him before?" Brows raised, she looks at the other girls, prompting them to answer. "Did he care that Tammy had a boyfriend? Nope. He sure didn't. And what happened when she broke up with him because she thought her and Levi were gonna be together?" she asks.

"He told her that she shouldn't have broken up with him. That it wasn't that serious," Kenna supplies.

"Yup. He sure did. And she wasn't the first to think that way. All I'm saying is do what you want, but don't do what you think Levi *wants* because he probably doesn't," Millie finishes with a sympathetic look on her face.

"You should talk to him before you make any decisions about anything. You never know, maybe he actually cares about you," Rae offers. "Stranger things have happened, and he has been acting differently. He doesn't treat you like he treats...the others," she says with a wince.

I shake my head. "There's nothing to talk about. It was a one-time thing, a lapse in judgment. Not a big deal at all. I'm not breaking up with my boyfriend for Levi. That would be the biggest mistake of my life." My words hold a confidence, a resolve, I don't quite feel. But I need to. God, do I need to.

## 21

## LEVI

I wonder if Saffie will be at Rae's game tonight? She's been back from her little trip for a couple of days now and has been avoiding me like it's her job. I even showed up at her practice this morning under the pretense of seeing my dad and she pretended she didn't see me. She saw me. Her back went ramrod straight, and her pitches erratic. My dad noticed and gave me a death glare before telling me to get my ass out of there. That's cool, though. She can't avoid me forever. I'm still her tutor.

My sister breaks into my thoughts. "Levi, did you bring Dad's parking pass?" Millie asks from the back seat where she, Maeve, and Benny are sitting.

"No. Should I have?" I act shocked, making Murphy snort-laugh.

"Oh, shut up." Millie hits the back of my seat.

"I got it, Mill. And the extra tickets," I reassure her as I whip my truck into the parking garage for the stadium. It's a good thing I grabbed it, too, because there wasn't a spot anywhere on the first two levels that weren't one of the reserved slots. The girl's hockey team was having a stellar season, and the games were packed, which was great to see. Women's hockey is badass. About time people noticed.

"Maeve and I will wait at the front gates with the extra tickets," Millie calls as she hops to the ground. "You can go with the boys," she says to Benny, shooing him away and taking the tickets from me.

With a laugh, Murphy slings his arm around Benny's shoulders. "Don't worry about it, eh? I'll hold your hand until she gets back. Just don't try to grab my butt like I saw you do to her earlier."

My head whips around to see Benny elbow Murphy in the gut, causing him to let out an, "Oomph."

"Can you try not to grope my sister in my presence, please?"

"Oh, shut up. You wouldn't even have known about it if it weren't for big mouth over here," Benny says, pushing Murph's arm off him as we pass through the metal detectors and hand our tickets to Gerry, the old guy at the door.

"How you boys doing tonight?" he asks as he hands the stubs back to us. "Odd seeing you on this side of things. You gonna be back on the ice at the next game, Levi?" This is said with a reprimanding look.

"Sure am, Ger. One-game suspension. First and last of the season," I promise.

"That's what I like to hear. You boys have fun," he tells us before taking the tickets from the family behind us. Gerry has been at every game since I started here at Fulton. Once he takes the tickets and everyone is in the stadium, he goes and stands with the ushers to watch the game. Then when the game ends, he comes down to the tunnel to let us out the back door, always with a word of encouragement or praise, and locks up behind us. He's a fixture here.

We weave through the crowd to our seats. My dad has season tickets for men's and women's hockey. Same section for both, on the glass, ten seats. Perks of being part of the athletic department. My parents couldn't make tonight's game, so we were giving the extra tickets to Rae's family, who doesn't have seats as good as these. Benny and Murphy make a beeline to the concessions.

"You want anything, Sexy?" Murph asks.

"Grab me a water." When he raises his arm above the throng of people to let me know that he heard me, I turn to go wait for my sisters and Rae's parents. God, I hope that Saffie is with them. Not having talked to her since my little revelation, I wasn't sure if she was gonna hit me with the ice queen Saffie or the sweet Saffie who let me kiss her. I'd love it if "just broke up with my boyfriend" Saffie showed the fuck up. My shoulder propped against the glass, I watch the ice as the girls do their drills, jerking my chin in greeting when Rae skates by. Her smile huge, she waves back with way more excitement than I'm used to. Takes me a second to realize she's not waving at me. Embarrassing. I turn to find my sisters, Rae's parents, along with another woman and Saffie making their way toward me. My eyes fix on Saffie as she comes down the steps. Her FU Fire hockey hoodie making her look like a proper hockey fan now. I wonder if it has my name on the back of it or if she got another one. I do my best to keep my face neutral, not wanting to let her see how happy I am that she came. I relax into the glass and wait for them to make it down to where I am. When they do, Saffie barely glances my way, instead standing back as Rae's mom gives me a big hug.

"Levi, it's so good to see you," Shelly French says, squeezing my cheek like I'm still a five-year-old kid.

"Good to see you too, Mrs. French." And it is. They've been friends of my parents for as long as I can remember. Always wicked nice.

I turn to Rae's dad, Doug, a huge guy who played hockey himself and almost made it to the show, a knee injury taking him out of the game. He takes the hand I offer and claps me on the shoulder. "Back on the ice tomorrow night?"

Seems to be the question of the day. "Yes, sir," I tell him, fighting the urge to look past him to where Saffie stands.

"Shit's changed so much since I played. You can't look at anyone sideways anymore without getting tossed." He shakes his head.

"Did you see the game?" I ask, figuring he didn't.

"I didn't, just heard from Shelly that you were suspended."

"Yeah, well, I did a little more than look at the guy sideways," I admit with a self-deprecating laugh.

He crosses his beefy arms over his chest. "Rough game?"

"More like he was playing like a hotheaded goon," Benny cuts in as he and Murphy join the group.

"That right?" Mr. French asks, brows raised in surprise. I'm an aggressive player, but not a goon. Typically.

Not able to deny the accusation, I shrug my shoulders and nod. "Something like that. I let myself get in my head about some shi—stuff." I correct, darting a glance at Rae's mom.

"It happens. Hockey is an emotional sport. Bunch of maniacs on blades." He chuckles. "Anyone hurt?"

"No. I drew a major for dropping the gloves over a little bump that I took issue with," I tell him. Thinking back on it makes me want to kick my own ass. "I deserved the suspension."

"Well, as long as you know it, all you can do is your best not to let your team down again this season," Mr. French says, clapping me on the back again. "Tell your dad we said thanks for the tickets." I nod, and he turns to his wife. "Let's make a concession run and get back so we don't miss the intro." They turn and go, leaving my view of Saffie unobstructed. She stands with my sisters and friends alongside the woman I don't recognize. She turns to say something to the group, and I can see my name across her shoulders under the hood of her sweatshirt, my number covering her back. I was hoping that she kept the stuff my ma had given her, even more so that she'd wear it. Just seeing her with my name on her feels like a flex. Knowing better than to mention it, I school my features into a more relaxed smile and walk over to them.

"Hey, Briggsy." I stand right beside her, not caring about invading her space.

"Hi, Levi," she responds a little cooly, not meeting my eyes. The woman behind her clears her throat, making Saffie glance at her over her shoulder. "Sorry. Mom, this is Millie and Maeve's brother, Levi. He's the one tutoring me," she says.

So she's at least mentioned me to her mom. That's good. I hold out a hand. "Great to finally meet you, Mrs. Briggs."

Taking my hand, she grins. "Please, call me Elisabeth."

"How was the drive over?" I ask, trying to make polite conversation.

"A nightmare, actually." She laughs. "And then to make matters worse, I got a flat tire just as I pulled into the drive."

"If you need me to, I can stop over after the game or in the morning and change it for you. It's no trouble." I make the offer without hesitation. She just lost her husband, and he's probably the one who handled all this shit for her like my dad does for my mom. Not that my ma couldn't do it.

"I have a service there now changing it. Thank you, though, that's very thoughtful of you." Elisabeth turns to Saffie. "If it doesn't work out with Landon, you should snag this one. He's a keeper," she tells her daughter with a wide smile.

"Oh my god, Mom!" Saffie admonishes.

"Beautiful and smart. Now I know where you get it." I flash her a dimpled smile. "You should listen to your mom, Briggsy."

Her mom laughs. "Oh, he's good."

"Please don't encourage him," she groans.

"Oh my god, Levi, leave my friend alone," Millie cuts in, wedging herself between us. "I apologize, Mrs. Briggs. He doesn't have an off button," Evil twin tells her, eliciting a laugh from Saffie's mom.

"He doesn't bother me." She pats my arm, making Saffie and Millie roll their eyes.

The music changes, and the countdown to the intro starts. We all turn hurriedly to settle into our seats, Rae's parents and Saffie's mom at the end of the row.

Saffie is just about to sit when Maeve says, "Saffie will you switch with me so I can be next to Benny?" At Saffie's murderous look, Maeve lays it on super thick. "Pretty pretty please?" She even adds in little praying hands. Nice touch. Saffron sighs and swaps seats with Maeve, putting her next to me. I grin at Maeve, making a mental note to tell her she's my favorite sister next chance I get.

"Don't worry, I don't bite," I promise her with a wicked grin before turning my attention to the ice and the team warming up. Not letting her scowl effect me. "Unless you want me to."

Millie leans across me to talk to Saffron, not giving her the chance to respond. "I forgot to ask you, how was your trip? Was Landon so excited to see you?" At the mention of his name, I stiffen in my seat, my eyes not leaving the players on the ice.

"It was great. I was so happy to be able to reconnect with him, you know?"

Turning to her, I ask, "Did something happen to make you feel un-connected?" I flash her a knowing grin. Ain't no damn way that trip was a coincidence.

"Not a thing." That's her too bright reply. Her sweet smile as fake as Duncan Keith's front teeth. The lie dripping from the pretty lips my eyes are fixed on.

Before I can respond, we're asked to stand for the national anthem. I remove my hat and wait as the singer makes her way to the microphone.

Saffie leans in and whispers, "Oh too bad that's not Whore-a singing. She's so amazing." She tsks with a roll of her eyes.

Loving that she's letting her jealousy slip out, I lower my mouth to her ear. "It's not her singing we like about her." Standing straight, my mouth kicked up in a grin I can just about feel the irritation rolling off Saffie. I probably shouldn't bait her, but I'm a dick and like the ice queen just as much as I like Sweet Saffie. At this point, I'll take whatever reaction she'll give me and run with it.

As if sitting next to Saffie, feeling her leg brush against mine, our shoulders bump every time we cheer, her laughter and scent surrounding me isn't torture enough, the game has just gone into OT. Nothing is more stressful than a game that goes into overtime except maybe sitting next to Saffie and not being able to touch her like I really want. We are all perched on the edge of our seats, literally. Out of my periphery, I can see Murphy's leg bouncing fast enough to take flight as he watches. Rae has just come off the bench for a shift change and gets the puck. Saffie grabs my arm, nails biting into my skin as her cousin moves up the ice in a breakaway with three Cranston players chasing after her. They aren't fast enough. Without slowing, Rae dangles left, making the goalie slide along the crease with her giving Rae room to put it up top, right over the goalie's shoulder. No time to react. The horn blares, signaling the goal. We all jump to our feet, the crowd roaring. Saffie yanks on my sleeve excitedly and launches into my arms when I turn to face her. Her head thrown back in excitement, arms wrapped around my neck, legs around my waist. My hands move across her back, holding her tightly and relishing in the feel of her crushed against me as we celebrate the win. Saffie's head rolls forward, gaze meeting mine. I know the moment she realizes what she did and that I have her in my arms. Pretty white teeth sink into her bottom lip, her breathing speeds up, nostrils flaring just slightly, pupils dilating so there's more black than gray as her eyes roam over every angle of my face. A good man would put her down and release us both from this torture, but I'm not that guy. Not today, not tomorrow, or any day after. We're jostled from behind, spurring Saffie into motion. She unwraps her legs and pushes against me to let her down. And I do. Slowly. Without really releasing my hold on her so that every part of her slides against every part of me. Teasing us both, doing my best to force her hand and make her realize she wants me as much as I want her. Because *that's* the guy I am. Today, tomorrow, and every day after.

## 22

## SAFFIE

"Can you pass the asparagus?" I ask my aunt, who does so with a smile. It's so surreal to be sitting at a table with my family, smiling and laughing with my mom after the last several months. It seems like forever since I've seen my mom look this carefree and...not sad. Maybe it was being here, outside of the home she shared with my dad, that allowed her to breathe. To smile freely. I know in a way it had allowed me to do so. Even though I hadn't lived with them in quite a while, walking into our family home caused a heaviness and sadness to settle across my shoulders. It happened the moment I stepped through the door. Without my dad, his booming laughter, cooking away in the kitchen, watching a game from his favorite spot on the couch, it wasn't a home anymore.

"I'm surprised you aren't eating at the Sexton's tonight," Uncle Doug says to Rae. "It's game night."

"I know, but with Auntie Beth here, I wanted to be home," my cousin answers. "I told them I'd see them at the game."

I glance up from my plate at that. I didn't realize she was going.

"Are you riding with us or is Saffie taking you?" my uncle asks, helping himself to the bowl of potatoes.

"I'm not going," I answer quickly.

"What do you mean? We're all going," he says around a bite of chicken.

"We-we are?"

Rae nudges me with her knee. "The Sextons gave my dad their extra tickets. It's a big game."

"Well, I'll just stay home with my mom so she won't be bored," I offer, happy to have a valid excuse.

"Oh, honey, I'm going too. I'm excited. Your uncle says that some of the boys on the team are moving on to the pros and that your friend Levi is something to see on the ice," my mother says, a smile tipping up the corners of her mouth.

"He's not my friend," I interject. "And since when do you like hockey?"

"I've always liked hockey, just never had a chance to really go. After watching Rae's game last night, I'm excited to see another one," she tells me as she fills up my glass of water.

"It's going to be a good game. Tough. Willette is at the top of the division this season right along with Fulton, and they'll be gunning for Levi and the boys tonight," my uncle says, nodding. "They're lucky Levi's suspension wasn't longer."

"We're lucky they had extra tickets. The game is completely sold out," Aunt Shelly says.

"Yay us," I mutter. I guess the plus side is that I wouldn't have to sit next to him again, and I for sure wouldn't find myself wrapped in his arms staring at his mouth.

Rae nudges me again. "Oh, come on. It will be fun. He'll need the support, and he shows up for us," she reminds me softly. And he does. In more ways than one. More than my own boyfriend has since I've been here, that's for sure.

My mom thankfully doesn't ask how he has and instead says, "He seems like such a nice young man. Handsome too."

"Not more handsome than Landon," I argue almost petulantly. "And he's not always nice either. He's a cocky pain in the ass who has girls following him around campus as if he's Tom Holland's hotter younger brother. And he has no boundaries. None. Not even one boundary! He doesn't care if you have a boyfriend either. Because he's Levi Sexton, hockey god." Abruptly, I stop speaking and roll my lips between my teeth and press down. Hopefully hard enough to keep from saying another damn word.

Rae stops chewing and stares at me wide-eyed as do my aunt and uncle. My mother, on the other hand, is doing her best to smother a smile. "Well, why don't you tell me how you really feel, Saffron Sauce?" She chuckles. "Although that does explain a couple of things."

Before I can ask her what that means, my phone vibrates in my pocket, saving me from my still staring family. I don't even bother looking at who it is calling and instead gesture to the buzzing phone and excuse myself from the table, answering it as I do.

"Hello?"

"Hey, baby! You miss me?"

"Landon." My voice is breathless, a nervous shake hanging to the end of his name.

"I'm on my way to Bud's to meet the guys for some food, but wanted to let you know that I'm coming up there this weekend."

My stomach dips at his words. Heat creeps across my face as I think of having him here. On the same campus as Levi. Shaking my head to rid myself of the thought, I clear my throat. "Oh my god, that's so awesome." I force excitement into my voice, unwilling to admit the real reason I'm nervous about him coming here. This is exactly what we need. What *I* need. I should have gone to see him when I had the chance, and maybe then I wouldn't be doing my best to avoid Levi. Which has proven to be nearly impossible. He seems to be everywhere, making it hard for me to ignore him. Especially when I do stupid things like jump into his arms and wrap myself around him like a stripper on a pole.

"Yeah, Grant is talking to some girl there and wants to go see her, so I figured I'd ride too. I mean, what are the chances he starts hooking up with someone at the same school you're at?" Landon asks. Without waiting for me to answer, he goes on. "Hey, I'm here, so I gotta go." His voice drops an octave, turning flirtatious. "Get that thing ready for me, baby. We're not leaving the bedroom the whole time I'm there."

"So Grant is bringing you up here to get laid?" I can't keep the snark from my voice.

"Don't be like that," he admonishes a bit exasperated. "I miss you, *and* that thing you do," Landon says suggestively, trying to be cute.

Which might have worked before, but I haven't seen him in forever, and he's planning a trip up here because his *friend* has found the time to come and visit some chick he's talking to. Something my longtime boyfriend hasn't done since I've been here, and I'm just supposed to fall all over myself and be excited? I don't think so.

"I've gotta go. My mom's here, and we're all going to the hockey game."

"Hockey? Bunch of caveman douchebags on ice." Landon snorts out a laugh, making my hair prick at the base of my skull, my anger rising. "Since when do you like hockey?" His voice holds an accusatory tone that makes me feel instantly guilty although I'm still pissed off at him.

"Since Rae likes it and wants me to go with," I tell him, my voice a bit softer though it still doesn't hold the warmth it typically would. "I'll talk to you later."

"Be good, babe. Don't go falling for any hockey player fuck

sticks." He chuckles, not realizing how *not* funny I find his words. Amazing how pissy guilt will make you.

~

Thirty minutes into the game and I'm on edge. My legs are bouncing, my heart is racing, and my breathing is labored. I feel like I've run a damn marathon. Why? Levi Sexton, that's why. Not only did he do his pregame skate-by complete with a flirty wave and a wink, but he's been crushed into the glass in front of us half a dozen times. Clotheslined once, although Rae said it wasn't quite a clothesline, though it should have been a penalty but wasn't called, and has been put into the bad boy box twice for something called roughing. It's been an eventful game, and it's only the second period. I don't know how his parents sit here and watch him be...basically beat up and look so calm. Although his mom did yell at the refs when he got clotheslined. Mr. Sexton just patted her arm and smiled gently as she screamed obscenities at them. It was wild.

"You doing okay?" Maeve leans over Rae and asks gently. Well as gently as she can over the noise in the arena.

"No!" I tell her. "These guys are bullies."

Maeve laughs and nods her head. "They are. All of them kind of are. But it's good hockey. You'll get used to it." She pats my knee like her dad had her mom and turns her attention back to the game just as another pair of hockey players crash into the glass, making it shake violently, and the crowd roars in approval.

At least this time it wasn't Levi. My mom looks over at me, a gleeful gleam in her eyes, and shouts, "This is a great game! Your uncle wasn't kidding. Levi is really something out there." I just nod, looking at her like I've never seen her before. My mother is a "docile, violence doesn't solve anything" type who just cheered and whistled when two of our players sandwiched one of theirs and made him fall like a ton of bricks. Okay, not gonna lie, I cheered at that too. I guess I don't care as much when it's not Levi and our guys getting crushed. The buzzer sounds, signaling the end of the period, and I exhale deeply, relieved that I'll get a few minutes of a reprieve. My anxiety has anxiety, and the third period is not going to be any easier on me and my frazzled nerves. Neither of these teams will go down without a fight. I wonder if anyone would notice if I sneak out and wait in the bathroom. The thought is fleeting as I realize that there's nowhere else I'd rather be right now than here, watching Levi do what he does, his name and number across my back and me on the edge of my seat hoping that he skates by and winks at me again. I flop back in my seat as it hits me as hard as the players out on the ice. I want Levi Sexton. Shit. Shit and double shit.

## 23

## LEVI

After the win against Willette, I skate by my family and the French's, pounding my fist against the glass as I pass them. Briggsy stands with her mom, who is clapping and whistling next to her daughter who looks a little dazed as she stares at me. I'm not sure what happened to put that look on her face, but I want to make sure it stays there, so I blow her a kiss to go with her wink, smirking when her eyes widen. Exiting through the tunnel, I bump fists with the fans, mostly little kids hanging over the glass as I make my way through. Not stopping to chat like I sometimes would, instead I'm eager to get out to the arena to see if Saffie hangs around to wait for me. Maybe I'll get lucky, and she'll even let me kiss her again. Just thinking about that kiss, my lips and hips pressed into her as I had her pinned against the boards, makes my dick uncomfortably hard behind my cup. Man, I hope Coach isn't in the mood for a long-drawn-out speech. The last thing I want to do is sit in the locker room, hard, while listening to him highlight the game. Thankfully, it's not my turn to do the interviews with the school press and whoever else is here asking questions tonight. Cubbie and Murphy didn't get so lucky, though, and would meet us at home later.

Coach kept us for twenty minutes, which is twenty minutes longer than I wanted to be in there. I usually don't mind the game rundowns after a win since they're a fuck ton better than the rundowns after a loss. But tonight I was ready to get out of there. Eager to see who would be waiting, I showered as fast as possible, not hanging back with the boys like I normally would. When we exit the locker room, Benny and I fall into step with each other, heading out into the opening where they allow family, girlfriends, or whoever to wait. "That game was brutal," he says, rubbing his shoulder. He took a nasty hit in the third that put him over the boards and onto our bench.

"Usually is with Willette, but tonight seemed different, right?" I spent more time in the penalty box tonight defending myself or my teammates than any other game all damn season.

"Oh, without a fucking doubt. They were out for blood." Benny winces. "I might need Maeve to give me a massa—"

"Stop. Don't say another fucking word." He laughs at my warning, but is smart and shuts up. I don't want to hear about my sister massaging him. It might cause me to beat his ass again.

Stepping out into the mouth of the tunnel, I see my sisters and their red hair first, then Rae and finally Saffie leaning against the wall. My lips kick up in a satisfied smile. If I didn't know any better, I would think that Saffron Briggs, the ice queen herself, is starting to like me. I better not bring it up, though, she'll just try to act like she doesn't.

Dimples on display, I walk up to their little group and stop right in front of Saffie. "Hey, ladies." I swing my gaze over to them before settling back on Saffie. All decked out in FU red and black, she has her hair pulled up in a messy bun and is wearing no makeup aside from some shiny gloss on her lips I would love to kiss off. "Briggsy." I swirl my finger over the numbers on the front of the jersey she's wearing. *My* numbers. Tracing them over and over, I feel her stomach quiver under my touch. I can hear the others talking and feel eyes on me as I watch my hand make its way up and over the sweep of the number three and then the straight line of the one. I'm not sure if they're Saffie's eyes on me or my sisters' and Benny's, but I don't really care. Let them see what they want. I know what I see. And that's Saffie, letting me touch her in front of people. She looks good with my name and number all over her. Seeing her in them does something to me that I can't explain. I never gave a shit before. But now, I want to fuck her wearing nothing but my sweater, bunched up around her waist as I drill into her. My breathing quickens at the image.

"Levi?" Saffie's voice, twinged with concern, breaks through the vision.

"Sorry. Was just thinking about...something."

"What something?" She tilts her head studying me. "Are you okay?"

"Why are you touching my friend? Did you hit your head?" Millie calls out, looking at me like I've lost my mind. Fuck. I have to get it together or get fucked because I feel like I *may* lose my mind if I don't get the chance to kiss her again soon.

"I'm fine, Mill. And I'm touching your friend because I want to." Arm on the wall, I do my best to block their view of Saffie. I rake my teeth over my bottom lip and tug on the sweater, pulling her into me just a bit so that I can whisper in her ear. "Have I told you how good you look with me all over you?" The hair escaping her bun tickles the side of my face when she shakes her head. Not giving her space, I lean back so I can see her face. The red creeping across her cheeks lets me know she's as affected as I am. What would happen if I kissed her right here? Just as I'm about to say "fuck it" and find out, Millie wedges herself between us and pushes me away, breaking whatever spell I had Saffie under that allowed me that close without her blowing me shit or running like she typically does. With my eyes still locked on her face, I watch as she breathes deeply, dropping her gaze and completely breaking our connection.

"Stop being weird. We have to go," my sister says as she tugs Saffie after her, leaving Rae scrambling to catch up.

"Where are you going?" I shove my hands in the pockets of my dress pants to try to relieve the pressure on my cock. It's mandatory that we wear suits on game day, and right now, my pants feel about two sizes too fucking small.

"Somewhere you're not," Millie calls over her shoulder, causing Rae to shrug apologetically at me. Benny and Maeve are slowly trailing us, in their own little world.

I've pushed my luck with Briggsy enough for one night. She won't even look at me. "We have to study tomorrow for your exam," I remind her, hoping that it's coming up this week.

"I have practice in the morning." She stops, Millie and Rae flanking her on either side. My sister looks impatient as all hell. Clearly, she doesn't want me talking to Saffie. She's worried I'll turn her little friend into a *hockey ho* and she should be.

"Meet me at the library after, I'll get our room."

"Oh good, I need to study too." Millie smiles smugly. "I'll come with."

My sister should know better. "If you think you being there to chaperone will stop me from hitting on your friend and trying to get her not to hate me, you're dead ass wrong. A cock block like you won't slow me down." I laugh at Millie's narrowed eyes and Saffie's gasp. She's been uncharacteristically quiet as she watches Millie's and my interaction. "See you two tomorrow." My steps are light as I turn away whistling, heading to the player's parking thinking of how I'll get rid of my sister so I can try to kiss her friend.

∽

I'M JUST PULLING up to the library for our study date when a text comes through.

> Briggsy: not gonna make it.

What the fuck. She's bailing on me?

> Sexy: Why? You scared?

> Briggsy: you're so dumb. I'm in the treatment room, your dad just brought me down.

> Sexy: what happened? Are you okay?

I put the truck in reverse while waiting for an answer and start the five-minute drive to the athletic building, which holds the treatment room complete with sauna, ice bath, and anything else athletes might need to keep their bodies in top-performing condition. As well as the gym and weight room and small theater to watch game tapes. Basically, anything we could ever need all in one spot to make life easier for us. I've still not received a reply from Briggsy as I'm putting the truck in park and hopping out. Fuck man, I hope she's not badly hurt. My dad bringing her here makes me nervous because he's not a coddler. He's a "rub some dirt in it" guy. I head straight for the treatment room when I enter, not allowing anyone to stop me along the way. The guys try calling out greetings and waving, the girls dragging hands over me as I walk by, touching wherever they can. Usually, I welcome it, encourage it, but today, I'm not even fazed.

When I don't see her in the main floor of the treatment room, I go to the back where closed rooms offer a little more privacy. Only one door is closed out of the four, so I start that way and intercept Aiden, one of the physical therapy assistants. "Hey, man, Saffron Briggs in there?"

He shakes his head at me. "You know I can't tell you that, bro."

His words say one thing but the look on his face says she is. "How bad is it?"

Aiden sighs. "Can't tell you that either, but I'm here and not Doc Grayson or one of the main PTs, so…"

"Two tickets in the box next home game if you just walk away and come back later. Much later." The box is where all the bigwigs sit. There's a buffet and servers and all kinds of fancy shit. My dad has seats he never uses because he would rather be down by the glass instead of up in the box away from the action.

A knowing smirk kicks up the corner of his mouth. "You're a fucking dog, Sexy. The new girl? Already? Two games and you can text me when it's safe for me to come back."

I probably shouldn't let him think Briggsy and I are smashing, but that's one less guy I have to worry about trying to hook up with her, so I don't correct him. "Fine, Two games."

"Deal. Text me," he says before walking away.

I don't bother knocking just enter the room quietly and groan inwardly when I see Briggsy on the table. She's on her stomach, resting her head on crossed arms. One side of her short shorts is rolled up and back, exposing the swell of her ass cheek, and a cold pack is strapped to the back of her upper thigh. I'm guessing she pulled a hammy. She doesn't raise her head when I walk in, so I take the opportunity to let my gaze travel over her. The mile of golden, toned legs and the curve of her hip in the silky shorts clinging to her body. She's wearing another FU Fire tank top, leaving her arms bare, with her blond hair in a ponytail draped across her back. I adjust my cock and take a step farther into the room.

"You didn't text me back."

Saffie gasps and jerks her head around, wincing at the sudden movement.

"My phone died. What are you doing here?" The way she's looking at me over her shoulder, mouth open in surprise... damn. "Levi?" She cuts through my dirty-ass thoughts of having her look at me like that while I pound into her from the back.

"Pulled hamstring?" My voice is rough as I try to swallow down my lust for her.

With a deep sigh, she turns around and puts her head back on her stacked arms. "Yeah. I didn't feel a pop, though, so we think it's just a strain, thankfully. First game of the season is next week. PT is gonna come in and stretch me out a bit."

"I know, that's why I'm here. They're short handed today." I'm not sure why the fuck I just said that other than the fact that the thought of Aiden stretching her out makes me want to hit shit.

"You?" There's a sense of panic in her tone with an underlying hint of confusion. Panic is probably because she knows I'll have my hands all over her, and she might like it as much as I do.

"Yeah. I've worked here at least one semester every year since I started here." And I have. I'm just not working here now. "We can study while I stretch you out. You'll be Bob."

She groans into her arms, the sound muffled. "Nothing good will come out of me being Bob."

At least she's admitting that much. Tossing my phone and keys onto the counter, I wash my hands, just as I would if she were any other patient. "You scared?" I goad.

"You always think I'm afraid of you. Like you're the Big Bad Wolf or something. I just don't like you as much as you think," she lies. There is zero conviction in her words.

With a chuckle, I shake my head, leaning back against the counter so I can see her fully. "I guess I'm not too different from the Big Bad Wolf. I'll eat you right up just like he would." My lips tip in a smirk, watching the way those words make her cheeks redden just like my touch did last night. "But like you said, you don't like me. So nothing to worry about, Briggsy. I can call up Millie, though, and have her come down if you feel like you might need her."

"Oh my god, shut up and just do whatever." She waves a hand in the air, flicking it over her body. How I fucking wish.

"How long have you had the ice on?" I'm eager to get my hands on her and stretch her out, but I also don't want to hurt her.

"About fifteen or twenty minutes now." She turns her head, resting her cheek on her folded hands and watching me as I walk over to the table.

"Can you stand so we can move over to the mat?"

"I think so." Pushing up on her elbows, she rolls to her side. I stand close, watching and waiting to help if she needs me. It's obviously not as easy as she thought if her pinched brow is anything to go by. Not able to watch her struggle, I move in closer.

"Here, put your arm around my neck, Briggsy." When she does as she's told, I slip an arm around her waist, my hand resting against her hip and her silky shorts. Straightening with her tucked into my side, I help her down from the table. Her scent surrounds me, the sweet honey scent clinging to my skin. I'm holding her so that her feet are barely touching the floor, bearing all the weight of her left side. Once we get to the mat, I snatch a large towel off the rack and toss it down so she has something to lay on since she'll be facedown.

"You trust me?" I ask, looking down at where she's nestled against my side.

She licks her lips, catching the bottom one between her teeth before answering me. "Yes, why?"

I honestly didn't expect her to say she trusted me. It makes my chest tighten, and my smile widen. Not bothering to answer, I pivot to stand in front of her, still taking her weight. "I'm going to help you get on the floor. Unless of course you feel you can bend your leg enough to do it yourself." I see the wheels turning as she tries to think of how this will work and whether she can do it on her own. She can't, not if she's not able to put weight on it yet. There's a hoist in here for just this thing, but then I can't put my hands all over her and make her trust me. Finally realizing she needs my help, she nods.

"What do you want me to do?"

I step around her so that her back is to my front and place my hands on her waist to steady her. When she tenses, I give her a squeeze. "Relax, Briggsy. This is going to be like a trust fall."

## 24

## LEVI

Her head whips around, her eyes wide. "What do you mean a trust fall? You're not going to drop me, right?"

"I thought you said you trusted me?" I jerk my chin, gesturing for her to turn around. "I promise I won't hurt you." She mumbles something that I can't make out. "What?" Lowering my head so I'm even closer, I wait for her to repeat what she said.

She doesn't. Instead, she pulls in a deep breath. "Nothing. Just tell me what to do."

If I push her now, I'll never be able to convince her to go along with the rest of my plan. "Just hold on to my arms and keep your leg straight and the hurt one off the floor. Lean into me and give me all your weight. I'm going to lower you into a sitting position and then you can get on your side or your stomach. Whichever is more comfortable."

Her hands move to my forearms and then she leans into me, nodding to let me know she's ready. Slowly, I start to lower her, but she tenses again and gives a little yelp. Not sure if it's because it hurts or because giving herself up to me and trusting me not to drop her is what caused the reaction. "Shhh...I got you, Briggsy. I promise I won't let you fall," I murmur against her ear, my voice low, my movements steady. I continue praising her as we get closer to the floor. "That's it, just a little lower. Easy. Like that. Good girl." The more I ease her through the motions, the harder I get. It doesn't help that I can see the goose bumps breaking out across her arms, and I know for damn sure she's not cold. It feels like it's one hundred degrees in here right now from the heat coming off our bodies. Fuck me. I might not survive the next half hour.

Once she's settled on her stomach again, the towel rolled into a pillow that she can bury her face into, I kneel beside her and start unwrapping the ice pack from her leg. My fingers brush the insides of her thighs as I unfasten the velcro. I do my best not to let my hands linger against the soft skin although I want nothing more. Removing the ice pack leaves her ass and leg completely exposed to me, a telltale sign she's either wearing a thong or nothing at all under those flimsy shorts. Swallowing back my groan, I toss the pack aside. My eyes glued to her ass, the skin pink from the ice. "Okay, Briggsy. Let's study." It comes out husky, my mouth dry, my hands itching to run up the back of her legs and grab her perfect ass.

Much to my dismay, she tugs her shorts into place. "Study? How?" It's as if she forgot I told her she was going to be Bob. Which she probably did or better yet, hoped I would forget.

"You have a test tomorrow, right? On the muscles this time?" She nods, not saying a word. "What better way to study the muscles than while we're working them out." Rubbing my hands together, I get on the mat, settling on my knees beside her. "I'll point out the muscle, and you tell me the name." She nods in agreement. I let my gaze roam over her, wondering where I should start. Probably shouldn't start with the gluteus maximus right from the jump, no matter how badly I want to. I decide to start at the top and work my way down. Hands going to the back of her head, burying them in the soft strands of hair, I massage her scalp. "This one is tricky. Everyone always forgets about it. What's it called?" The way she rests her forehead on the makeshift pillow, I can see her profile, eyes squeezed shut, allowing me to look without her talking shit.

"Ummmm..." Her mouth twists in thought. "The occipital?" she hedges.

"Close, it's the occipitalis."

Her fist clenches. "Dammit," she mutters, making me laugh. I move my hand down to her nape, my thumb, index, and middle fingers gently digging into either side of her neck. She arches, pushing into my touch. "I don't know what that one is, but it might be my favorite," Saffie murmurs.

"I promise, it's not your favorite. We haven't made it to that one yet." I rub in circles, smiling at the flush crawling up her cheeks. "This is the splenius capitis." I lower to her upper shoulder area, kneading there as well.

"I know this one!" The excitement in her voice makes me smile. She's always so cool and collected. "Traps," she says proudly.

"Ah, ah, ah. You need to know the proper medical term. Canerday won't give you credit if it's not."

"Seriously?" She huffs.

"Seriously, Briggsy. I don't make the rules. I just break them."

"Because you have no boundaries," she mutters before she answers. "Trapezius. Next."

My hands curve over her shoulders. "As a pitcher, I know you know this one."

"Deltoid." I touch a spot lower. "Teres minor, major is right under."

"Good. And this?" I press my thumbs into the middle of her back on either side of her spine.

"Mmm…" The moan slips out, but she cuts it off abruptly like she doesn't want to encourage me.

"I'm not sure that's what it's called, but do it again anyway," I tell her playfully. I must fucking like slow torture. My dick is hard, she's moaning, and I haven't even gotten to the good bits yet or the stretching.

"Lats—no wait, latissimus dorsi. Right?"

"Right." I curl my hands around her waist, my fingers dipping between her and the mat. "These?"

"External obliques." Her breathing quickens, and I'm not sure if it's because she feels the same anticipation that I feel—knowing what muscles are next on my exploration.

Slowly, I let my fingers skim over the curve of her hips until they land on her ass. With my breath held, I trace the bottom of her cheek, the crease where her ass meets her thigh. Back and forth under the hem of her shorts, I rub her bare skin, waiting for her to tell me to stop. When she doesn't, I move to palm her ass and squeeze. "And this?" My voice is gravelly. I don't even recognize it as my own.

"Gluteus maximus." The answer comes out on an exhale, barely audible.

"Good girl," I praise, letting my hands drift to the backs of her thighs, her skin so soft under my rough hands. "Spread your legs, Saffie." She tenses but then does as I ask. I shift so that I'm kneeling between her legs now. I'm not able to see her face from here, but I don't need to. I can see how having me this close is affecting her. Her body is telling me all I need to know. Her shoulders rise and fall more rapidly now. She's braced on her elbows, head hanging down, her body radiating heat. "Do you know the three muscles that make up the hamstring, Brigsy?" I sound much more calm than I am. While I wait for her to answer, I trail my fingers up the backs of her thighs, letting them skim her inner thighs before retreating and running them down the outer edges. Over and over, I follow the same path, dipping deeper each pass over her inner thighs. It's pure fucking torture.

"I-I'm not sure. I can't think with you doing that," Saffie admits. Even as she does, she spreads her legs just a bit farther. An invitation? Subconsciously needing my hands on the spot I am so very close to yet not close enough?

"Doing what?" I ask nonchalantly, not missing the opportunity to take advantage of the space she's given me. It would take nothing to smooth a finger right over her pussy. Press against her clit. I bet I'd find her wet. The thought has me biting back a groan.

"Semitendinosous, biceps femoris, an-and semimembranosus," Saffie rattles off quickly, mindlessly.

I nod although she can't see me and slide my thumbs between her thighs and press on the smooth skin there. "Which is this?"

"Semimembranosus. Can we stretch now? I think I've got the muscles down."

I have her on edge, trying to run from the way I'm making her feel, but she can't. And stretching instead of "studying" is running right into the fire, not the safety she's thinking it will be. Reluctantly, I pull my hands back and move to her side again. "If you think you've studied enough, sure. You need help rolling over?"

"Nope. I've got it. Easy peasy." Oh, she's cute. Playing like this is all just whatever and that her skin isn't still tingling everywhere my hands just were. I can see the goose bumps skattered across the expanse of her bare skin.

Bottom lip clamped between my teeth, I watch her as she gingerly rolls to her back. My eyes instantly fall to her tits and the pebbled nipples I can see through her tank. When I tear my eyes away and bring them to her face, Saffie's eyes are fixed on the front of my sweats and the rock-hard cock punching against the soft material. Oh, we are so fucked. Pretending I didn't catch her eye fucking my dick and knowing I need to defuse the tension in the room, I move over her and straddle her right leg, standing in a lunge. Gently I take the ankle of her injured leg and push her leg toward her chest, her ankle resting on my knee. Saffie hisses out a breath, her forehead creased. "You okay, Briggsy?" She nods. "Tell me when you feel it stretch, and I won't push, okay?" She just nods again, letting me go a little further before she stops me.

"There."

"We'll hold it for thirty seconds and then relax." Her eyes are closed, arms thrown up above her head, and all I can picture is me pinning her that way while I fuck her. It's really not helping the state of my hard-on right now, but I can't help it. This close to her, touching her, the smell of her all around me, and all I can think about is fucking her. When the time is up, I release her leg and do the same thing to the other side just to rest her injured leg before starting the exercise again.

"You ready for the big stretch now?" Not waiting for an answer, I move into position between her thighs, lifting her leg and placing her ankle on my shoulder. It's at that moment Saffie realizes that this wasn't the safe bet she thought it was. I see it in her eyes as they flare wide, a look of panic flashing through them. "Same way, Briggsy. I push, and when you feel the pull, you tell me to stop." The way we're aligned, my dick is pressed up to the back of her thigh, my hand grasping her calf and applying pressure. "Keep your hips on the ground," I grit out, my barely there control about to snap when she whimpers. It's not in pain. No. This is an *"I need you to fuck me and make me come because this foreplay has gone on long e-fucking-nough"* whimper. Unable to help it, I subtly grind my cock into her, just a nudge to try to find some relief. My gaze finds hers when she melts into that touch, and the panic isn't there anymore. Instead, her gray eyes have gone soft with a lust-filled haze that I'm sure mirrors mine. Fuck me. "Tell me when to stop." My voice is barely above a whisper, rough with the need I have to plow into her. I tell her to tell me when to stop, but I don't know whether I mean for her to tell me when to stop pushing her leg up or to stop trying to dry fuck her on the floor of the treatment room. God, why did I tell her to keep her hips on the ground? If she would just raise them slightly, I could shift and...ah, fuck. My hold on her leg tightens when she raises her hips, just slightly but enough for me to press into her center, the ridge of my hard cock tight against her pussy, making her gasp and a bead of sweat snake down my spine. I could come so fucking easily right now. I've gone longer in the past few weeks without sex than I have since my first time, and the sight of her under me, the feel of her skin and the heat of her pussy pressed against the soft cotton of my sweats is enough to push me right over the edge.

Must be for her too because she rocks against me, my name falling from her lips. "Levi, please."

Just as I'm about to melt the ice queen, there's a knock on the door, and Charlie, the main physical therapist on staff, walks in whistling a song that is clearly the cock blocker's anthem.

## 25

## SAFFIE

I've been pacing around stiff-legged in my dorm room for the past thirty minutes. My leg is killing me, but Landon is supposed to be here today, and I have to tell him what happened with Levi. What I *almost* let him do. What I *begged* him to do. "Gahhh, what was I thinking?" Frustrated, I tug at the messy bun on top of my head just to gather it all back up again and tie it in an even messier 'do. I know what I was thinking. I was thinking that he had spent a half hour running his hands all over my body, the clean, icy scent of his cologne surrounding me and then those damn gray sweatpants. They really put me right over the edge. There was no hiding his massive hard-on the entire time he was helping me *study*. I kept stealing peeks at him out of the corner of my eye. And then when I rushed him into stretching me out, and I felt the hardness against the softness of my thigh...I was a goner. Never in my life have I wanted someone more. I didn't care that we were on the floor in the treatment room. I didn't care that I had a boyfriend. I didn't care one bit that this was Levi and that I wasn't supposed to like him. My tutor, hockey god, and campus player. Nope. All I cared about was that he made me feel so damn good, and he hadn't even really done anything more than give me a light massage. I'm an athlete. I get rubbed down and stretched all the time and never ever in the history of ever had I wanted whomever was doing the rubbing and stretching to fuck me. And that's where my problems begin. I have to tell Landon, but what am I hoping for? Do I want to break up with him? Do I want him to forgive me and move on like it never happened? But if that's the case, can I promise it won't happen again. *That* is the million-dollar question. I mean, this is Sexy. He doesn't do relationships. He does hookups and hockey. He's said so himself. But is that all I want from him? I'm going to break up with my boyfriend for a quick hookup with Levi and then what? He moves on to the next chick and that's it? Do I even want to date him? Maybe it's not Levi at all. Maybe it's just that I haven't had sex in so long. As soon as I think it, I know it's a lie. The look on Levi's face when Charlie walked into the room reflected what I was feeling. Frustration. Disappointment. And a shit ton of want. Levi had left, and Charlie had finished up with the stretches, and I didn't get all hot and bothered with him, so, yeah. It was one hundred percent Levi Sexton that my body craved.

A knock on my door has me freezing in place. Landon isn't supposed to be here for hours yet. I'm not ready. I'm about to answer when the door opens, and the twins and Rae come in. "Sorry, we weren't sure if you were in here with someone," Rae says, flopping down on the bed.

"He's not supposed to be here for a while."

"Are you so excited to see him and finally get laid?" Millie asks as she sits next to my cousin on the bed.

The knot in my stomach tightens at her words. Maeve must see something cross my face at the question because she interjects before I can answer. "We wanted to see if you wanted to grab a coffee with us at Spun. Figured it would be better than sitting around here and waiting."

"Unless you need to get...ready." Millie waggles her eyebrows suggestively.

"Oh my god, Mill, you have a one-track mind." Rae laughs and gets to her feet. "Let's go, cuzzo. You look like you need a drink...or three. Coffee will have to do until later, though. I have to be at the outdoor rink in a bit to help with the tournament the boy's team is running." She links her arm through mine and leads me to the door, walking slowly to accommodate my hobble.

"I'm not going to the rink, though. Just coffee." I'm in no way ready to see Levi just yet.

"That's fine. Maeve and I are going to support the boys." She pats my hand.

Relief floods through me. "Grab my keys, Maeve. I can't walk all the way to Spun with my leg."

"You should really get that stretched out," Millie calls out as she gets off the bed to follow us. I nearly stumble at her words. If she only freaking knew.

Spun is crazy busy all the time. A combination coffee, book, and yarn shop, it's already a campus favorite. The owners just opened this location and weren't sure how it would do with the college crowd. I mean, the coffee was a given since we basically live on caffeine, but the books and yarn had them unsure. They needn't have worried. The place is jamming, and the vibe is incredible. The knitting and crocheting classes are always full. I'm struck by the heavenly smell of coffee and cupcakes the moment we step inside. Glancing around, I see Kenna and Lakyn sitting at a round table in front of the fireplace, waving us over.

"I thought we were going to have to fight people over this table," Kenna says, pulling a chair out for me. "Sit, girl. You look like you're in pain."

Millie nods. "I told her she needs to get it stretched out."

"Oh, I heard she got it stretched out reeeeeaaalll good," Lakyn sing-songs. My head whips in her direction. What? How could she possibly know anything?

"Wait, what?" Millie's eyes are wide as her gaze ping-pongs between Lakyn and me.

"Come on, let's get our coffee first," Maeve coaxes as she grabs Millie, dragging her and Rae away. "Same as always, Saffie?"

"Yes, please." The minute they're out of earshot, I turn to Lakyn, who is watching me. Her pretty golden eyes full of mischief.

Kenna leans forward, bouncing in her seat. "Spill. We know you probably don't want to say anything in front of the twins, so you have about five minutes, and we need the tea, girl."

"I-I don't know what you mean," I lie, wishing like hell I would've stayed behind and continued pacing and panicking in the comfort of my room.

Lakyn sucks her teeth. "Nuh-uh, baby. That won't fly here. Aidan told Kenna that Sexy bribed him with box tickets to disappear so you guys could...be alone in the treatment room the other day." She smirks.

My eyes widen in disbelief. "He did what now?" Oh my god, I might die of embarrassment.

"Mm-hmm. I knew he was supposed to be working, and when he showed up at my dorm looking to hook up, I asked him why he wasn't at the center. And that's when he told me that he was covered until Sexy texted him that he could come back." She boops my nose, her face split in a grin.

"He told me they were short-staffed, and he was helping out," I say, confused.

Lakyn hoots out a laugh, leaning across the table. "So you did smash! I knew it!" She and Kenna high-five each other like a couple of teenage boys.

"No. We did not smash," I hiss, glancing around to see who might overhear us.

The crestfallen look on Kenna's face is almost comical. "So nothing happened?" She pouts.

I can feel the heat creep up my neck and across my cheeks, and it doesn't get past Lakyn either. "Oh, shit. *Something* happened." She and Kenna move closer. "Seriously, Saffie, the tea."

I slump back in the chair and run my hands over my face. There's no way they're going to let this drop, and I'd rather talk about it now than when the twins and my cousin get back. "We-we were just studying," I try lamely." Kenna rolls her eyes, and Lakyn makes a gimme gesture, her sparkly painted nails clacking together. "We were. But it was more of...a show-and-tell type of study session," I admit.

"Wait. Isn't he your anatomy and physiology tutor?" Kenna practically screeches.

Shushing her, I nod. "Yes. I had a test on the muscular system that I had to study for. And-and he helped me by pointing out the muscles on my body and having me name them," I say hurriedly. There. That was the truth, and I didn't have to go into any details about how every spot he touched felt like a million watts of electricity followed by an overflow of magma. When his hands skated over my inner thighs...it took everything in me not to squeeze my legs together and trap his hand against me for some delicious, much-needed friction.

"If you could see your face right now, you'd know that we know you're full of shit. You look like you just creamed your damn panties." Lakyn grins smugly, pointing a finger at my face.

I hadn't just now, but I certainly had at the time, and having to finish the PT session with Charlie knowing that my panties were soaked was mortifying. "Okay, okay fine!" I whisper shout. "He nearly made me come just from putting his hands on me.

It was so hot even though it wasn't anything really. Just Levi and his hands on my arms and back and thighs..." I trail off. "And then I suggested we be done with that portion of the study session and move on to the stretching of my hamstring because if he touched the inside of my thigh one more time, I was going to embarrass us both." I shake my head at how dumb that was. "I mean, what did I think was going to happen once I was on my back?"

"You thought that would be better?" Kenna snort-laughs. "Girl, you so dumbbbbb." Her and Lakyn break into a fit of giggles.

"Yeah, I am because it was torture. He literally had my leg thrown over his shoulder, you guys," I whine. "And then him and his stupid gray sweatpants were all up on me, and I'm pretty sure I begged him to fuck me." The last bit comes out a little louder than I intended, making me cringe.

"So did he? Because there's no way in hell that you asked Sexy to fuck you, and he didn't come through," Kenna says, crossing her arms over her chest.

"For real. Sexy has been trying to smash you since day one! Ain't no way he didn't."

I shake my head at them, my face flaming. "Charlie walked in before we had a chance—"

"What did Charlie walk in on?" Rae asks as she puts my coffee down in front of me.

"Oh nothing, only her and their brother about to smash," Lakyn says nonchalantly.

Millie shoots her iced coffee out of her nose at the same time as my cousin yelps and Maeve claps her hands excitedly.

Burying my face in my hands, I pray for the ground to just swallow me right now. "Not cool, Lakyn. Not cool," I mutter.

"Oh, stop it. That boy is so fucking fine. If you're not related to him, you'd be dumb not to want to hit that. It can't be helped. You're a mere mortal, Saffron Briggs. You can't fight his pull.

He's a god. A hockey god with big dick energy. You're forgiven, my child." She makes the sign of the cross in the air in front of me.

"Lalalalala, I am not listening to any of this!" Millie practically screeches as she dabs at her face, trying to clean the coffee off her. "I feel like we just had this conversation, and you said you wouldn't kiss him again! You lying little hockey hoe," she chastises, tossing the napkin on the table.

"I'm not a lying little hockey hoe!" I correct her, "I didn't kiss him. I only may have maybe asked him to...to..."

"To fuck her," Kenna supplies happily.

"Oh gooodddddd whhhyyy?" Mill moans dramatically.

"You know why." Lakyn tsks, reveling in Millie's misery.

Maeve pats her sister's back like a little mother hen. "Okay, okay. Calm down my little drama llama. So Charlie interrupted, and then what?"

Raegan pulls her chair closer, slurping at her frozen Chai latte. "Yeah, did he toss Levi out or what?"

"No. No. Nothing like that. I'm sure it all looked normal from where he was standing. I mean, we were fully clothed and kind of in the right position for some hamstring stretches."

This makes Kenna burst into a fit of giggles. "Ahem. Sorry," she lies.

"Anyway, Charlie walked in and said that he would finish up so he could file the report with Coach, set me up with my treatment plan, and then I could get out of there. Levi left and Charlie helped me with some stretches and that was it."

Rae's mouth hangs open. "Was Levi waiting for you?"

I shake my head, and I don't tell them how disappointed I had been at that.

"And have you spoken since then?" Maeve asks, genuinely curious. I think she would love to see me and her brother together. Now that her and Benny are a thing, I swear she's walking around like Cupid with hearts in her eyes.

"No. We don't typically talk every day, though, unless we're planning a study date or you guys drag me to a game," I admit.

"Guess you don't gotta talk to be DTF." Lakyn snickers behind her hand.

I glare at her. "You're not helping."

"Baby, you don't need help. You need dick. Sexy's dick." She twirls one of her braids around her finger, her smile wide.

Maeve puts a hand up. "Please. Please do not say those two words together in front of me again. I think I threw up in my mouth."

"So what now?" Rae asks. "Landon is coming tonight, right?"

I nod.

"You're telling him, right?" My cousin is no fan of Landon, never has been. "I mean, I don't give a shit about him, but I just think if you and Levi are kissing and…stuff, and you're trying to convince yourself that you don't like him just so you don't admit that you're into him, then it's probably time to end things with Landon." She holds up her hand just as Millie had. "And not for him. But for you. Because even if whatever this thing with Levi is or isn't, Landon is a tool, and I hate the hell out of him for you." That's the first time she's ever come right out and said that she didn't like him.

"Tell me how you really feel, Rae." I grimace.

"I don't even know him, and I don't like him." Maeve shrugs.

"And Maeve is like Beiber's mama and likes everyone." Kenna nods like if Mama Maeve says he's no good that's gospel.

I sigh deeply, cupping my hands around my coffee. "Yeah. I'm going to tell him. I just don't know what I want to happen after that. You know?" I glance at the faces around the table, my friends. Friends I've come to love and depend on in such a short amount of time. They've come through for me again and again. More than I can say about my friends back at St. Claire since I've been here and especially about my boyfriend. "Maybe once I see Landon, I'll know exactly what I'm supposed to do."

"Maybe," Rae says encouragingly. She opens her mouth to say something else but is interrupted when Nora stops at our table.

"You look like shit, Saffron." That's her greeting. And I'm sure I do. Especially compared to her and her perfectly made-up face and cute little workout clothes that have probably never even seen a gym.

"Yet she has my brother *and* her boyfriend trying to hit that," Millie says, surprising the hell out of me. Not that she came to my defense but that she used her brother to do it. She must *really* want to piss Nora off.

It works. Nora's eyes narrow to slits. "*Yet,*" she mocks, "I don't see either one of them here."

"Levi is at the rink, and her boyfriend is on his way here as we speak." Millie stands. "In fact, we have to go so she can get ready. So many hookups, so little time. You know how that is, don't you, Nora?" Millie's words drip with scathing innuendo.

Not giving Nora an opportunity to respond, Millie turns her back, effectively blocking her from the table. "Come on, gimpy. I'll help you back to your dorm while they go to the outdoor rink." She looks over her shoulder, watching as Nora stomps out of the coffee shop.

"Fucking *whore-a*," Rae mutters, making us all laugh.

∼

> Rae: Party at Hockey House. Meet us over there. Levi told me to tell you.

I LOOK AT THE MESSAGE, and the thought of going over there and seeing Levi has my insides jumping. He told my cousin to tell me? Why didn't he just text me himself? Because he knew you'd probably ignore his text but not Rae's.

> Me: It's the middle of the day!

It's Hockey House, they do what they want there, but they've never had a day party since I've been here.

> Rae: I know. They have that tourney all weekend, though, so they decided to have one now.

> Me: I'm not coming over there before Landon gets here. I'm already confused enough.

> Rae: Fair

Immediately after she sends that, another text comes through.

> Landon: Hey babe. Not gonna make it. I'm super fucking sick and Grant's girl canceled on him anyway.

I had assumed he left already, and he's just now telling me he's not coming?

> Me: That's convenient.

I can't help my pissy reply, though I'm not sure who it's convenient for. Him or me? And then I feel instantly guilty with the next message.

> Landon: I wish you were here to take care of me like you always used to. I would still come up there, but I don't want to get you sick.

Dammit. I should really give him a break. It's not his fault

I'm all over the place. In fact I should be extra nice to him given what I've been doing up here.

> Me: I'm sorry you don't feel well. I'll have your favorite soup delivered from Connie's.

> Landon: Nah. That's okay. I don't even think I can get out of bed to answer the door *sick face emoji*

He never did handle being sick well at all. Landon was the definition of man flu

> Me: Go and get some rest. You'll feel better in the morning I'm sure. We can talk then.

> Landon: Luv u

> Me: *heart emoji*

God, I'm a terrible person. I mean, what did it say about me that I couldn't even text back that I loved him? When did shit get so messed up? Do I still love him? Do you fall out of love with someone just like that? No. I'm just confused.

*"Are we going to talk about that kiss or just pretend it never happened?"* I hear Levi's voice in my head. I groan and roll off my bed. Going to my closet, I throw some clothes in my duffel bag, scoop my toiletries from the bathroom, and toss those in too. I cannot put off talking to Landon about this anymore. I'll bring him some soup to soften the blow and help him feel better. He can't be *that* sick. He texted me yesterday and never mentioned not feeling well. But sick or not, I can't go on feeling this way. My insides feel like someone is in there with an ax just hacking away. I can't deal.

With all my stuff in hand, I walk out to my truck and jump in. Opening up the maps app on my phone, I punch in

Landon's address. It will take about three, three and a half hours to get there. "Uggghh, I hate road trips," I mutter. Pulling out of the lot, I flip my blinker on to turn right, but at the last second, I turn left...toward Hockey House. I feel a clawing need to see Levi and tell him that I'm going to talk to Landon. That I'm going to tell him everything. Why it seems so important, I'm not sure. Maybe I need to see how he reacts. What if he tells me not to, that it's not like that? I hadn't thought about that. It makes stopping there even more important. Will I break up with Landon if Levi tells me not to? "Shit." It was so much easier when I hated him. It only takes a few minutes before I'm pulling into the driveway. A ton of cars are already here, but I'm not surprised. Their parties are always lit. Even in the middle of the day, apparently. Checking my appearance in the rearview mirror, I'm glad I at least got myself somewhat together in preparation for Landon coming. I don't look like the hot mess I did this morning. Jumping out of the truck, I head to the front door and go inside. Doing my best not to draw attention to myself, I take the steps up to Levi's room. I don't want the whole damn campus knowing I'm here to see him. Reaching his door, I knock loud enough to be heard over the music, though it's not that loud up here, tapping my foot nervously as I wait for him to answer. One beat. Two. I knock again, and this time the door flies open. Levi stands there looking irritated as hell. Probably at the interruption since sitting on the bed behind him is a smug-looking Nora.

## 26

## LEVI

"Briggsy?" I'm surprised to see her here. Especially because Rae told me she wasn't coming because she had plans. Plans that Nora just told me were to hook up with her boyfriend who was coming into town for the fucking weekend to see her. I'm not sure how the hell she knew. Maybe she made it up. It's not like her and Saffie are friends. Far from it. I hope to hell she made it up because the thought of him here with her has put me in a shitty ass mood.

"I-I just came to tell you that I was leaving for the weekend," she stammers nervously. Her tongue darts out to wet her lips, glancing behind me to where Nora is sitting on my bed. Shit. I should probably tell her that I didn't invite her here, and she isn't fucking staying. But before I do, her eyes come back to land on me, the gray flashing hot with anger. Her chin lifts, and with a hint of defiance, she drops a bomb on me. "To see Landon." She bites the inside of her cheek as she holds my gaze, almost as if she's daring me to say something about it.

My insides churn. I hate this fucking guy. So Nora wasn't wrong about them spending the weekend together, she just had the semantics wrong. "Does he know you're coming?"

"No. I'm going to surprise him. He was supposed to come here, but he's sick."

I step into the hall and close my door behind me. I don't need Nora hearing our conversation, and I'd bet my favorite hockey stick she was listening. "Not a good idea, Briggsy. Call first," I warn. As much as I would love for her to catch this asshole cheating, I don't want to see her get hurt.

"What's that supposed to mean?" she demands angrily.

"It's not supposed to mean anything. It means to call first because if you don't, you're not gonna like what you find."

"You know, not every one is like you, Levi. Not all guys have commitment issues," she hisses, the ice queen out in full force. Good, because I feel like fighting with her.

"That's where you're wrong, sweetheart." She all but snarls at me at the condescending name. "When it comes to shit like this, we are all the same. I'm just more open about it. Guys like your precious Landon aren't. They'll sneak around behind your back until they get caught. Then they'll act like it was all a mistake, a one-time thing. How they're sorry, and it won't happen again. But they're full of shit." I shrug. "I would love for you to prove me wrong for your sake, but you won't. You put that much ass in front of a frat boy golfer or whatever he is who thinks he's hot shit on campus and then send his girl a couple of hundred miles away? Yeah, you better call." There's no way he's not cheating on her up there. Hell, I'd bet my *other* favorite stick on it.

"You think just because you're up front about it that it makes it okay?" She's missing the point and focusing on me and what a douche that makes me. Because deep down, she knows I'm right.

"Be mad at me all you want. I don't pretend to be something I'm not. I like sex. A lot. I like fucking, and nobody gets hurt, unless they want to, because they know going in that's all it is. Fantastic. No-strings fucking." I grin slowly at her flushed face, and her lip caught between her teeth. It reminds me of how she looked when she was soft and pliant underneath me the other day. Using my thumb, I tug at that lip. She swats my hand away, coming to her senses and shaking off her reaction to my words. "I'm not with anybody because, until now, I didn't want to be. Nobody gets hurt. Nobody gets played that way. That's not a commitment issue. Fucking around on your girl or your man..." I smirk, flashing my dimples at her. "*That* sounds like a commitment issue." If she caught the little "until now," she doesn't seem surprised. Not about that or about the dig that she's the one with commitment issues, not me since she's the one committed.

Saffie snorts indelicately, taking a step backward and putting some distance between us. "Yeah, right. Until now. Says the guy who would've fucked me the other day yet has another girl in his room right now."

And there it is.

"So let me get this straight. You don't want me, but you don't want anyone else to have me either? How's that fair, Saffie? Hmm? You have your fancy Ivy League boyfriend, and I get no one? Is that how it is?"

"I didn't say that." She huffs.

Pushing away from the door, I move closer. She turns her head, eyes averted, looking anywhere but at me. I keep walking. Saffie takes one step back to every one of mine forward until her back hits the wall, and she has nowhere left to go. Grasping her chin, I force her to look at me. "You didn't have to say it, Saffie." My gaze roams over her face, the need to kiss her so fucking strong. Instead, I step into her, invading her space even more, forcing her to acknowledge me. "I saw it. I saw it in your eyes, the way they flashed fire when the door opened, and you saw Nora in my room. I heard it in that pissy little tone you use when you're fighting yourself from wanting me. And the way you bit the inside of your cheek to keep from saying anything more that might let me know that you actually like me. Reealllyy like me." I place my palms flat against the wall on either side of her head and lean in even closer, our thighs touching, my cock, hard from sparring with her nudging against her belly. Taking a second to breathe in the honey scent of her before brushing my lips against the shell of her ear. "Tell me you don't want me to touch anyone else, Saffie. Tell me you want me, and I'm yours." I nip her lobe, catching the little gold hoop she's wearing between my teeth before releasing it to say softly, "Just one word, and I'll make you forget his name." She trembles against me, at my words, my touch, causing me to smirk. She can play hard to get all she wants. I know this isn't one-sided. I know this fire I feel, this need to have her, isn't all me. She feels it. She's just too good to admit it. I'm not. I couldn't give a single fuck less about her boyfriend. Not one single fuck.

She shakes her head, her teeth grazing across her reddened bottom lip. Stubborn as fuck. "Say it or I'm going back in there and I'm gonna fuck Nora," I threaten. "I'm not a saint, and I won't act like some pussy-whipped asshole while you go and visit your little boyfriend and let him finish what I started in the treatment center. I'm not that guy." I clench my teeth so hard I swear I can hear the molars grind against each other in danger of shattering, the muscle in my jaw pulsing in time with my racing heart. I don't bother to tell her that the last thing I want to do is fuck Nora. That's information she doesn't need. All she needs to know is that it's in her hands. All she has to do is say the fucking word.

"You're an asshole," she hisses, ducking under my arm and running down the stairs. I hear the front door slam, and the murmur of voices as the party goes on like Saffie didn't just come up here and manhandle the shit out of my feelings, no fucking penalty called.

Slamming my fist against the wall making the plaster cave

under the force of it, I turn and stalk to my room. Throwing the door open, I growl in frustration when I see that not only is Nora in my bed but she's now naked, her hands trailing over her tits in slow circles as she watches me. I close the door, leaning against it, watching, willing my dick to do something. I haven't fucked Nora or anyone else in a long fucking while. Long for me, at least. And now's my chance. Saffie is on her way to Connecticut to fuck her little boyfriend, so why shouldn't I do the same and fuck Nora? All Saffie had to do was tell me not to. I asked her to tell me not to. Nora, growing bolder from me watching, unaware of my inner battle of wills, opens her legs wide and dips her fingers into her pussy, moaning at the invasion. My cock stirs but doesn't come to life. I was harder fighting with Saffie than I am right now, and Nora is really putting on a show, writhing and moaning dramatically. I know fingering herself isn't that fucking good. My irritation at the situation grows. Any other time, this would have had me hard and ready to fuck Nora and whatever one of her friends she brought up here with her. But now? Now I just want her the fuck out of my room so I can drive myself insane wondering what the hell Saffie is doing with her boyfriend while I'm back here like some pussy, pining after the ice queen. Without saying a word, I open the door and walk out, slamming it behind me and leaving Nora to finish whatever she started by herself. On my way out my front door, I snag Cubbie. "Get Nora out of my room and lock it behind you."

He looks at me confused. "She's in your room? And you're leaving? You sick, Sexy?"

"Nah, bro. Just don't want to deal with her shit. Fuck her if you want, just don't do it in my room."

Cubbie grins, nodding his head. "Saffie." He says her name like it's an epiphany. I don't bother answering him. What's there to say? She made her choice tonight.

## 27

## SAFFIE

The drive here felt like the longest ride of my damn life. I was stuck in awful bumper-to-bumper traffic most of the way, and all I could think about was Levi with Nora. It took me, miserable in the truck all by myself, to figure out that I had gone to Hockey House eager to tell him that I was going to talk to Landon to gauge his reaction. I had been certain that he would give me the answers I needed to help clear up any confusion I was feeling. He cleared up the confusion all right. It's crystal clear now that Levi is Levi, and I was stupid to think, even for a second, we could be anything more than what we were. Or that I would be satisfied with being just another one of his hockey hoes. I've come to the realization that I had wanted him to want me, only me. A part of me wanted to be the one who brought Sexy to his knees. I know that isn't fair since I'm still with Landon, but on the almost five-hour ride that should have been three hours, that's the conclusion I've come to. Shitty-ass timing, but there it is. And now? I have no clue what to do with any of that. The pain I felt when I saw Nora in his room and when he gave me that ultimatum *"Say it or I'm going back in there and I'm gonna fuck Nora."* It was like someone had punched me right in the gut. Did he make good on that promise? Of course he did. He's Levi. He said it himself. He likes sex, a lot. And Nora was there and willing. *But he was asking you to choose him, and you didn't.* I shoot that thought down because I can't deal with that right now. I need to talk with Landon before anything else. Levi might not care that I have a boyfriend, but I do. I've already done way more than I should have been doing, both emotionally and physically.

Shaking my head to rid myself of that thought, I turn into the lot of Connie's, a little mom-and-pop place near St. Claire's campus that serves the best comfort foods, making it a favorite with college kids away from home. I scan over the cars parked around me, hoping I don't run into anyone I know. I'm not in the mood to people right now. I just want to get Landon his soup and get out. It's still early, just after five, so the clientele should be of the early bird variety right now. The bells chime as I walk in, heading right for the takeout counter and not making eye contact with anyone in the dining room. Thankfully, the girl at the window isn't anyone I recognize, and I'm able to get the order I called in and get out of there without incident. It's not until I'm unlocking my truck that someone calls my name. Groaning inwardly, I turn to see who caught me. "Brett, hi." He's one of Landon's friends. They roomed together freshman year in the dorm until Landon pledged and moved into the frat house.

"I didn't know you were in town," he says, hugging me. "Are you headed over to the Green?" That's what they call Alpha Phi Alpha house because it's on the back half of the golf course.

"Yeah, just grabbing some soup. Landon isn't feeling well."

His brows shoot up into his hairline. "Oh! You've seen him already?"

"Not yet. He was supposed to come to Boston for the weekend but got sick."

"Aah, so you're here instead. Does he know you're coming?"

What is it with guys asking that question? Not wanting to get into it with Brett the way I did with Levi and get a lecture of the correct way to surprise your boyfriend, I just nod and open the truck door. "Yep, he's expecting me. Talk to you later, Brett," I say hurriedly, ready to just get out of there.

He looks relieved. "Oh, good. Right. I've got to go too. It was good to see you, Saffron. Don't be a stranger."

I lift a hand and wave as I climb into the truck and pull out before anyone else decides to stop me. I'm already regretting coming here, and I haven't even got to the hard part of talking to Landon yet. It takes me about five minutes to get to the Green. I breathe a sigh of relief when I see only Landon's Range Rover in the drive and Grant's Jeep. I wasn't up for a crowd, and though this isn't a typical party house, a lot of the APA guys were golfers and would meet back here after golfing. Not to mention that they had four other roommates. With a shaky breath, I flip down the visor to check my face in the little mirror, hoping I don't look as bad as I feel. Satisfied that I don't, I gather the soup and my phone and hop out. The house has a keypad at the front door that unlocks the doors. Hopefully, they haven't changed the code since I left. Punching in the numbers, I'm relieved when I hear the lock click open. I feel a little guilty using the keypad, but Landon had said he was too sick to get out of bed, so I didn't want to bother him and have him come open the door. Quietly, I swing the door open and enter the foyer. The Green is the opposite of Hockey House in every way. For one, there's not a never-ending orgy happening in the family room, and where Hockey House is homey, the Green is a little less inviting. You would never even know it was a frat house. Then again, they did have a housekeeper who came out three days a week. The APA guys were a bit spoiled. I toe my shoes off at the door since the entire upstairs is sand-colored carpeting and head up the flight of stairs to the bedrooms. Landon's bedroom has the same kind of keypad lock, so punching in the numbers, our anniversary, I ease the door open, not wanting to wake him if he's sleeping. The moment the door opens, it's clear I needn't have worried because Landon is wide awake and not sick at all. In fact, he's railing the hell out of Cassidy Winston, the drink cart girl from the golf course. I make a strangled noise in my throat and the bag holding the soup falls from my hands, thudding quietly on the carpeted floor as I gawk in disbelief.

"Grant I said you'd have to wa—" Landon starts before looking over his shoulder and seeing me standing there. He yelps as if he's been bit in the ass...or caught fucking around. "Saffron! Fuck. Baby, this isn't—this is. Fuck!" The panic on his face as he climbs off Cassidy, who doesn't even have the decency to look sorry but instead looks put out like I've ruined *her* day by fucking *her* boyfriend, is almost comical. Or is the funny part the fact that both of the men in my life are busy fucking other women tonight, and I can't seem to stop walking in on them?

"Landon! Bro! Brett just called and said Saff—" Grant comes barreling into the room, coming to an abrupt stop when he sees me standing there. "Oh, shit," leaves his mouth in a whoosh.

As I stand there, it's almost as if I can feel the thrum of my heartbeat everywhere. In my neck, my chest, even the tips of my fingers are pulsing as I watch Landon scramble to find clothes, his now limp dick looking smaller than I remembered. Grant is talking to me, but I can't really hear him. I feel like I'm standing outside a window and looking in on someone else's life. How did I get here, to this place, in this situation, and why am I so calm? I have yet to say a single word to any of them. Why aren't I screaming? Crying? With a shake of my head, I break the daze I'm in and move past Grant to leave the room.

"Saffron, wait! Grant, stop her!" I can hear Landon order frantically. Cassidy says something in a whiny voice that I can't make out. Probably wondering if he's coming back or if she should just finish by herself.

"What do you want me to do, hold her down?" Grant asks his dumbass friend in a tone that indicates he also thinks he's a giant dumbass.

I have got to get out of here before Landon finds clothes. I'm not going to discuss anything with him smelling like sex and begging for forgiveness. Dammit. Levi was right. I should have called. Luckily, I make it to my truck before anyone catches up to me. I had planned to stay at my house tonight since my mom is in Boston and nobody would be there, but I can't now. That's the first place Landon would look. Once I'm out on the road, I slam a hand on my steering wheel. "Think, Saffie," I mutter, glancing behind me to be sure there's not a Range Rover following. My phone starts ringing from my pocket and then connecting with the Bluetooth in the truck to ring in stereo. "Landon Lover" flashes across the screen on the dash. I send it to voicemail, and it immediately starts ringing again. Again I send it to voicemail. It takes about thirty seconds for the texts to start coming. Knowing he won't stop, I power the phone down so I can think. I don't give a shit what he has to say. There's no explanation for what I saw other than exactly what I saw, and right now, I don't want to hear excuses or apologies. I just want to focus on where the hell I'm going. Then I can deal with my feelings. Or lack thereof because right now, I feel numb. Empty. Without realizing it, I'm heading back to the ramp to get onto I-84 toward Boston. I look at the clock. It's not even six. How did all of that happen in less than an hour's time? If traffic is cleared up, I can make it back to FU by eight, but where will I go then? He'll show up at my dorm. I don't want to go to my aunt and uncle's, where my mom is staying. I'm not ready to face people and explain what I don't even understand. Turning on my phone again, I wait for it to do its thing and start cringing when it starts pinging, alerting me of thirty missed calls and just as many texts. Not looking at any of them, I call my cousin.

"Heeeyyyyy, girl!" Rae answers, the music loud in the background. Shit, I forgot that she had been at Hockey House when I'd left.

"You still at Levi's?" I clear my throat, trying to rid my voice of the tightness.

"Yeah. Are you okay? You with Landon?" she asks, sounding confused.

A wry laugh slips out before I can stop it. "No. No I'm not."

I hear the music fading, "Saffie, what's going on? Shhh," she hisses at someone or someones. Probably the twins. "I thought Landon was at your place?"

So Levi hadn't told them. He and Nora probably haven't come out of his room the whole time I've been gone. Why the thought of that hurts me so much more than the sight of Landon with Cassidy makes me so damn angry. Fuck them both! Fuck them all!

"No. He didn't show, so I drove to St. Claire to see him. I'm on my way back now. Can I stay with you at your dorm tonight?" I don't explain any more. They'll drill me enough when I get there wanting to know everything.

"I'm staying with the twins tonight because my roommate's boyfriend is in town. Whatever, that doesn't matter. Just come here," she insists.

"I'm not going there, I don't want to see Levi," I admit.

"You won't. We'll wait outside for you. Millie has been drinking, and Maeve is somewhere with Benny. Murphy is supposed to be driving us home later." There's more shushing on her side. "I can't believe you drove and are driving back. Are you okay? Like you're awake and alert, right?" I didn't mean to worry her.

"Yeah, I'm fine. Just…I'm fine." Tears clog my throat, the last fine coming out a bit strangled.

"Saffron Theodora Briggs! Are you crying?" Rae shouts a little panicked.

"I'm fine. It's just been a day. First, Levi and Nora and then Landon and Cassidy..." A sob causes my voice to break, the tears streaming down my face in rivers now.

"Levi and Landon? What happened? Saffie? Are you okay, should you pull over?" They must have found Maeve. Her gentle mothering makes me cry harder. I don't even know why. I'm not entirely sure what it is I'm crying about. Landon or Levi? Both of them? Neither of them? No, my heart hurts, and my insides feel like they just went a round with Mike Tyson, and I think that's on both of them. They've put me through it today.

"I-I'm fine," I say again. "I'm g-gonna go. I'll be there in a couple of hours. Please don't make me look for you. I can't see him right now. Especially not with her," I plead, rambling and not caring if they know what I'm talking about. Swiping at the tears on my face, I'm aggravated with myself for allowing this moment of weakness when neither of them deserves it.

"We won't." They answer in unison. I must be on speaker so they can hear my meltdown in stereo.

"I'll text you when I'm close."

"Okay. Be careful," Maeve calls out.

"I will," I answer before I disconnect the call. Glad I know my way back and don't need the phone for navigation, I power it back off again so nobody can call or text me. I have a couple of hours to figure out my feelings, and I don't think it will be nearly enough time.

## 28

## LEVI

The party is still in full swing when I pull into the drive. Groaning I get out of my truck and head to the side door so I can hopefully avoid as many people as possible. It doesn't work. The house is packed. Some of these people have been here since noon when the party kicked off. Whose fucking idea was that anyway? When I agreed to it, I think I was just looking for a way to get Saffie here and thought a party might work. Carefully picking my way through the house, stepping around bodies, giving nods as I go, I look for one of my roommates. Finally spotting Murphy, I make a wrap-it-up motion with my hand to let him know the party is over. He nods in understanding, thankfully not pushing back because I don't want to have to fight him tonight, and I would because I just want everyone gone. Taking the stairs two at a time, I don't stop until I'm at my room, happy to find the door locked, which means Cubbie did what I asked and got Nora the fuck out of there. Hopefully, he got her out of the fucking house and not just my room. Flipping on the lights and tossing my keys on the dresser, I walk right over to my bed and start stripping the bedding. I don't want to be in it after she was rolling around on my sheets. I'm just tossing the sheets on the floor when my door flies open, crashing against the wall. I whip my head in that direction, ready to kick someone's ass and hoping like hell it isn't Nora. "What the fu—" My sisters and Rae are standing in the doorway, looking pissed as hell. "What's wrong? Are you guys okay?" I take a step in their direction, scanning over them to be sure they're not hurt.

Millie slams the door behind her. "What did you do to her, Levi?" she demands.

I'm confused, and my brows slam down, creasing my forehead. "To who? What the hell are you talking about, Mill?"

"To Saffie. She just called Rae. She's wicked upset and crying," Maeve says, her tone just as accusatory as Millie's.

"Crying? What did she say? Where is she?" I go to step past them and out the door, but Maeve stops me.

"She's not here yet. She's on her way." When she doesn't say more, I look between the three of them expectantly.

"One of you better tell me what the fuck is going on," I snap.

"She called me on the way home from Connecticut. She was crying and said something about you and Nora and Landon and some Clarissa chick," Rae explains.

Fuck. "She's on her way back already?"

"You knew she was going?" Millie stands up straighter, her eyes narrowing.

Running my hands through my hair, I tug until I feel the sting against my scalp. I drop onto the edge of my bed, the girls close in on me but don't sit. "Yeah. She came here and said she was going to surprise the golfer fuck because he didn't show up here like he was supposed to."

"She was going to surprise him?" Maeve asks.

"Oh shit." Rae groans.

"Yeah." I nod. "I told her not to just show up, to make sure she called first."

"Bet she walked in on him banging that Clarissa bitch," Millie says.

"That poor thing." Maeve's face creases. "But what does that have to do with you and Nora?"

I grimace. This is not going to go over well even though I didn't stay.

"Oh, Levi, what did you do?" The disappointment in Maeve's tone is mirrored on her face.

"Nora came to my room talking shit about how Saffie's boyfriend was coming here to spend the weekend, and I didn't believe her until Rae texted me that she said she had plans and wasn't coming to the party." I stand and go over to the closet, grabbing the clean bedding, needing to do something with my hands before I start punching shit. Rae and Maeve help me put the sheet on, waiting for me to continue telling them how I'd fucked up. Mille stands with her arms crossed, glaring daggers at me. "And?" she prompts, rolling her hand at me to keep going.

"And she was sitting on my bed when Briggsy got here to tell me that she was going to surprise the fuck stick." I plant my hands on my hips, feet spread wide in defense. This next part might get me jumped by these three. "Then I gave her an ultimatum."

"What kind of ultimatum?" Rae drags out the words slowly.

"Basically, I told her if she didn't stay here with me instead of going to him, I was gonna fuck Nora." As soon as the words leave my mouth, the three of them are on me with a chorus of "Levi!" I knew they weren't going to like that part.

"Tell me you fucking didn't, Levi," Millie hisses, jabbing her pointy finger into my chest. She's not at all bothered that I outweigh her by nearly a hundred pounds or that I tower over her. We're toe-to-toe, and she's not backing down. "I swear if you did, I'm calling Ma and telling her!" she threatens.

"Calm down, short stack, I didn't touch Nora. I actually left her here and went and spent the afternoon with Ma."

"But Saffie doesn't know that." Rae shakes her head. "She doesn't like you most days and will never believe that you didn't."

I know she's right. Saffie likes to convince herself that she doesn't like me even when she does, but she will one hundred percent think the worst of me on this, and that's on me. I've never regretted my reputation until now. Until her.

"Ma will vouch for you if it comes to that," Maeve reassures.

"So let me get this straight." Millie starts shoving the pillows into fresh cases. "Her boyfriend stands her up, she comes here, and you have Nora in your room, you give her some shit-ass ultimatum, *then* you let her leave thinking you're going to follow through on it, she drives hours to, most likely, catch her boyfriend smashing some other chick and is now driving back here thinking that you and Nora were doing the same thing?"

Fuck, man, when she lays it all out like that, it sounds fucking awful.

"That about sums it up." I sigh.

"Poor, Saffie. No wonder she was crying," Rae says sadly.

"How long before she's here?"

"She said she'd text us," Maeve tells me, taking the comforter from my hands and spreading it over the bed.

"When did she call?"

"About an hour and a half ago. We were watching for you to come back," Millie tells me, throwing the pillows onto the bed with more force than necessary. "I can't believe that I'm going to say this, but...you have to fix this, Levi. And not with more ultimatums." She points a finger at me in warning.

"I know. She's not going to talk to me, though." I walk over to my dresser and grab clothes out. "I have to take a shower. Ma had me doing manual labor. You guys can hang in here until she gets here and then you can help me figure out how to get her up here so that I can talk to her."

Maeve balls up the dirty bedding from the floor and stuffs it into the hamper. "We will. But we aren't going to trick her or anything, Levi. She's been through enough tonight. She's going to be exhausted too. That's a long drive by yourself."

I nod, wondering if she's okay. Leaving the girls in my room and going to the bathroom, I lock the door behind and pull out my phone. My thumbs hover over the keyboard, wondering if I should text her, just to check to be sure she's okay or if I should leave her be until she gets here? I hate this feeling. The feeling of uncertainty. I'm never uncertain about shit. To the point of being overly cocky but still not uncertain. Not in hockey, or school, and for sure never with chicks. Then again, I've never caught feelings before, either.

*Me: Be careful, Briggsy*

That's all I say. Everything else needs to be said in person. If she ever talks to me again.

∼

MAEVE LEFT us a little while ago to talk to Benny, making us promise to text her when Briggsy got here. In the meantime, Millie, Rae, and I have been playing video games and checking Rae's phone every three minutes. Finally, Rae's phone dings at nine thirty.

"She's here." They both look at me expectantly.

"She's going to be pissed at you," I remind them. I'd finally convinced Maeve to let me just go down and meet her and see if I could get her to agree to talk to me. I'm not thrilled that the three of them have been here to witness my pussification over their friend, but fuck if anything could be done about it.

"We know." Rae nods. "Come on, Mill. Let's go find Maeve. Text us and let us know what you tell her."

With a nod, I grab my FU Fire hat, put it on my head backward, slip my shoes on, and walk with the girls out of the room.

"Is that on purpose?" Millie asks, her eyebrow cocked.

"Is what on purpose?"

"That." She gestures, flicking her hand from head to toe in front of me. "Gray sweats, backward hat, white shirt, and gold chain? That's lady catnip, brother. Don't act like you don't know."

"I'm Sexy, everything I wear is lady catnip." I wink and move past them to head down the steps, eager to see Briggsy. The house is mostly empty now, thank fuck. Nora still hasn't popped up, so I'm hoping she's long gone or locked away in Cubbie's room.

"Don't fuck it up," Rae calls over the railing in warning before she and Millie knock on Benny's door and slip in.

I'd feel sorry for him if it weren't my other sister in the room that he's trying to...spend quality time with. Sorry not sorry, fucker. I use the side door again so Saffie doesn't see me walking out the front door. It had started to snow about thirty minutes ago, big fat white flakes coming down like crazy making me worry about her driving even more. Her truck idles at the curb when I open the door and slide into the passenger seat as if it were the most natural thing in the world. Saffie startles, then stiffens. The flash from the dome light allows me to see that her pretty eyes are puffy from crying, before I close the door and put us in darkness. I don't mention her eyes.

"Hey, Briggsy," I say softly, my hands twitching to reach for her. I want to pull her onto my lap and hold her until she's back to her typical sassy *"I don't even like you"* self.

"Levi, I'm not doing this right now. I'm exhausted and hungry, in desperate need of a shower, and I have to pee. Please. I cannot deal with any more fuckery today." Her head thumps on the steering wheel, eye squeezed shut for a beat before she turns to face me. "What the shit are you trying to do?"

I hold out my hands in front of me in a sign of surrender. "I'm not trying to do anything, I saw you pull up and came out." The little white lie will hopefully keep the girls out of trouble.

"Yeah, well you shouldn't have. I'm not staying. So I guess you can go fuck Nora again since that's what you do when you don't get your way." The words hit their mark, making me wince.

"I deserved that. I'd much rather talk to you, though." I reach out to touch the soft golden strands of hair hanging over her shoulder. She moves farther toward her window, trying to break the contact.

"I'd much rather *not* talk to you," she replies. "I'm just here to pick up your sisters and my cousin."

"They're sleeping. Fell asleep watching movies. Problem solved, now you can come talk to me." When she turns her glare on me again, I flash her my dimples. It only makes her angrier. Her gray eyes are icier than ever with a dangerous glint to them. "We are talking, Briggsy, so you might as well cut the shit and come inside." I'm not sure this tough-love tactic will work, but I'm willing to try.

"No." She crosses her arms over her chest defiantly.

Okay, so this is how we're doing this. I reach over and turn the truck off, quickly pocketing the keys. Her eyes widen in disbelief, her mouth falling open and then snapping shut, her glare downright belligerent now. "That's not funny. Give them back," Saffie demands, holding her hand out.

"Come and get them." Not giving her the chance to kill me in the truck, I hop out and walk away. When I get halfway up the sidewalk, I turn to see if she's coming, walking backward as I watch her struggle with herself inside the truck. I know I've got her when, through the falling snow, I see her slam her fist against the steering wheel and throw the door open. "Gotcha," I murmur to myself as she stomps toward me. She truly looks like the ice queen right now. The snow blows around her, whipping her long blond hair across her face. Her cheeks are reddened, probably from wanting to beat my ass, and her pretty lips slashed in a frown and cursing my name. She's fucking perfect, even if she does hate me.

## 29

## SAFFIE

I cannot even believe this is my life right now. I should have just gone straight to my dorm. It would have been better than being held hostage by Levi. I hurry after him into the house, wanting to scream at him to just give me my damn keys so I can leave but not wanting to attract any attention from the people still hanging around. The infuriating asshole isn't even saying anything just casually jogging up the stairs like he didn't just steal my keys to get me to come in and talk to him. The first chance I get, I'm taking them back and getting the hell out of here. I don't want to hear anything he has to say, same as I didn't want to hear anything Landon had to say. I know it makes me a hypocrite to be mad at the two of them when I haven't necessarily been acting with the best of intentions, but what the fuck? Both of them? And why did Levi have to be right about Landon? He's just going to rub it in, and I'm really, *really* not in the mood for that. Plus if I have to see Nora after this afternoon, I will probably flip my shit and square up. That's where I'm at right now.

Levi opens his door and leads us in, locking it behind me.

"Are you hungry? I ordered some pizza," Levi offers. My

stomach nearly rumbles at the mention of food. I hadn't wanted to stop on the way, eager to just get back here.

"I'm not going to be here long enough to eat," I inform him.

He chuckles, those bastard dimples flashing in his cheek. "Oh you think?"

"I do."

"It's cute that you think I'm letting you out of here." Levi walks into his closet, messing with something on the shelf just out of my view and then comes back into the room stopping right in front of me.

"You can't just keep me here, Levi. Besides, Nora wouldn't like that." Her name tastes sour in my mouth.

"I don't give a fuck what Nora likes. I care what you like, Briggsy." His mouth is pressed into an angry line. "Are you okay?" He surprises me with the compassion and empathy in his voice. Rae must have told him. My cousin is always throwing me to the wolves, the *wolves* being Levi. What is her deal?

"Oh don't act like you're not happy that you were right. I should have called. I went there, and he was fucking Cassidy Winston. She's the drink girl from the golf course, so I'm sure this wasn't the first time. So yeah, you were right. He was there fucking Cassidy while you were here fucking Nora, yet I'm the one who really got fucked, didn't I?" I laugh sardonically, frustration tightening my throat. "Landon is just like the rest of you. Happy?" I ask bitterly. Angry tears pricking at my eyes.

"Happy that he broke your heart? No. Fuck no, Briggsy. But I am happy that maybe now you'll give me a chance," he says quietly, locking eyes with me, his gaze steady.

He can't be serious. Damn the flutter of excitement that his words caused. "What do you mean give you a chance? I'm not looking for a hookup, Levi. And I'm definitely not trying to be another one of your hockey hoes."

"Neither am I."

I snort in disbelief.

Levi shakes his head at me. "Don't do that, Briggs. Don't pretend you don't know I'm into you. Like I haven't been doing my damnedest to get you to see me for more than just the fuck boy hockey stud you've got me pegged as. Not that I haven't been exactly that since I got here, but I haven't touched a single person since I had you up against the boards. Before that even. Can you say the same?"

What? There's no way. He's going to try to gaslight me now? He remembers that I was here today, right? That I saw him and heard what he said. Loud and clear. *"Say it or I'm going back in there and I'm gonna fuck Nora."* My brow creases in confusion that he has the audacity. "You were with Nora today. She was in your room, and you told me—*you* told me you were going to fuck her," I remind him, poking him in the chest. "You gave me that stupid damn ultimatum, and I left. And you f—"

"And I left right after you. Sent Cubbie to come up here and deal with Nora." Taking the hand I was just poking him with and pulling me closer to him, he makes it so there's no space between us. My mind is reeling, flashing through all of our interactions over the past few weeks. All the times I've seen him. Could he be telling the truth? He's Sexy. There are girls constantly around. Nora is always around, warning me off him. But was *he* ever around them? I can't remember seeing him with anyone specific, they just always seemed to be where he was. Which I can understand. Most days, I'm not even sure that I like him and still I want to be where he is. To be in his orbit. I can't help but gravitate toward him. Even if it's just to pretend I don't like him.

"You left? You and Nora didn't...?" I hate the uncertainty and hope in my voice. A part of me wants to believe him so badly. The other part doesn't trust herself to believe him.

"I walked in, she was naked, and I walked out. Then when I came back here after spending the afternoon with the most important woman in my life." When I give him a *"see, I knew it look,"* he just shakes his head at me. "My ma." His smile is smug. "I came back here, and my sisters and Rae helped me change all the bedding while they glared daggers at me and threatened bodily harm because I let you leave today thinking that I was going to fuck Nora."

They might be willing to throw me to the wolves, but at least they had my back when it mattered.

Levi's hand glides up the side of my neck over my runaway pulse to circle my nape. "I was never going to touch her. I shouldn't have said that but I was so mad that you were going to see him, and well, I don't give a fuck about fighting fair, especially when I want something, and I thought that maybe that would've worked on you. But it didn't," he admits, wincing at the memory. "I shouldn't have let you leave, though." Levi's thumb brushes against my skin, his touch causing jolts of electricity with every swipe.

I'm not able to think when he's this close. *"Especially when I want something."* Am I that something? I step back, breaking our connection to get a little clarity. "So you're telling me that you haven't hooked up or anything with anyone since that day at the outdoor rink?" I ask with my arms wrapped around myself, trying to keep all the confusion and pent-up emotions from spilling out. I guess crying for the three-hour ride here wasn't enough because they're bubbling at the surface, leaving me feeling raw and weak. I'm not a fan.

"Since before that." He nods, stopping me from moving any further by hooking our fingers together. It's such a simple, innocent touch, but it leaves me feeling just this side of on fire.

"That was weeks ago, Levi."

"Tell me about it." A groan rumbles from his throat.

"Why?" I ask, trying to understand. Hoping the answer will be what I so desperately want it to be, though had you asked me a week ago my answer would have been very different. Wouldn't it have been? Maybe not.

"Because for some reason, this pain-in-the-ass, hot-as-fuck softball player who pretends she doesn't like me has me by the balls. Thinking about shit I've never thought about and not wanting to hook up with anyone else because the thought of being inside anyone but her isn't even remotely fucking appealing."

"It's not?" Shocked at his admission, the question falls from my lips in a barely audible whisper.

"Not even a fucking little." His eyes drop from mine down to my mouth and back up again. The heat in his gaze making my lips tingle. "I almost went crazy thinking about you there with him," he admits, his voice gruff. "I've never in my life given a fuck about who people I was hooking up with were also hooking up with. As long as I was wrapping it up, I honestly didn't care. But you? I haven't even touched you yet, and I was ready to follow you and throw you over my shoulder. *After I beat his ass on principle.*"

My lips tilt up in a small smile at the thought. "On what principle?"

"That you chose him." Levi shrugs, not looking the least bit embarrassed about that.

"I didn't choose him," I tell him quietly, my smile falling.

"I'm pretty sure you did, Briggsy." It's his turn to laugh humorlessly. "Even faced with a fucked-up ultimatum you thought for sure I would act on, you chose him."

"I didn't choose him." I nervously run my free hand, the one Levi is not currently holding on to, through my hair. My teeth latch onto my bottom lip, the sting from my teeth helping to center me. "I was going there to tell him about what had been going on here"—I gesture back and forth between him and me —"with us because even though I'm not sure exactly what it is, I knew it was time to tell him. My feelings are all over the place.

The more time we spent together, the less I hated you and the more I wanted to be around you, no matter how much I told myself I didn't want that. Or you. My feelings toward Landon were just as confusing. I'd been avoiding his calls, not that there were many, out of guilt. I knew it wasn't fair. Not after the other day at the treatment center. Because had Charlie not come into that room..." I trail off, my face on fire from the memory and from admitting to him that I know what would have happened next if we hadn't been interrupted. I shake my head. "I wasn't being fair. Not to him and not to you or me."

Levi uses his hold on my fingers to pull me against him, not stopping until our bodies are flush. My hand rests against his chest, the cotton of his white T-shirt soft under my hands. He's so tall I have to crane my neck back to look up when he starts speaking. "Fuck him. You don't have to be fair to him." His hands flex at my waist, his fingers sinking into the fleshy part of my hips. "I know what would have happened that day, what I wanted to happen. But no matter how good I would have made you feel, and trust me, I would have"—he smirks, confidence pouring off him—"you would have left there pissed off at me for making you lose control like that, and for making you do it there." He's not wrong. It's a little unnerving how well he knows me. "But now?" His eyes land on my mouth again.

"But now?" I prompt, my breaths coming faster.

I watch as his tongue slowly glides along his bottom lip before he sucks it between his teeth, all the while his gaze fixed on my mouth. Bringing a hand up he skates the back of his fingers over my cheek and along my jaw, hooking my chin. "Now? Now I'm going to kiss you, feed you and then we're going to get into that bed over there," he drags his nose along my ear before whispering "and...sleep," he says as he moves so his mouth hovers just above my lips, his minty breath cool against them.

Blinking rapidly, I try to bring him into focus. "Sleep? You want to sleep?"

His lips graze against mine when he smiles, pecking softly and much too briefly. "I thought you were exhausted?" I was. I am. But I also know that more than food or sleep or anything else, I need Levi Sexton to kiss me.

## 30

## LEVI

God, she's killing me. The disappointment that fell across her face when I said that we were going to sleep. I'm trying to give her what she needs, which is sleep and food. She looks so tired and doesn't even notice she's swaying on her feet. I've heard her stomach growl twice now. But first, I have to kiss her. Whether that's what she needs the most or not, it's what I fucking need.

Drawing her tighter to me, I splay my hand low on her back, teasing the very top of her ass. She's almost a foot shorter, so tiny against me, yet her soft curves press into my hard angles. Curves on curves that I can't wait to fill my hands with. I brush the softest kiss against her mouth, teasing both of us. Her lashes flutter against her cheeks, a soft sigh escaping past her lips as she leans into me, tilting her face up to mine. A blatant invitation that I intend to take. This time, there's nothing soft about the way I kiss her. It's hungry and a little desperate. My teeth nip at her bottom lip, my tongue slipping inside her mouth when she gasps. There's no tentativeness. No hesitation. I kiss her like I've been kissing her forever. Lips and teeth and tongue. My hands finding her curves, lifting her into me, dragging her onto tiptoes giving me the access I need. "Briggsy. Fuck." I groan against her lips. I need to slow this down. I want to take care of her. To show her that, with her, I'm about more than fucking. That I want more from her. Tearing my mouth from hers is the hardest thing I think I've ever done. Both of us panting, I rest my forehead to hers. "I need you to go take a shower, I'll warm you up some food." My voice sounds strangled even to my own ears.

"Levi?" She asks uncertain, probably confused that I'm putting a stop to this. Grabbing her wrist, I put her hand over my cock, straining against my sweatpants, and squeeze, growling at the tingling sensations that shoot down my spine at the feel of her small hand pressed against me.

"You feel that? That's me being about ten seconds away from not being able to stop because I want you so fucking bad. I've wanted you since the first moment I saw you when you gave me shit and told me I wasn't your type." A low chuckle escapes at the memory. "But when I have you, you will need your energy, baby. You think I play hockey like a god? You ain't seen nothing yet. I have big *stick* energy on *and* off the ice." I wink and drop her hand, smirking at her dazed expression. "Go. I'll get your food and try not to think about you naked and wet in my shower." Groaning at my dirty-ass conjurings, I give her one final squeeze before releasing her and stepping away. Afraid that if I don't, I'll follow her into the bathroom and get her so damn dirty she'll have to shower twice.

"I don't have my bag up here," Saffie says as she walks to the bathroom.

"I'll grab you a shirt and some boxers for now. It's snowing like a bitch out there. I'll go grab your bag in the morning," I promise as I get clothes for her out of my dresser.

"The morning? I can't stay here all night, Levi. My cousin—"

I cut her off. "Knows you're with me and that I'm not letting you leave." I hand her the clothes, an FU hockey shirt with my name and number on it because I love seeing them on her, and place a kiss to her cheek, right at the corner of her mouth. "You're not gonna win this one, Briggsy. Remember, I fight dirty." With a gentle shove toward the bathroom, I take a moment to admire her ass before she closes the door, shutting her in and away from me. Giving myself a second to get my dick under control, I whip out my phone and text my sisters and Rae and then I go in search of sustenance for Saffie. She's gonna fucking need it.

Showered and fed, Saffie looks like she is going to fall asleep sitting up. "Let's go, Briggsy." I hold out my hand to help her from the chair where she'd been eating. She refused to just eat in the bed, saying she hated sleeping with crumbs.

"Let me clean this stuff up," she mumbles around a yawn.

I chuckle. "Leave it alone, sleeping beauty." I guide her to the bed, pulling back the covers on the right side and waiting for her to slide in. Once she's settled on the pillows, I pull the blanket over her, going back over to the coffee table and our mess. Making quick work of the plates, I strip down to my boxer briefs and climb into bed beside a nearly asleep Saffie, doing my best not to jostle her. As soon as I'm under the covers, she rolls my way, draping her leg over me. Her thighs bare, skin soft, and smelling like my shower gel. Pulling up the smart app on my phone, I turn off all the lights and read the text that my sisters and Rae sent in response to my earlier text asking if they needed a ride home because I was keeping their friend. Murphy had taken them home, thankfully. I slide my arms around Briggsy, bringing her even closer, her tits pressed against my side, thigh thrown across my half-hard cock, silky hair tickling my chin. She sighs and snuggles closer, and the dumbass I am, I settle my hand high on her exposed skin, keeping her in place and testing my willpower. It's going to be a long fucking night.

∼

SUNLIGHT TRICKLES THROUGH THE CURTAINS, bathing the room in an early morning glow. Not ready to be up yet, I carefully ease out of the bed to shut the curtains all the way and detour to the bathroom really quick. While in there, I brush my teeth, pulling out the new toothbrush my ma had stuck in my stocking, just in case Briggsy wants one. As quietly as I can, I climb back into bed, not hesitating to gather her up in my arms and tuck her back into me. She literally slept fused to me all night, and while my sleep was fitful because of the hard-on I was trying to sleep with, it was worth it. The rise and fall of her chest and her even breathing have me settling back into sleep, my eyes drifting closed when she does the softball ass wiggle. Cracking an eye open, I see that she's awake, watching me over her shoulder.

"Morning," she says sleepily.

"Morning, Briggsy."

"What time is it? I left my phone in the truck."

"It's too early to be worrying about what time it is. Go back to sleep," I grumble, pulling us farther into the warm blankets.

"I have to go to the bathroom first. Be right back." I tighten my hold on her not letting her out of the bed and making her giggle. "I'll be right back, I promise.

"Ugh, fine. Just hurry back. It's cold."

"Cold? I thought you were the hockey god with big *stick* energy? You're not supposed to get cold. You live on the ice," she teases.

"The ice is a different cold than my bed when my hot snuggle buddy gets out," I grumble

Saffie laughs and tucks me into bed, pulling the blanket to my chin. "Be right back." I watch as she walks away, the hem of my shirt covering more of her than I'd like. I do love watching her walk away, though. Her ass is high and round with the perfect little sway with each step, even with the slight limp she's rocking right now. Tanned thighs that are toned and thick and that I now know are so damn smooth. I swallow a groan, my dick hardening to the point of pain. Suddenly, I'm too hot under this blanket when just a minute ago I was cold. Pushing it down, I roll to my back and throw my arm across my eyes, running through hockey stats in my mind trying to will my dick down. It doesn't work. I don't hear her leave the bathroom over the blood rushing through my ears, but I smell her sweet scent and feel the bed dip when she gets in it. I lift my arm just enough to peek at her.

"Thought you were going back to sleep. What are you doing?"

"Hockey stats," I mumble, letting my arm fall to my side, staring up at the ceiling for a minute before looking at her. She's lying on her side, head propped on her hand, hair, bed messed and hanging over her shoulder and arm. Eyes narrowed and face scrunched up in confusion, she asks, "Hockey stats, why?"

Instead of answering with words, I roll us, tucking her beneath me. Without prompting her legs fall open, and I settle between them, my hard cock pressing against her. Her eyes widen as understanding dawns.

"Oh."

"Yeah, oh." I grin. "I've been fighting it all night long, but watching you walk away, which might be my favorite fucking thing to do, got me so damn hard." I emphasize my words with a little hip roll that causes her eyes to flutter closed. "You like that?" My eyes roam over her face. Her features are soft, mouth open just a little. Just enough to slip my tongue past her full lips. Instead, I roll my hips again, watching her reaction. Saffie lets out a breathy gasp at the same time as I press my lips to hers and swallow the sound. Not because I'm afraid someone will hear, but because I want to breathe her in. Take all of her and keep it for myself. My tongue slides against hers before I retreat, nipping at her plump top lip, then flicking it with the pointed tip of my tongue just as I would if it were her clit.

I don't want to stop, but I know if I keep this dry fucking up, I'll make us both come, but it won't be nearly as satisfying as it would be if I were inside her. And I've waited too fucking long to have her. I'm not rushing this. Moving so that I'm on my knees between her legs, I look down at her, face flushed, hair splayed out against the pillow, eyes bright and full of the same heat I'm feeling. "Tell me you want this, Briggsy. It all stops if you're not ready, but I gotta tell you, I hope like hell you are because I've never been more ready in my life." My shirt is bunched around her hips, my fingers skimming over the waistband of the borrowed boxer briefs, slipping farther under the elastic with each pass. And with each pass, she raises her hips, chasing after my fingers.

"Don't stop." Saffie's voice is sexy, throaty. "Make me forget his name," she murmurs, reminding me of the promise I made and spreading her legs even wider.

No hesitation I tug at the shorts, dragging them down her legs, my eyes glued to every inch of skin I reveal. "Baby, I'm going to make you forget *your* own damn name," I promise, laser-focused on the bare pussy I've just uncovered. Placing my hands on the inside of her knees, I gently press her legs open so I don't hurt her strained muscles. "Goddamn, Briggsy, that is a beautiful fucking pussy." My hand falls over my cock, squeezing through my boxer briefs as I take in her wet slit. When she squirms under my attention, I bring my gaze to her face, loving the flush across her cheeks.

"Please, Levi. I need you," she pleads, and it's music to my ears because I need her too. To taste her, to fuck her, to cover her in my scent, my sweat, and my come.

"I got you, baby." When I move down the bed, she raises up on her elbows to watch me as I position myself, my shoulders almost too wide for the narrow space between her thighs. Pushing her legs back against the bed, I place a wet, open-mouthed kiss on the inside of her thigh, loving the slight tremble underneath my lips, then do the same to the other and get the same reaction. Nipping at her soft flesh, I inhale her scent. The smell of her arousal mixed with the sweet honey that she always smells of is hot as hell. Teasing us both, I go back and forth between her thighs, laving attention to both of them but skipping over where she wants me the most. When she whimpers in frustrated need, I have mercy on us and finally close my mouth around her clit. Sucking it deeply into my mouth, I cause her to fall back on the bed, watching forgotten.

"Goooddd, yes," she moans, making me smile against her pussy. Hands sliding under her, I grab her ass and drag her closer, using my hold on her to move her over my face. My tongue dips deep to taste her. "Fuck, Briggsy, you taste so fucking good. Smell so fucking good." I swipe my nose through her center, latching onto her clit again, biting and sucking until she's writhing against my mouth before pulling away, kissing across her thighs, not ready for her to come yet.

"Leeevviiii," she groans. "You're such a tease."

Grinning, I slide a finger into her pussy, groaning, "You're so tight." I press in up to my knuckle, curling my finger to press against her, knowing I've found her spot when she shudders underneath me. Adding another finger, I do it again. Never taking my eyes off her face, even as I pull her clit back into my mouth. Using teeth and tongue while my fingers work in and out of her, I take cues from her sounds and the way she raises her hips, rolling them against my face and hand. Flattening my tongue against her, I let her ride it, setting her own pace, switching up only when I know she's close and wanting to prolong her orgasm just a little bit longer. A low rumbled growl leaves me, vibrating against her pussy as I pump my fingers into her, curling and twisting. When she grabs my head, tangling her fingers into my hair and holding me in place, I know I can't make her wait any longer. She's too close.

"That's it. Don't stop, please fuck, don't stop. Make me come, Sexy. All over your face. I want to so bad." She thrashes her head, and the words and low moans tumbling from her mouth have me grinding my cock against the mattress desperate for some relief of my own. Saffie tenses beneath me, her back bowing almost knocking me off her. "Yesss, ahhh, yesss." Long and hard, she comes against my hands and face as I lick her, savoring every bit of it, the taste of her come exploding on my tongue, her scent already clinging to my skin. When she comes back down to Earth, her body trembling slightly, I slip my fingers from her, loving the sound her pussy makes as I pull them from her body.

"You're fucking perfect," I tell her. And she is. So responsive and hot and wet and wicked fucking tight. Knowing that I have to take the edge off before I even think of fucking her, I take my boxers off and move up her body, pulling my shirt off her and kissing as I go, leaving a wet trail along the way and slowing only to take a nipple into my mouth. Her tits are perfect, just like the rest of her. I can't wait to spend more time on them. But not yet. Reluctantly, I release her with a pop, and she watches as I make my way up, stopping when I'm straddling her chest, careful to keep my weight off her. I place pillows beneath her head for better positioning, then take my cock in hand, stroking over the head and down the shaft, the tip brushing against her lips, leaving a glistening line of pre-come. "Open your mouth, Briggsy." Without hesitation, she does, her pink tongue flicking against the underside of my cock. "You've got me so fucking close just from the way you just came all over my face that I need you to suck me off. Now it's my turn. Let me fuck your face and come down your throat, baby." With one hand grasping the top of the headboard, the other still wrapped around my cock, I slide myself over her tongue, moaning as she looks up at me.

Her gray eyes and long lashes sucking me in as easily as her mouth does my cock. When her lips wrap around me, my head falls back between my shoulder blades, and I hiss out a breath. "Fuuuuccccckkkkkk. So good. Your mouth is so good." Lifting my head so that I can watch my cock disappear, I tighten my core and pump into her mouth, shallow thrusts at first until she plants her palms against my ass and urges me deeper. Teeth gritted against the pleasure ricocheting through my body, I press farther, harder, faster, watching her and testing her limits. Both of my hands grip the headboard now as my hips piston against her face. I feel as if the cool wood might crack under my strength when I hit the back of her throat, and she gags but then she swallows, constricting around me. "You're a goddamn beauty, baby. A fucking dime. But with my cock in your mouth? You know what you look like? Mine. You look like mine." I growl as she takes me to the back of her throat again. In and out I pump, never taking my eyes off hers, tears trailing from the corners and into her hair but pulling me closer when I back up. The tightening in my balls is intense, the tingling in my spine zinging. "I'm going to come in your mouth, Briggsy, and you're going to take it all and swallow it like a good girl," I demand, not giving her a choice. The choice was taken from both of us the moment I slid past her lips. Wrapping my fist in her hair, I use it to give me better leverage as I glide in and out of her mouth. My pace is frenzied as I chase the orgasm dragging its icy fingers down over each vertebra until I'm exploding down her throat. "That's it, baby. That's it." I watch as she struggles to swallow all of my come but not able to let up on my punishing pace. She slows once she's milked every last drop from me and lets me fall from her mouth. Saffie places a kiss over the head of my cock before I move off her and reach for the nightstand and the condoms in the drawer. I flash her a wicked grin. "Now that we got that out of the way, I can work on making you forget shit."

## 31

## SAFFIE

My whole body is still tingling and a little boneless from the orgasm Levi gave me *before* he had his, and he's ready for round two? He's not human. With heavy lids, I watch as he rolls a condom onto his still very hard, very, very large dick. "You can't fall asleep on me yet, Briggsy." He grins, and his dimples come out to play. Unable to help myself, I touch his face, dipping into the indentation.

"These don't make you look innocent like they do other people," I inform him. "In fact, I think they make you look like trouble. Pure one hundred percent trouble. There's not a damn thing innocent about you." The taste of him lingering on my tongue is a testament to that. And the fact he just gave me the sexiest face fucking of my life. Even if I was worried about how it would work when he first straddled me.

On his knees between my legs, he smiles wider, more mischievous if that's possible. "I'll have you know these dimples have gotten me out of a world of shit in my life."

"And into it, I'd bet." I stretch my arms over my head, my whole body feeling languid. The movement draws Levi's attention, his gaze landing on my tits because this position pushes them higher into the air. Before I can drop my arms to my sides again, he clasps my wrists in one big hand, holding me there. His grip tightens a fraction, and the strength of his hold makes my pussy pulse in time with my heartbeat. It has me wishing I could cross my legs to put pressure where I need it most, or that he would do it for me.

"They've got me into...things." He bends over me, holding himself up on his forearm as he licks across my nipple. A long, slow swipe of his tongue. He moves across my chest from one nipple to the other, never taking his mouth from my skin. Just making his way lazily, licking and sucking the skin, I'm sure leaving love bites along the way, until he takes the whole tip of my tit into his mouth. The wet heat and pressure make me bow against him, unabashedly begging. "You have the most perfect tits, Briggsy." His eyes feast on me, taking in the skin, glistening from his mouth, and I can't look away from him. All taut skin and muscle, tiny scars, and bruises scattered across his chest and arms and the one through his lip begging to be kissed. The gold chain around his neck glinting in the morning sunlight.

*Beautiful, perfect, mine*...all words he's said to me with reverence and sincerity. He made me feel every one of those things. More in these moments in his bed than I ever have with anyone else. "I'm going to love coming all over them." Levi breaks into my thoughts with his filthy words, excitement arcing through me at what that would look like.

"Okay," I answer. Not even understanding why I wanted him to, just that I did. A fucking lot. I've never had or even wanted, anyone to before Levi but he makes me feel feral. He could literally get me to do anything he wanted right now and he's not even touching me aside from holding my wrists. That makes him dangerous. And that is the most fitting word I could use to describe him. Dangerous to my well-being, to my body and my self-control.

"Okay."

He nods. "But not this time. This time, I'm coming buried inside you. Deep inside you." His tongue swipes along my bottom lip, pulling it between his teeth and then releasing it, my lips parting and giving him the opening he needs. Mouth hovering above mine, his hand wanders down my belly, stopping just before he gets to my pussy. "Are you wet for me, Briggsy?" His breath feathers across my lips. I nod that I am, and he rewards me with a kiss. His tongue licking at the inside of my mouth, making me moan at the taste of me on his tongue mingling with the taste of him on mine. Levi's hand dips lower and slides through my lips to find me not just wet for him but fucking soaked. Groaning low in his throat, he drops his forehead to mine. "God, I hope you're this wet every time I fucking touch you. If you aren't, I'll never stop trying to get you to this right here." Levi slips one finger inside me, twisting when I clamp around him and then adding another and bringing his palm up to press against my clit as he pushes them in deep, making me shudder when he hits my spot. How he already knows my body and what I like is beyond me, but ever since he put his hands on me, he's been touching me like he's been doing it forever. He's learned things about me and what I need that I didn't even know myself. It takes absolutely no time at all, and he has me ready to explode.

"Levi, don't stop. Please don't stop," I beg.

"Are you gonna come all over my fingers already?" His low and husky voice is filled with excitement.

"Yes, god yes."

"Open your eyes, Briggsy. I want you to see who it is making you come. Again. I want to watch you come apart on my fingers like you did on my face." Jesus this man and his mouth. Nobody has ever spoken to me like this. And maybe I wouldn't have liked it if they did. But right now? With Levi? It's elevated every one of my senses. With every word, I can feel them on my skin, taste him in my mouth, hear my need echoed back at me, and see how it affects us both.

My eyes find him as my hips rock against his hand, my pace desperate. "Fuck my hand, baby. Take what you want, and I'll give you everything you need," he promises. "Come for me, Briggsy," Levi demands. The command makes me shatter into what feels like a million pieces, my body convulsing around his fingers as he continues to move them inside me—pulling every ounce of pleasure from me.

"Yes. Yes. Yes." I chant almost to myself. I'm still floating on the high of the most intense orgasm of my life when I feel the head of his cock replace his fingers. Sliding through my come, he covers himself in it and circles my clit before doing it all again. Down, up, around. I can't even think straight because it feels so good. My overly sensitive skin quivers under his touch.

"I've dreamed of this. Of you. Of how it would feel when I finally slide inside you." He guides the tip of his cock into me painfully slow. Inch by inch, he gives us both time to adjust. "It was never this good in my dreams, though." Pushing farther, he sucks in a breath between his teeth. Balanced on his forearms, his hands now buried in my hair, gripping tight enough to cause my scalp to sting. I loved it. Yet one more thing he's taught me about myself tonight. "Are you okay? You're so tight I don't want to hurt you, baby."

My body count is pretty low, but even I know that Levi is bigger than most guys are and that he wasn't kidding about his big *stick* energy. "I'm good. I want more. I want all of it," I encourage, curling my leg higher on his hip to take him deeper.

Growling, Levi sits up on his knees, dragging me to meet his thrust as he seats himself deep. Pleasure twinged with pain ripples through me.

"Again," I demand. He obeys, thrusting twice, each time giving me more of him. He's so fucking big. On the third thrust, he bottoms out, making me cry out.

"That's it, baby. You take me so fucking good. This pussy was made for my cock. Never been this fucking good," he groans when he retreats, my walls tightening around him. Levi pulls my leg over so that my knees are together across his legs, it's like missionary and doggie style at the same time. He grabs a hold of my ass, spreading me as he drives forward. This new angle allows him to hit my G-spot with each thrust, which I wasn't sure existed before tonight. My back arches damn near off the bed, thrusting my chest into the air. He doesn't need more invitation than that, grabbing my tit and rolling the tight nipple between his fingers.

"Mmmmm, Levi, ahhhhh." I moan my words becoming incoherent as he drills into me, skin slapping, his grip on my nipple now becoming leverage as he fills his palm with my tit. I'm not even trying to be quiet. I don't care who's in this house or who I wake up. I feel like my soul is leaving my body with every thrust, and I couldn't give a single fuck if everyone on campus knows I'm in here letting Sexy fuck me. He swivels his hips every time he pulls back, and it has me seeing stars as I explode all around him, his name leaving my mouth on a moan so loud I'm positive even his neighbors heard me come. I pry my eyes open to see him smirking smugly.

"What's your name?" Levi asks as he backs out of me and moves to stand at the edge of the bed, grabbing my legs and dragging me to him. My startled yelp turns into a laugh when he flips me to my stomach. Smoothly hooking his arm around my waist, he lifts so I'm on my knees, ass in the air. "Do you remember what it is?" he asks as he kneads the globes of my ass, making me melt into his touch.

"Saffron Theodora Briggs. Better keep trying," I tease.

"A name shouldn't be so fucking sexy." Giving my ass a slap, he leans in and places a kiss over the spot, then bites it, making me shoot forward from the onslaught of sensations those three actions just caused. He stops my escape. "You're not going anywhere, Briggsy. I'm not even close to done with you." With a hand in the middle of my back, he pushes down so that my chest and cheek are against the bed. He then takes my arms and moves them to my legs. "Hold on to your ankles and don't let go," Levi commands. My breaths leaving me in pants now. Not even sure why him being so bossy is so damn hot. "Are you okay? You're not in any pain, right?" he asks, running a calloused palm up the back of my hurt leg.

"No. I feel too good to feel any pain right now." It's the truth. Every inch of me.

"Let's see if we can make you feel better than good, Briggsy." I can hear the smile in his voice. His hand glides from the center of my back up to the back of my neck, holding me in place. My nails dig into the skin of my ankles as pleasure ripples through me at the possessiveness of it. Levi enters me in one hard thrust, making me whimper at the invasion yet pushing back against him for more. "God, I love that you like it rough. I just want to be all the way in-fucking-side you," he hisses through gritted teeth. The fingers of his left hand curl tighter around my nape while his right hand latches onto my clit. He pinches, then rubs as he rocks into me with such force that if he wasn't holding me up, I would have gone sprawling. "I want to get so deep that you'll feel me here for fucking days." His movements become more urgent, steady but faster, harder and impossibly deeper. There's no way I won't still feel him here. He's touching parts of me nobody ever has. They belong to him now, and that should scare the shit out of me, but I'm on the verge of coming again and can't find it in me to care right now. Hands still locked on my ankles, I bounce against his every thrust, the pain turning to pleasure with every flick of my clit. "I know you're almost there again, Briggsy. I can feel you getting even tighter around me." Both his hands land on my waist, and he lifts his foot onto the bed, which changes the angle and has him tapping that magic spot over and over, taking me right to the edge and shooting me into the stratosphere, and I take him along with me. He growls my name as I moan his, mingling with the sound of our skin slapping together and our panting breaths. Levi's movements slow but don't stop completely, making sure he milks every last drop of pleasure from us both. When he's satisfied, he slips from inside me, chuckling when I collapse almost immediately. He steps away for a moment to take care of the condom and then pulls me up the bed to settle against his chest, blanket draped on our lower halves.

I may not love Levi's reputation, but fuck if I don't understand it now.

After a few minutes, my heart rate returns to a more normal pace and my breathing evens out. I run my finger along his gold chain and circle over the St. Sebastian charm, gathering the courage to ask a very important question. "You made me forget his name, but who will make me forget yours?" I murmur against his chest, completely sated, my insides feeling effervescent.

"Nobody," Levi answers, pressing a kiss to the top of my head.

And I'm afraid he's right.

## 32

## LEVI

Wet. Warm. Gentle. Firm. My eyes pop open as the sensations roll through me and lock with Saffie's as she deep throats my cock. She pulls me from her mouth. "Morning, again."

I grunt out a laugh. "Morning, Briggsy." A smile slides across my face as I stack my hands under my head to give myself a better view. I lift my hips. "Don't let me stop you," I encourage. "I'm not sure what I did to deserve this kind of wake up, but you'll have to tell me so I can do it all the time."

A smile plays on her lips as she licks the head of my cock nonchalantly like it's nothing more than an ice cream cone. "Well, I figured since you made me come—"

"Four times." I interrupt, my smug smile bringing with it a flash of dimples.

She rolls her eyes, but she can't deny it. "As I was saying." *Lick.* "Since you made me come four times." *Lick* "I owe you a couple." She pairs this lick with a twist of her hand, making me thrust involuntarily.

"We're not keeping score, Briggsy. You don't owe me shit," I grit out as she takes more of me into her mouth.

Raising her head, she arches her eyebrow. "Oh so you want me to stop?" she asks saucily.

"Not a fucking chance." I nudge her with my foot. "Suck my cock, Saffie. I want to come all over your tits." The thought has me throbbing in her hand, pre-come already seeping from the slit. She swipes her tongue over it.

"Not in my mouth?" Her hand slides up and down my shaft slowly, waiting for my answer.

"Your mouth, your tits, your pussy. I'm going to paint you in my come, Briggsy." I jerk my head, motioning for her. "Get on your knees." She pauses for just a moment before backing off the bed. Before I follow, I admire the sway of her tits as she moves, the arch of her back and curve of her hip. If I'm not careful, it'll be me forgetting my damn name. I move to stand at the edge of the bed, grabbing a pillow and dropping it on the floor between my spread feet for her.

"Such a gentleman," she teases as she settles on the pillow and takes me into her soft hands.

I snort. "Tell me that when you're covered in my come." The look she gives me is pure fire as she puts her mouth on me. I do my best to let her set the pace since I didn't show her any mercy earlier when I was fucking her face like a madman. I hum in approval as she fists my shaft and swallows as much of my length as she can. Her hand pumps up, down, and over the head in a delicious pattern. Twisting and squeezing as she sucks, her cheeks hallowing out, making a vacuum that has me embarrassingly close already.

A sexy little purr vibrates over my cock. My eyes locked on her, I watch as her hand snakes between her legs, eyes closed, mouth working me in tandem with her other hand. My low rumbled groan has her opening her eyes. She starts to pull her hand away. "Don't you dare. You know how fucking hot it is knowing that sucking me off has you hot?" My hand swipes the hair back from her face, her pace slowing. "Make us both come," I demand, gripping her hair and pushing her head down gently, making her take me deeper but still letting her set the pace. Groaning as I watch my cock disappear into her mouth, the tendons in her arm rippling as she plays with her pussy, her movements becoming faster, more deliberate. "That's it, baby. Eyes on me. I want to see you when you make yourself come." She does as I say, looking up at me, lashes spiky with tears from taking me so deep. "God, you're fucking beautiful," I whisper, bending slightly to palm one of her swaying tits. Her pink nipple is hard as I press against it, making her moan around me. Seeing that she likes that, I do it again, the sounds of her pleasure causing my balls to tighten. This might be the quickest blow job she's ever given if she keeps it up. I can usually last much longer, especially after coming twice already, but her hand and mouth combo paired with the way she's working her clit right now has me at the edge, fighting it. Her eyes start to flutter closed, and her rhythm slips. "You ready to come, baby?" I ask, my voice raspy, my chest rising and falling quicker. She nods her head as much as she can with me in her mouth. I pull out, taking my cock in hand, pumping up and down the shaft covered in her saliva. "So fucking hot," I mutter as I watch her watch my hand work over myself, holding back for her to come first. "Come, Briggsy. Come on your fingers so I can come on you." That's all the encouragement she needs, her mouth falls open in a silent scream. Hissing out a string of curses I pump harder, the first ribbons of come shooting right into her open mouth. She groans as she takes it, curling her tongue to keep it from falling from her lips. I cover her tits and then lean back to hit her pussy just like I said I would. We're both breathing as if we've just been double shifted in the third. Unable to help myself, I reach out and smear my come all over her chest, covering her nipples in the silky wetness. "You look fucking perfect covered in my come," I rasp out, offering my clean hand to help her up.

Before she's even steady on her feet, there's pounding on my bedroom door. "Yo, Sexy! I'm really sorry to break this smashapalooza of yours up, but we have to be at the rink in a little over an hour, and you're gonna be so trashed," Cubbie yells, making Briggsy jump.

Chuckling, I hand her my shirt to put back on. "Shut up, you pigeon! We'll be down in a minute."

She looks at me in confusion as she slips the shirt on and steps into her leggings from yesterday. "Pigeon?"

"Hockey lingo means he sucks and can only score off my misses, basically." I shrug. "I'll teach you all the words, Briggsy." Leaning down to kiss her, I don't give myself time to linger. "You wanna go grab your bag while I jump in the shower really quick?" She follows me as I go into the closet and stops in her tracks as I punch in the code on my safe and grab her keys.

"You put my keys in a safe?" Her mouth hangs open in disbelief. Hooking my finger underneath her chin, I close it for her.

"Bet your sweet ass I did. I wasn't letting you leave here, and I wasn't sure you wouldn't go looking for them the moment I left you alone." I'm not even a little bit sorry, and it's apparent.

"I'd say that I can't believe you, but I can." She shakes her head, thrusting her hand at me, palm up. "Gimme so I can do the walk of shame covered in your..." Her face flushes red, shy in the brightly lit closet all of a sudden.

I snake an arm around her waist and pull her into my still naked body. "Come. Covered in my come. And sweat and my scent. All over you." I bury my nose in her tangled hair, inhaling deeply. "Smells almost better than hockey." She pushes back, a look of utter disgust on her face making me laugh.

"I better not smell like hockey! Hockey smells terrible." Nose scrunched up, she makes a gagging noise as she walks away, doing her best to tame her hair as she goes. And again I'm left standing with a hard dick as I watch her walk away.

She's gone all of two minutes when Murphy texts me.

**Murphy:** *We've got trouble. Get down here now.*

Not bothering to answer, I yank on my sweats and head out of the room, taking the stairs two at a time. I hear voices, more than just my roommates.

"Ronnie, I've been looking all over for you. You wouldn't answer my calls. You have to let me explain."

Coming to an abrupt stop, I curse. "This motherfucker." Stepping into the room, I see them, and he's standing way too close.

"Landon? What are you doing here? How did you know I was here?" Saffie sounds confused, wary.

"One of your friends brought me."

He glances around the living room and the small crowd that's now gathered to find out who the fuck the dude in my house is calling Saffie "Ronnie." One of those people being Nora, who I'm assuming is the "friend." She's getting banned from Hockey House. I don't give a fuck what anyone says.

"Can we please go somewhere private to talk?"

My jaw tightens as I watch her face. The way it softens tells me that she's thinking about it. Thinking about it even as she stands there in my fucking shirt. My come still on her skin, the smell of me clinging to her. Like hell this was happening. Landon must see the softening too because he takes a step closer to her, reaching out to tuck a piece of escaped hair back behind her ear and talks in a low voice. He uses the only weapon he has like the pussy he is. "I love you, Ronnie." When she shakes her head and goes to step away from him, he holds on to her and dips his head, taking her mouth in a desperate kiss. My hands open and close into fists, my temple throbbing with the knowledge that I can't hit him like I want to while he's kissing her because I don't want to hurt Briggsy.

She pushes against him, and the second he breaks away, I can see that he thinks he's won. Not today, motherfucker.

"How's my dick taste?" I feel every set of eyes on me now, but I'm only looking at Landon. His are wide with confusion.

"What was that?"

"I said, how. Does. My. Dick. Taste?" I enunciate every syllable slowly so there's no confusion this time, though I'm pretty sure there wasn't the first time I said it. Saffie lets out a horrified gasp. She'll hate me for this and might not forgive me, but I'm sick of this little bitch constantly getting in the way of what she and I could have.

"Who the fuck are you?"

"I'm him." I shrug.

"Him who?" He looks so fucking confused.

"The guy who makes her forget your name. The rebound guy?" I shrug. "Although I've been here working on her for a while now. So I'm not sure I can be considered the rebound guy. Can I?" My head is cocked to the side, my tone thoughtful like I'm actually asking him. It throws him off.

"Levi." Briggsy cuts in, her voice heavy with warning.

"Levi? The tutor?" Landon asks incredulously. His voice at least two octaves higher than it was. Obviously I'm not what he was picturing when she told him she was being tutored.

"I guess I have taught her a few things," I respond smugly, letting the innuendo hang there between us.

"That's enough, Levi," Saffie says, moving in my direction.

I'm still watching him, though. I know once I look at her, it's game over. I won't be able to be the dick I am right now. One look and she'll have me. Talk about a pussy. When he snakes an arm out and yanks her back to him, me, Murphy, and Cubbie all take a step forward. Landon puts that fancy education to work, sensing he's gonna be in trouble in about two fucking seconds if he doesn't take his hands off her. He does it as if he's not afraid of us but that letting go of her was his plan all along.

Not only did he come here alone, he came to Hockey House, and as I look around, I notice that quite a few of our teammates are here just waiting for the gloves to drop.

"What's he talking about? Have you been up here sleeping with this asshole the whole time?" I don't even care about the dig. I am an asshole, but I don't like his fucking tone, and clearly, neither does Briggsy.

"No, Landon. Unlike you, I've been faithful to you the whole time I've been here," Saffie spits out.

Has she, though? That's debatable. Not that I'm going to argue with her right now.

"So you didn't fuck him?" There's hope in his voice that I can't wait to piss all over.

"Ask her whose shirt she has on," I whisper conspiratorially. A cocky grin slides over my lips when he looks down at the shirt as if it might bite him. If he only knew what she was wearing on her skin underneath it.

## 33

## SAFFIE

Is he kidding me right now? This situation is already a shit show. Levi doesn't need to add to it. He for sure doesn't need to rub it in Landon's face that we were just having sex. I'm not trying to spare his feelings. I'm just not trying to make a bigger spectacle.

"So you're fucking him?" Landon's accusatory tone makes me bristle.

"You gave up the right to ask me that when you slept with Cassidy," I inform him calmly.

"It was just that one time, I swear!" Levi chuckles, making me close my eyes and pray for patience. He said that Landon would say that exact thing, and he did. Of course he did.

"One time or twelve, it doesn't matter. We're over."

"Ronnie—" God, I hate that nickname. He smiles gently. "I can forgive you for him." He jerks a thumb in Levi's direction.

"I'm not asking for forgiveness. I didn't sleep with Levi to get back at you. I slept with him because I wanted to," I tell him truthfully. The crestfallen look on his face gives me a pang of guilt, but I tamp it down. "Listen, we tried the long-distance thing, and it didn't work, and that's on both of us. I was coming to tell you yesterday that I wanted to break up. You just made it all a lot easier." I shrug. "While I didn't cheat on you physically, I was cheating on you emotionally, and that's not any better."

Landon's brow furrows. "What are you saying?"

"I'm saying that I checked out of this relationship before I walked in on you yesterday and that it's over." Having this very honest conversation with him while I'm sticky from Levi's come and with an audience is not the way I would have chosen to do this. But here we are.

"So that's it?" he asks a bit incredulously. "I gave you two years, and you're breaking up with me for this douchebag?"

Thankfully, Levi doesn't react to the name-calling. That was very brave of Landon, seeing as how he's in Levi's house along with half the damn hockey team.

I don't bother to tell him that I'm not breaking up with him for Levi but because of him. If I'd really loved Landon, Levi and all his charm wouldn't have mattered. But it did. I was swayed. Epically. And the only thing I'm sorry about is that I fought it for as long as I did out of a sense of stubborn nobility or something. "You should go," I say gently. I didn't want to cause an even bigger scene than we already have and have nothing left to say. I'm tired of being on display, and I desperately need a shower so that I can fight with Levi for being a giant dick and embarrassing me. Not gonna lie, his whole alpha man douchebaggery was a little hot, but I'm not letting him know that.

"You're a real bitch you know that, right?" Landon shocks me with the venom behind his words. Where the hell did this come from? His cool demeanor gone, the good guy mask is slipping. I can practically feel Levi's anger from where he's standing behind me. "You made me wait months and months before giving it up, and this guy barely has to work for it? When he gets tired of you and you come crawling back to me, I won't make it easy on you. I'll make you beg for another chance."

I don't even have a chance to respond. Levi barrels forward, snatches Landon up by the front of his shirt, literally off his feet, and walks him to the door that Murphy opens wide. Levi tosses him outside and stands with his fists clenched at his sides, probably to keep from hitting him. "Briggsy isn't begging you for shit, you dumb fuck. Not now, not ever." Landon stands straight, fixing his shirt and squaring up with Levi, who has a good four inches and thirty pounds of muscle on him. "Don't call her or text her. Don't even think about her. And if you do think about her, remember it's me she's with now, and she'll never need shit from your sorry ass again. I'm giving her everything she needs. And I'll end you if you come back here looking for her."

His words make me feel all types of ways. Clearly, we have a lot to talk about.

"Fuck you," Landon spits out.

"Nah, I'd rather fuck her." That's Levi's cocky reply right before he slams the door. But he's not done. He turns and narrows in on Nora. "You bring him here?"

She raises her chin. "He was looking for his girlfriend. I thought I would help."

Levi nods his mouth drawn down. "Yeah, I bet you did. I'm gonna tell you the same thing I told him. I'm with Briggsy now. Do not come back here. Not for nothing. Not for me, not for anyone else on the team, and not to start shit with her."

"What? You can't just ban me from coming here." Nora huffs, arms crossed.

"Oh, I absolutely can, and I did. Right, Murph?"

"Yup," Murphy calls out.

"Benny, Cubbie?" They murmur their agreement, her face turning molten.

"Looks like you're gonna have to find another ride to the show," Levi tells her, jerking his chin at Murphy who opens the door once again.

"Bye, Nora," the giant goalie says gleefully, slamming the door behind her when she stomps out.

I'm standing there a little shell-shocked at everything that just went down in this family room when Levi takes my hand and leads me out of the room.

"We'll meet you guys at the rink," he calls over his shoulder as we head up the stairs. Once we make it to the safety of his room, I take a deep breath. That was…a lot. "You okay, Briggsy?" Levi asks, trailing a finger down my cheek.

I shove his hand away. "You're an asshole, you know that?"

Surprising me even further, he agrees, "I know."

"You know?" I ask suspiciously as if he's trying to trick me.

"I do. I couldn't help it. I went all over-the-top possessive but being in the same room with him, knowing that he's touched you. Tasted you." He shakes his head. "Made me fucking crazy. Then I had to *watch* him kiss you and put his hands on you. He's lucky he left walking because I was ready to rip off his arms and legs and beat him with them," he admits, throwing me for yet another loop.

"You know how ridiculous that sounds when I'm constantly surrounded by people you've slept with, right?" I point out.

"I know it's not rational, Briggsy, but nothing is when it comes to you." He runs a hand through his messed hair, the blond strands falling over his forehead and eye. "But I meant what I said. If he comes back here, I'll end his punk ass, same with Nora, but I'll have Millie handle her. She'd love that." Levi smiles at the thought. He's right, though. His sister and my cousin, for that matter, would be all over the opportunity to kick Nora's ass.

"He's not going to come back here. He was pretty pissed." I start pacing a path to the bathroom and back. There is so much I'm trying to sift through in my mind, so many things Levi said down there that I have to unpack. Did he mean it? Does he realize what he was saying? "Levi. Just because we've slept together doesn't mean we're together," I say tentatively, fully expecting him to laugh and agree at how silly the notion is.

"That's bullshit, and you know it," he answers defiantly. His arms cross over his bare chest, drawing my eyes to the expanse of skin before I bring them back to his face.

"I'm sorry? What's bullshit?"

"That we're not together." His mouth is set in a determined line.

"Since when does that make people a couple?" I ask incredulously. "Especially you. Have you even ever been in a relationship?" I demand.

"Since you." He comes closer, stopping my pacing. "I'm twenty-one, Saffie. Never had a serious relationship, let alone wanted one before you. I'm not going to pretend that I know what the fuck forever is. But I'll tell you this. When I think of my future, I see two things clearly. You and hockey. And lately, as insane to me as it is, you're what pops in my head first. Does that scare the shit out of me? Fuck yes, it does. But it is what it is. You're what I want. Two of the most important things in my life, and you're one of them. That's gotta mean something, right? To you? Because it sure as fuck does to me." Gently, he tucks the hair that refuses to stay in place behind my ear. He lets his touch linger as his eyes trace over my face. "What are you thinking?"

"I'm scared," I admit. Walking away from him, I'm ready to escape to the bathroom. It's always so hard to think with him this close. "I'm scared because you're *Sexy,* and I don't want to get burned." Leaning heavily against the doorframe, I look at my bare feet, feeling much too vulnerable.

"I get it. I do. And I'm telling you, I'm gonna fuck up." My eyes go wide, but he holds up a hand to stop me from saying anything as he moves to stand in front of me. "I'm gonna fuck up because I've never been a boyfriend, but I won't fuck up like that. I can promise you that." He sounds so sure.

"How? How can you promise something like that?" I hate how small my voice sounds.

"Because the thought of you hurt for any reason whatsoever hurts me. Physically fucking hurts me. And I don't ever want to be the cause of that. I know that makes me sound like a pussy, but I'll only ever be a pussy over you." He flashes me his dimples and grips the top of the doorframe, leaning in and effectively trapping me when he wraps his other arm around my waist. If I thought I couldn't think with how close he was before, I really can't think now. The muscles in his arm above me are as distracting as his six-pack abs and bare chest. The gold chain he's never without, sexier than it should be lying against his smooth skin. My pulse flutters when he brushes his lips against the shell of my ear. "Give me a chance, Briggsy. Let me show you how well I can melt the ice queen?" His cocky grin is a reminder of just how he made me melt this morning.

Never in a million years did I imagine Levi Sexy Sexton asking for a chance at anything. But maybe I shouldn't be surprised. He's gone out of his way to prove that he's honest, dependable and caring, even when I didn't want to see or admit it. "I don't even like you," I tell him, smiling coyly, knowing he's got me and there's no use fighting it.

"Whatever you gotta tell yourself, Briggsy." Levi lowers his head and kisses me softly, his hand traveling from my waist to the nape of my neck, making me melt into him. "I know what you do like, though." He grins confidently, dimples and all. "My big *stick* energy."

He's not wrong about that.

The End

# EPILOGUE

Saffie
One Year Later

The Garden is packed, the energy is insane, and it's probably one of my favorite arenas I've been to. Tonight's game is special, though. It's the first time Levi has played back in Boston since the season started in Chicago. I've learned a ton about hockey since then. And sexting. And sexy FaceTime. And how to do long distance the right way. It's not always easy, but when he's not on the road, the time he's at home is that much sweeter, and I've never been happier. Tonight is also the first time that he, Benny, and Murphy will be on the ice together since they played for FU. They've been texting back and forth, talking shit all week. Maeve and I are taking bets on who will hit who first. My money is on Murph taking them both out. Looking to my left, I can't help but smile. Mr. Sexton insisted we sit on the glass just like we always did at Fulton, although tickets had to be astronomical here. Yet here we all were, my mom, aunt, and uncle included. All of us wore our Chicago sweaters with Levi's name and number on the back. Well, except for Maeve, who was rocking her Boston sweater for Benny. I told her we would have to make her a half Chicago, half Boston one for when they played each other. We even had Stella sitting with us to show support for our FU boys. They were doing a tribute to them before the game. Levi said it was because this was their home town, and they went out on such a high last year, winning the championship. Levi even took home a special trophy he said basically makes him a hockey god, but that I could just call him Sexy. Some things never change. The skaters come out of the tunnels for warm-ups. Levi, Benny, and Murphy meet at center ice to give each other taps with their sticks, laughing and then skating over to where we are for a quick hello. I wave excitedly at Murphy, who winks at Rae, and Benny is on his way over to Maeve. It's so great to see them on the ice together again, even if they're playing against each other.

Rae sits next to me practically vibrating with excitement. "I still can't believe they're playing in the NHL. It's so surreal." She hasn't been able to see Levi in a live game since the season started and has been counting down to this one since they released the schedule.

"I know. I mean, hockey is hockey is hockey to me, but it does seem crazy that my boyfriend is a pro athlete," I admit.

"Don't you ever let Levi hear you say that hockey is hockey bullshit. He might break up with you." Her face is deadly serious. "We don't play when it comes to hockey."

I just shrug and watch as he skates away. The last one to come over is Jason, who blows a kiss to a beaming Stella and waves to the rest of us. Since coming to Chicago after graduation, I've spent a lot of time with Stella and Jason. In fact, Stella got me into the softball program at the same school she teaches and coaches at. I've been coaching there and training the team in the off-season. I thought about pursuing pro softball. Mr. Sexton encouraged me and offered to help, but I decided I didn't want to do that. I'd rather help the next generation of ballers. Stella and I did join a park district league, though, just for shits and giggles to keep us busy when the guys were on the road. It's been huge having her with me to help with the transition to live-in girlfriend with a hotshot hockey player.

They're not out there long before the players return to the tunnel, and the lights dim while the Jumbotron plays the pregame montage. I reach over and shake Maeve's leg when I recognize Benny up there. Her smile takes over her whole face. They are literally the cutest. "There's Murph," I point out to Rae unnecessarily. Smiling at the way she tries to act all nonchalant about it when I know for certain she's been crushing on him for years. The countdown begins, and the place explodes when it gets to zero, and they begin introducing the starting players.

Standing, I wait for Levi to do his skate by. I have my palm on the glass, which is now our thing, and he touches his to it, winking and mouthing, "I love you," as he skates by to where his dad is, giving him his fist bump and his ma her Shaka followed by the rest of the fam. It's all so sweet and has become my favorite part of every game. Though I usually don't sit on the glass when I go to his games, I do walk down to it for our ritual before going back up to where the other wives, girlfriends, and family members sit. Sitting down, I stay perched on the edge of my seat, watching him move. I'll never understand how someone so big can be so damn graceful with knives strapped to their feet.

"Do you know when they're doing the tribute thing?" I ask Rae, shouting to be heard over the noise in the arena. "I just assumed they would do it in the pregame."

My cousin shrugs. "No clue." Just as she says that, the lights change, and the spotlights go wild over the ice.

"Ladddiieesss and genttellemeen! Before tonight's game, we

have something special for the hometown crowd," the announcer booms as the Jumbotron lights up and another countdown starts.

"This must be it," I say excitedly, my eyes never leaving the screen. When it hits zero, a message that reads "Welcome home to Fulton University's very own..." with their names and then a sequence of pictures start flashing on the screen. Levi in his FU uniform, then Benny and Murphy. Them on the ice at practice and at the outdoor rink. One by one, the pictures flash, the crowd cheering louder and louder when they come to the last game they played at Fulton, hoisting the trophy over their heads, helmets, sticks, and gloves scattered across the ice, which I've learned is called a yard sale. And then one more picture...Levi on one knee holding a ring box with a flashing banner across the bottom that says "Saffron Briggs, Will You Marry Me?" The crowd erupts in deafening catcalls and whistles. My gaze is glued to the Jumbotron in shock. Is he for real? The way my heart is thundering in my chest I might pass out before I ever find out. I'm pulled from my stupor when Rae elbows me to gain my attention. I look over at her, mouth agape, eyes wide, and she points over my shoulder to where an usher awaits me. She nudges me toward him, and I stumble in my dazed state, righting myself before being embarrassed and face planting. When I reach him, he takes me over to one of the doors at the glass where Levi is standing. A smile so wide it even makes his dimples disappear. All I can do is shake my head at him in disbelief, certain there's no way he could hear me over the roar of the crowd. When he drops to his knee and holds out the ring, I burst into tears, screaming, "Yes!" Knowing he still can't hear me, I launch myself at him, which is not the smartest move, considering he's on ice. Thankfully, he's good on skates and somehow manages to catch me and keep us both from falling to the ice.

"Is that a yes, then?" Levi shouts, his smile teasing. I nod, and he slips the ring on my finger. I don't even look at it, taking his face in my trembling hands and kissing him to the cheers of nearly twenty thousand people.

Two massive bodies tackle hug us from each side. Benny and Murphy yell excitedly.

"Man, I'm really gonna hate beating you after that. Serves you right, though, you asshole. There's no way I can top this!" Benny says, shaking his head as the lights in the arena change for the national anthem so we can start the game. They skate away, and Levi helps me off the ice, kissing me one last time. "One for me and two for your mom!" I yell, earning a wink from him before he skates back to the bench amid a raucous chorus of stick tapping.

This proposal is the most Levi thing ever. His two loves, me and hockey. I wouldn't have it any other way.

READ on for more from Mandi Beck. Chapter One of Love Hurts is next!

# MORE FROM MANDI BECK

Read the Prologue and Chapter One from Love Hurts, available now on Amazon.

Prologue
Deacon

NOTHING CAN KILL a mood faster than having your cock in some chick's mouth when the woman you love is calling. I sit in the chair, head thrown back, thinking about whether I should answer the call or not. I haven't heard that ringtone in two months. Never did I think that I would miss hearing Iggy Azalea telling me how fucking "Fancy" I am. That's my girl though—she's got jokes.

Two months, two fucking months, and she calls *now*? Snorting, I shake my head, debating how badly I want to hear her voice and know what she has to say. Bad enough to kick this bitch out? I don't know who I'm trying to bullshit. There's nothing—nothing—I want more than to talk to her, to hear that raspy, sexy voice that I've missed so much. Fuck, just thinking about it is making me harder than I've been all night. I need to make a decision before this chick thinks that it's her that has me going solid in her mouth.

My mind made up, I sigh. We've gone long enough without speaking. I just want to talk to my girl, see where her head's at. I don't even care if she's calling to bitch at me, as long as she's calling. Does that make me a pussy? Oh well if it does. I need her and clearly she needs me.

## Chapter One
### Deacon

"I CAN'T BELIEVE that you're allowing this to happen, Deacon."

"It's the Princess, Mav. She loves all of this shit. Always has, no matter how hard we tried to beat it out of her growing up," I tell him, shrugging in acceptance, thankful that we didn't succeed.

"Yeah, but she also likes cool stuff. Like sports. Indie couldn't do a hockey-themed party?" he snorts, mildly disgusted.

Shaking my head, I slap him on the back and walk away, heading into the house. Let him tell Indie he doesn't like the party. I'd have one less brother, but it might be worth it to see how *that* whole conversation plays out. I'm not even sure what the theme is supposed to be. There's lace. A lot of lace and feathers...and leather? All over my house. How the fuck does she come up with this shit? Not that I'm complaining. It's actually really sexy. I don't have time to explain that to my dumbass brothers though.

I bound up the stairs two at a time, needing to get ready for this party. I hope like hell that I'm able to stay cool. Today is not the day for me to beat the shit out of Frankie's douchebag boyfriend. It's getting harder and harder for me to see them together. I've always struggled seeing her with other guys, but I couldn't do shit about it. Not without coming clean about how I feel about her, so I've just learned to grin and fucking bear it. Well, that noise is getting old and I'm getting sick as fuck of fighting the urge to claim her ass.

I'm not weak, but this thing with Frankie has me frustrated as hell. I've been a total prick to be around lately and don't have time for any of the bullshit right now. I'm leaving for my next series of fights and the Elite Warriors Federation doesn't give a fuck if I have sand in my vagina over a woman or not. I am a professional MMA fighter and they expect me to act like it. I can't afford any distractions right now—not even the Princess, who is a *huge* distraction.

Striding into my bedroom, I go straight for my music system, firing it up and setting it to shuffle. I enter the bathroom knowing Indie is going to be pissed. I'm sure my playlist isn't what she had in mind for her little sex-themed party.

Jumping out of the shower, towel slung low on my hips, I head back into my room and the walk-in closet, rubbing another towel over my head, drying my hair. After being in the military and told that I had to wear my hair short, I've rebelled since I was discharged and now wear it long. Even though it's kind of a pain in my ass, especially in the cage where fuckers like to pull it like a bunch of girls. I pull a pair of boxer briefs out of my dresser, slip into them, and finish dressing before throwing my boots on. I see that Frankie is at it again when I open the vanity drawer.

Shaking my head, I grab one of the pink hair ties she has

replaced my black ones with, yet again, and shove it into my front pocket along with my phone. Checking my watch, I realize that guests are probably arriving and head to the safe in my office to grab Frankie's present. I look in the bag with the two blue boxes that I picked up earlier in the week and smile as I flick the light off and head downstairs. Indie is at the landing, stabbing her fingers at the panel that controls the sound system.

"What are you doing, woman? Why are you being so rough with my shit?" I growl at her, swatting her hands away.

"The DJ is trying to set up and do a sound check but all anyone can hear is your shitty music!" she shouts.

Glancing down at the bag I hold, she jerks her chin in my direction.

"Is that her gift?"

"Yep."

"You gonna show me?"

"Nope," I say as I walk past whistling.

"Are you wearing that? You know he'll be in a suit, right?"

I don't even bother looking down at my worn jeans and plain, black Henley. I don't need to dress up in a fucking suit in order to look good or impress anyone. Who the fuck wears a suit to an outdoor party at the end of May anyway? Douchebags, that's who.

I keep walking but yell over my shoulder, "You say that shit like it matters, Jones!" Running a hand through my still-damp hair, I flex for her, causing my shirt to strain against the muscles rippling beneath. "Doesn't matter what he wears. I'll still look better."

She rolls her eyes, shaking her head in exasperation. Laughing, I wink and make my way outside.

Two hours later, the DJ has all of Frankie's favorites playing. Some of it I love, some I tolerate, and some makes me want to put a bullet in my brain. The Princess has really eclectic taste in music—probably because she's a dancer. Not a stripper, but an actual trained dancer. She did teach a pole dancing class at the gym for a while though, which I found to be fucking hot as hell. She's amazing -- she has a studio in the gym our dads own, teaches classes, and even competes, though not as much as she used to.

Looking around at all of the milling guests and the ones still arriving, I still don't see Frankie. Mav and Sonny are at the bar that's set up on the patio, talking to Indie and one of her friends that I've met but has one of those names that you can never remember. I make my way over to them and ask, "Where's the Princess?"

"Apparently, Annnddrreewww had something important come up at the office. Some hush hush important client or some shit," Indie snarls.

Seething in anger, I begin to shake, "Fuck that! Fuck him! It's her birthday, this is her damn party!"

I grab my phone from my pocket and toss it to Indie. "Call Frankie and tell her I'm on my way!" I turn but before I get very far Indie grabs my arm and holds up her hand to shut me up when I go to speak.

"Slow down, hero." She places the phone in my hand but doesn't let go, forcing me to stay put. "I already called and she's on her way now. That was about five or ten minutes ago, so she should be here any minute."

Slipping my phone back into my pants, I try to reel in my aggravation. I fucking hate this guy!

"God, he's such a fucking tool," Sonny says, before he takes a pull from his beer.

Everyone nods in agreement, but I don't say anything, just grab my drink from the bartender and break away from the group and head back toward the house. I want to be the one to greet her when she arrives.

The kitchen door opens and I see her. She stands there before me and takes my breath away. *Jesus fuck.* I stop my advance and take her in. She's fucking gorgeous. Her long, blonde hair is pulled to the side in some fancy ass braid which falls over her shoulder. Icy eyes done up with dark makeup, making them look smoky, almost as if they're glowing, blue flames. She has this short, gray dress on that hugs every single one of her curves. And my girl has curves on her tight little dancer's body. I don't know what the material is, nor do I give a fuck, but it looks soft and drapes off of her shoulder. The way it hangs leaves the skin there bare, with glimpses of her tattoo playing peekaboo.

Continuing my perusal, I let my gaze linger on the hottest set of legs I've ever seen. For someone that's only five-foot-two, her legs are unreal. On her tiny feet are light pink, fuck-me heels that make my dick instantly hard. I'm so fucked. Bringing my gaze back up, I rest on her face,

"Hey, Princess! I was getting worried about my birthday girl," I tell her, not acknowledging the prick standing beside her.

"I know. I should've called, Deacon, but I didn't think we would be this late," she says apologetically.

Not even glancing at him, I gesture with my head.

"Come, give me some love."

Arms open wide, I smile when she lets go of Andrew's arm and walks right into mine. Wrapping my body around her tiny frame, I look Drew right in the eyes and smirk. I pull back just far enough to grab her wrist, making sure that he's watching as I bring it up to my mouth and place a kiss there.

*Take that, fucker.*

I watch him watching us for a second longer. To say that he is pissed would be putting it mildly. My smirk morphs into a smile as I look down at my girl. "Happy birthday, Frankie," I say, squeezing her tighter to me.

"Thanks, Deacon. I really am sorry that we're late," she says in that throaty, sexy as fuck rasp of hers.

"No worries, babe. It's your party and doesn't start 'til you get here, yeah?"

I loosen my hold on her, allowing her to step back next to Andrew, who immediately pulls her into his side making the muscle in my jaw tick. I still haven't said shit to him. I guess he's a bigger man than me though because he's the one to finally break the silence.

"Yes, I apologize. I had something that couldn't wait come up at the office and it took longer than I would have liked. I'm in the middle of a very important case." Glancing distastefully around the room, he continues in that pompous ass voice of his, "Thank you for throwing this party for Francesca. I have been so busy at work lately that there was no way I would have been able to throw something together." The condescending tone he uses makes me want to break his fucking face.

Turning away, I lead us through the house and toward the party. Stopping on the patio I turn back to them.

"Yeah, well, we can't all be a prosecutor for the D.A., can we? No worries though, I wouldn't have let you anyway, Drew." He hates when I call him that, which only makes me use it as often as possible. "This is a tradition and you don't fuck with tradition. I've been throwing Frankie her birthday party for as long as I can remember. Wouldn't have it any other way," I say as I glance over at Frankie and wink before I swing my gaze back to his beady, hate-filled eyes.

I love to remind him of my place in her life every chance I get. Meeting his cold stare unblinkingly, I convey my message, *That's right, asshole, you may be here with her, but make no mistake about whose girl she is.* He breaks eye contact and I smile.

Point one for The Hitman.

Sitting at the bar, where it appears my brother has taken up residence, I take stock. The party is going really well -- they always do. Frankie loves everything that Indie has chosen, just like she does every year. If there are two people that know her, it's me and Indie. There is no question that she would like anything that we put together. I did however hear Drew say something about it being crass or risqué or some shit like that. Fucking prude. He probably fucks with his socks on and the lights off. Fuck. I don't even want to think about it.

I look over at Sonny drinking his bottle of *Furious*. "What the fuck does she see in that guy?" I ask, shaking my head in confusion.

"I don't know, brother. She's never really had a type. Even still, he's definitely not right for her. Indie said that Frankie told her that Drew hates her tattoos. Wants the Princess to get them removed—even offered to pay for it," Sonny conveys, tossing a handful of peanuts into his mouth.

"You're kidding me, right? She's not going to do it, is she?"

Chewing thoughtfully, he swivels his stool in my direction.

"I don't know. I don't think so. Indie said that she flew off the handle at Frankie, was telling her what bullshit it was and all that. Frankie said that she'd think about it. Indie thinks that he's trying to mold her into some country clubber so that she fits in with his associates down at the State Attorney's office or something."

That pisses me off on every level. I've been the one to take Frankie for all of her ink. It's our thing and some of my fondest memories. I have more of my body covered in ink than not, and so many of them have something to do with her or a memory that includes her. When she told me that she wanted some work done, I jumped at the chance to share that bond with her.

Now this asshole wants to erase it like it's dirty or something? *No fucking way! Not on my watch!*

I'm lost in thought when I see Andrew make his way to the DJ and say something to him. The DJ nods his head and pulls out a mic, handing it to him.

*What the fuck is he doing?*

When the song ends, the DJ waves his hand as if to say "All yours." Drew clears his throat, thanks the DJ, and starts talking.

"Francesca, can you please come up here, darling?"

*"Darling?" Really? I hate this motherfucker. I. Hate. Him.*

All I can hear is the blood pounding in my ears, drowning out everything around me. My eyes following her every move, I watch Frankie glide up to the stage. As soon as she reaches him, he takes her hand and smiles at her. Then he drops to one knee.

*What the holy fuck is going on right now?*

I don't even realize that I've taken a step toward them until I feel both Mav and Sonny press their hands to either side of my chest and push back a little. I don't acknowledge them, or anyone else for that matter. I just stare at the train wreck in front of me, feeling my heart race, threatening to beat right the fuck out of my chest. I can see his lips move, imagine what he's saying, the promises, but I can't actually make out the words. Still, I hear nothing but the sound of my own blood, a deafening roar through my head, and to myself I just keep repeating, "Please don't say yes. Please don't say yes." I see her nod her head yes and watch him slip the ring on her finger, stand up, and wrap his arms around her, kissing her. I'm not sure whether I want someone to kill me or I want to be the one doing the killing. No, I know what I want. And it's not his pretty boy ass standing next to her, where I should be.

# ACKNOWLEDGMENTS

First, I need to thank my boys. I'm a wife and mom before all else. My husband is my rock. He believes in me and encourages me to chase this dream. He just smiles at me and tells me, "It's okay, Sug", when the house is a wreck, the laundry isn't folded, and we're eating takeout for the third night in a row because I'm on deadline or we were at hockey practice four times this week. I would be completely lost without you, Ran. Love you more than you'll ever know.

And to the other Beck boys, I love you to infinity and beyond. Thank you for giving me a reason to chase my dreams.

Addy: Without you, this book would never have happened. Hell, none of them would! You're the best friend I could ever ask for, and your faith in me makes me believe that I can REALLY do this. Thank you from the bottom of my little black heart for putting up with me and my petty. Love you forever.

Melissa: I pity you for having to wrangle me, but you do it so well! You're my right hand and I'd be lost without you. I love our lunches and chats and that you don't quit on me—even when some days you probably should.

To the members of Mandi Beck's Books: Thank you. Thank you for your undying support. For being a safe space and for sticking with me when you didn't have to. My cup runneth over.

Stephy Poo: Always in my corner, I don't know how I'd release a book without you! Thank you for your friendship and support. Love you lots.

Kristy: Thank you for being so patient with me. Your help is invaluable, and I appreciate you with every fiber of my being! I left you hanging on this story for months at a time and you never quit me. You're the real MVP.

To the bloggers both big and small: You guys are the heart and soul of the book world. Nobody works harder. Thank you for all that you do and for taking a chance on me.

Candi Kane PR: My Southside friend! Thank you so much for always taking me on and always being so patient with me. You and your team are incredible, and I love the hell out of you.

Lauren: Your talent never ceases to amaze me. Every time I'm just in awe of your work. I'm incredibly lucky to call you my friend, and I cherish our friendship more than you know! Love you a ton!

Letita: Thank you for being so amazing and for not killing me when I'm sure you want to. You created magic with this series! Love your face, girl!

# ABOUT THE AUTHOR

USA Today Bestselling author, Mandi Beck has been an avid reader all of her life. A deep love for books always had her jotting down little stories on napkins, notebooks, and her hand. As an adult she was further submerged into the book world through book clubs and the epicness of social media. It was then that she graduated to writing her stories on her phone and then finally on a proper computer.

A wife, mother to two rambunctious and somewhat rotten boys, and stepmom to two great girls away at college, she shares her time with her husband in Chicago where she was born and raised. Mandi is a diehard hockey fan and blames the Blackhawks when her deadlines are not met. Ask her who her favorite hockey player is though, and she'll tell you that he calls her...mom.

You can find all of her books and sign up for her newsletter on her website.

Printed in Great Britain
by Amazon